TOMB
TRAVELLERS

ROY POND
TOMB TRAVELLERS

Beyond the gateways and guardians
of Egypt's underworld

AN ALBATROSS BOOK

© Roy Pond 1991

Published in Australia and New Zealand by
Albatross Books Pty Ltd
PO Box 320, Sutherland
NSW 2232, Australia
in the United States of America by
Albatross Books
PO Box 131, Claremont
CA 91711, USA
and in the United Kingdom by
Lion Publishing
Peter's Way, Sandy Lane West
Littlemore, Oxford OX4 5HG, England

First edition 1991
Reprinted 1992

National Library of Australia
Cataloguing-in-Publication data

Tomb Travellers

ISBN 0 86760 133 7 (Albatross)
ISBN 0 7459 2184 1 (Lion)

I. Title

A823.3

Cover illustration: Michael Mucci
Printed and bound by The Book Printer, Victoria

Contents

1

The ibis bird

PHILLIP'S UNCLE, AN ARCHAEOLOGIST, mailed him a four-thousand-year-old mummy for his birthday. It wasn't the body of a pharaoh; it wasn't even a person. It was a dried-up ibis bird from ancient Egypt and it flew in — special delivery — from Cairo in the Arab Republic of Egypt.

Phillip signed for the package at the door while the dog barked excitedly. He thanked the delivery man, took the box from him and closed the door with the toe of a new pair of sneakers. The box felt disappointingly light for its size. Phillip gave it a shake next to his ear. He heard a dry rattle inside.

He knelt on the polished timber floor of the hallway, peeling off the masking tape that sealed the cardboard box. 'What do you reckon, Dogstar?' he said to the dog who drew near, sniffing, to investigate. 'What's Uncle William going to surprise me with this time?'

Phillip pulled out some protective plastic wrapping and uncovered a square object inside. He lifted it out. It was a glass case stuffed with what appeared to be cloth packing material, badly discoloured. The dog sniffed inquisitively at the case, then dropped its tail between its legs and backed away, rumbling in an offended manner. Phillip held up the glass case to look inside. It couldn't be packing material. Packing wouldn't be so tightly wadded or wound so evenly. It was an object bound up with very old bandages. Holding it all together were hoops of fibre. Papyrus strips? he wondered.

He saw a label attached to the glass case and recognised the marching-ants scrawl of Uncle William's hand. He read it out aloud:

For my dear nephew and archaeological partner, Phillip: I've always enjoyed giving you the bird, so here's one that's 4 000 years old — a mummified ibis bird! Just the thing for a boy of your advanced years. Hope it brings you good fortune. These sacred ibis birds are rich in magical significance. The ibis, you will remember, symbolised the bird-headed god Thoth. He was the god of wisdom, magic and writing and was also the author of Egypt's Book of the Dead. Happy fifteenth birthday. Love, Uncle William.

'Oh, wow!' Phillip said.

He felt bathed in a warm glow of good fortune, as if a shaft of favourable sunlight had fallen on him. Housed in the glass case was a genuine, mummified ibis bird. There was no mistaking the ancient stain of decay on the wrappings, a peculiar, rusty flush like sunset. He couldn't have been more grateful if his uncle had sent him the treasures of Tutankhamen, even though it was hard to tell that it had once been a beautiful white ibis bird and was only vaguely bird-shaped, looking more like an old, stuffed sock in a basket.

He showed the mummy bird to his father and mother who greeted his good fortune with remarkable restraint.

Phillip generously decided to put the bandaged bird on exhibition where the whole family could enjoy it.

When his parents weren't looking, he sat the glass case next to an ornamental mirror on the mantelpiece in the living room of their double-storey, red brick home. He glimpsed his own reflection in the mirror as he adjusted the bird to a favourable angle. His blue eyes, normally thoughtful and faraway-looking, held the avid gleam of an enthusiast. The dog growled as Phillip stood back to admire the bird.

'What's bugging you, Dogstar?' Phillip said. The animal bared its teeth. Perhaps it recognised the long dead creature on the mantelpiece or sensed its history. Dogstar, Phillip's dog, was itself an animal of ancient Egyptian descent, a tall, sleek running dog known as a pharaoh hound, white in colour with rich tan markings, a sharp face and pointed ears that were spear-shaped like a jackal's. Dogstar had also been a present from Uncle William, given to Phillip when it was a puppy. It shrank away, growling.

'What's got into your dog, Phillip?' his mother said, coming into the room and noticing the dog's behaviour. She went to the mirror to tidy her hair. She saw the mummified ibis bird on the mantelpiece and shrieked. 'Phillip, get that dead duck out of here!'

'It isn't a dead duck. It's a sacred ibis bird and it's survived for around four thousand years.'

'P-h-i-l-l-i-p! It won't last another four seconds if you don't get it out of here.'

'Do as your mother tells you, Phillip,' his father said gravely, following her into the room. 'It isn't right to keep dead pets in the living room.'

'It isn't a dead pet, either; it's a precious antiquity.' To them it was just a dried-up old bird, but not to Phillip. He shared his Uncle William's obsession with the mysterious and the wonderful. 'This particular bird was probably worshipped in ancient Egypt,' he said.

'Well, it's not worshipped here. We don't care for it.'

'It's ghastly,' his mother said, clutching her thin, nervy hands. 'Why don't you be a good boy, Phillip, and throw it out?'

'I can't throw out a valuable bird.'

'Then give it to an animal home or something.'

'Animal homes don't want dead birds.'

'Neither do we,' his father said, dropping into a comfortable leather chair that creaked under his big frame.

'Surely you can find a good home for it,' his mother said. 'Donate it to a museum.'

'It has a good home. Mine. It's my birthday present from my uncle.'

'We know that, Phillip, but please put it somewhere else,' she said. 'In the garage or the garden shed.'

'If you don't want it, I'll put it in my bedroom,' he said firmly. 'I'll put it on my bookcase as a prize exhibit. Some people appreciate ancient history.'

His mother was aghast. 'You want that thing sitting in your bedroom staring at you?'

'It isn't staring. Its eyes are covered with bandages.' He held up the bird in its case to show her. 'See.'

His mother squeaked faintly. 'That's even worse. I can't see where it's looking. Don't expect me to go into your room with that thing sitting there.'

Dogstar gave another growl, underlining Phillip's mother's distaste. He carried the bird out of the room with an injured air. Anything that kept a mother out of a teenager's bedroom must possess some magical properties, he thought, consoling himself as he went upstairs to his room. Dogstar followed him, slinking up the stairs at a distance.

Phillip brightened when another use for the mummified bird occurred to him. He could take it to school for a history project the following week. It would fascinate his history teacher, Miss Harrison, and send a few shivers of admiration through Julia, a girl in his class whom he liked to impress.

In the privacy of his book-lined bedroom, a room dominated by a framed poster of the Great Pyramid and a wall map of ancient Egypt, he took the bird out of its glass case, rehearsing how he might reveal it in class and parade it in front of their astonished eyes. He hefted the bird in one hand.

The bird, swathed in powdery, dry wrappings, felt amazingly light. Light enough to fly, he thought, giving it a playful swish through the air. Sadly, this one hadn't felt the breeze under its wings since the age of the pyramid builders. Imagine his mother calling it a dead duck!

He put the bird on his bed and chose a book from a shelf, paging through it to find a picture to illustrate his talk. He stopped at a colour plate of an ibis bird. It showed a white bird with a black head, neck and tail and a long, curved beak. It was wading, hunched in a thoughtful way, among reeds on a riverbank. That would do nicely. Phillip imagined himself standing in front of the class, with Miss Harrison looking on approvingly.

'This is a white, sacred ibis bird,' he said to a room that was empty except for Dogstar who lay near the door at a wary distance. 'Not to be confused with an ibis falcinellus which has brown plumage or a crested ibis which has bronze. . .' Phillip held up the book and turned it to reveal it to the imaginary class.

That was when the mummified ibis bird sitting on his bed took off. It flew off in the jaws of Dogstar and it could hardly have moved more swiftly if it had been swooping on the wing in the time of the pharaohs.

'Dogstar! Drop that bird or you're in dead trouble!'
The pharaoh hound, relative of today's greyhound,
streaked out of the bedroom and down the stairs in an
elastic, body-pouring run. Phillip pounded down the
stairs after it, almost tripping and falling.

Dogstar, unlike him, had no trouble with stairs. Not
much could stop Dogstar. The dog was agile and could
even run up a ladder, a trick Phillip had taught it. It
disappeared around a corner.

Phillip knew it had reached the lounge when he heard
his mother's scream. Phillip ran past his mother through
the lounge and down the hallway. The dog found that
the front door was closed. It wheeled and cut past him
to the kitchen. The dog ran with the bird in its jaws like
a retriever going in the wrong direction, but unlike a
retriever it wasn't intent on salvaging a bird for its master;
it was tossing its head in an attempt to shake the thing
to pieces.

'Stop it, Dogstar! You're shaking the life out of it!'
Phillip yelled. Dogstar tried the back door next. That,
too, was locked, it discovered. Dogstar switched direction. Phillip followed. He cornered it in the pantry.

'Drop it right there, 'Star boy — now! Don't shake it
like that!' Phillip edged closer. Dogstar's rumbling
growl seemed to begin in its belly. It shook the dog. In
the gloom of the pantry, its eyes sparked like metal pieces
on a grinding wheel.

Phillip made a dive. Dogstar bounded clear of him.
It ran back to Phillip's mother. The dog knew where to
create the maximum amount of confusion. When Phillip
gave chase, it ran like a whirlwind around her. His
mother spun in a tight circle, making a moaning noise
like a child's musical spinning top. Dogstar gained ac-
celeration around her spinning body like a space satellite

making use of the slingshot effect to launch itself on to the next planet. It went into the laundry room. Phillip lunged after it, cutting it off.

'Got you, hound,' he thought. He stood in the doorway, gasping, catching his breath, his legs spread wide to block the dog's exit. Dogstar came forward, innocently wagging its tail in a lazy, friendly motion, its mouth empty, panting. 'You've hidden it, you devil,' Phillip said.

He let the dog go by and went inside the laundry room to search. The bird wasn't behind the washing machine. It wasn't under the sink. It wasn't among some cardboard grocery boxes stored in a corner. Think like a dog. Where would a dog put it? There was nowhere else to look, unless the dog could open a spin-drier door. Impossible. It couldn't work the catch, unless. . . if the door had already been open, it could have put the bird inside and then nudged the door shut with its nose.

The lean, wily Dogstar was clever. Phillip opened the door and peered into the stainless steel drum of the spin-drier. 'You sly dog,' he said, his voice batting around in the confined space of the drum. 'Here it is!' He reached in and took out the bird. He made a quick inspection. It was a bit damp and dented from Dogstar's mouth, but it was still in one piece.

It was Julia, his classmate, on the telephone.

'Happy birthday, Phillip.'

'Thanks.'

'First, the important question. What did you get for your birthday?'

'Clothes, a new pair of sneakers and one very special present,' he said mysteriously.

'What's that?'

'You're not going to believe it — my Uncle William

in Egypt has sent me a mummy. It's four thousand years old.'

'I don't believe it. What kind of uncle would send his nephew a creepy, dead pharaoh for his birthday?'

'It isn't a pharaoh. It's a mummified sacred ibis bird. Isn't that brilliant?'

There was a dubious silence like a vacuum on the line. She must have covered the mouthpiece with her hand. The line cleared again like a lid coming off a jar. 'If you think so, Phillip.'

'I thought I'd bring it to school one day for a history lesson.'

'Um, great. Look, what are you doing today? I take it you're not having a party?'

'Not me. You know me and parties.'

'Yes I do.' She sounded relieved. She would have been hurt not to have been invited to his party. 'Why don't we go to town?' she said. 'The festival's on in the park and we could hang around.'

'You know me and crowds.'

'Well, you can't sit around in the house. It's the weekend and it's your birthday. Come with me.'

He had an idea. 'We could go to the museum. It's right next to the park.'

'You want to spend your birthday in a dusty old museum?' Her voice rose in protest. 'You're supposed to have fun, Phillip. Remember fun?'

'Museums are fun, Julia. They are treasure-houses of the past and crammed with secrets and mysteries. I'd like to visit the Egyptian antiquities section. . .'

'You must have been there thousands of times.'

'. . . and compare mummies. . .'

'You're a weird one, Phillip.'

'It's my birthday.'

She gave in. 'Well all right, as long as we can visit the

festival afterwards. I'll meet you near the entrance to the park.'

The parkland was ablaze with tents like an outburst of gaudy wildflowers and it swarmed with crowds in colourful clothes. A band in a clearing blew blasts of brassy summer sunshine through trumpets and tubas and horns. Flags promoting Festival Week fluttered from flagpoles.

Phillip walked along a pavement on the fringe of it, resisting its call. His eyes were fixed ahead on the museum, a building of classic, pillared geometry that rose imposingly behind the tree-lined park. He longed to leave the bright sunlight and enter its cool gloom.

A treasure-house of the past, he thought. It called to him with a mysterious, sad voice that made the sounds of the festival jar in his ears. His mind crowded with images of mummies in glass cases, bound hand and foot in the sleep of eternity, of scarab-beetle amulets, winking jewellery, statues, bas-relief carvings and slender Egyptian vases. He pictured his mummified ibis bird sitting on his bookcase at home.

Four thousand years ago, it would have waded among the reeds of the Nile on a bright summer's day like this. Did the sun, in ancient times, shine the way it did today? He imagined ancient Egypt looking golden, diffused and dreamlike, as if seen through gauze.

A white-faced clown on a unicycle reeled out from the park and spun in wobbly circles on the pavement. Phillip changed course to avoid him. He gave the clown a momentary frown, but couldn't help parting with a smile. Other people on the pavement stopped to watch the cyclist's antics.

Phillip kept going, checking his wristwatch as he walked. He was a few minutes late. He hoped he hadn't kept Julia waiting. He quickened his pace.

He heard a lazy clapping sound coming from under some trees at the edge of the park. He half turned his head, expecting to see a busker entertaining a sleepy afternoon audience.

It was Julia entertaining a crowd. She stood on a giant chequered chessboard — a public venue for chess matches — under the dappled light of some spreading trees, surrounded by chess pieces and by a ring of on-lookers. She was holding an outsize white bishop the size of a fire hydrant in her hands. She walked with it diagonally along a line of white squares and deposited it emphatically in front of her opponent, a thin, scholarly man with a dark beard and glasses that flashed with surprise at her move.

Trust Julia.

She spotted Phillip. She gave him a wave. 'Hi, Phillip, won't be long,' she said, stepping off the painted squares. Julia was a clean, bright-faced girl who wore her blonde hair tied in plaits at the side of her face and she was made even more pretty by an imperfection, a slight gap in her smile. 'Give me two minutes.'

'I like your confidence!' the bearded man called out, overhearing.

'You won't beat my dad,' a small boy in the crowd told Julia. 'He's a maths teacher and he's president of the chess club.'

'Is he? Good,' Julia said with relief. 'I want it to be a fair match.' Phillip went closer and stood beside the boy to watch Julia in action.

Julia was the school's and a state junior chess cham-pion and the world's worst person to play board games against, Phillip believed. Whether you played Checkers, Monopoly, Scrabble, Trivial Pursuit or Backgammon, it ended the same way. Julia won.

Julia narrowed her attention to focus on the match.

When she played a board game, she went into combat with a deadly intensity that did not soften until she had wiped her opponent off the board. Julia never believed in taking prisoners, Phillip recalled. She was so good at chess that she could memorise the board and play blindfolded — and still win.

She was no different today. In less than a dozen moves it was all over. Julia clapped her hands as if shaking the dust off them. 'Thanks for the game,' she said to her opponent. 'You are a very resourceful player.'

The man's glasses flashed like glaring mirrors. The ring of spectators gave Julia a round of applause. The man's son threw a scowl at Julia. She gave him a sweet smile in return. 'Well done, Julia,' Phillip said. 'He was pretty brave to challenge you.'

'He didn't. I challenged him. He laughed at the idea at first.'

'He isn't laughing now.'

'Isn't it a beautiful day, Phillip? I wish we didn't have to go to the museum!'

'You said you would.'

She wrinkled her nose. 'Come on then, let's get it over with. The sooner we've been, the sooner we can join in the fun.'

'But Julia, museums are fun,' Phillip said again. It surprised him that Julia couldn't see it. 'Don't you like a little mystery in your life?'

'I've got plenty of mysteries in my life. And you're one of them, Phillip.'

'Thanks. What time do you have to be home?'

She shrugged. 'It doesn't matter.'

'What did you tell your folks?'

'What do they care?'

Julia was adopted and she always hinted that she felt unloved by her adoptive parents. She envied friends who had their own parents. Phillip couldn't understand why. Her parents turned love on her like the sun, but it made no difference. She believed that her real parents had abandoned her and she couldn't forgive them.

'I've bought you a little present,' she said, dipping into the pocket of her blue dress. She handed him a small object wrapped in tissue. He opened it. It was a tiny beetle made of glazed green pottery.

'Oh, wow! A scarab beetle!'

'I don't want to encourage your obsession with ancient Egypt, Phillip, but I thought you'd like it. I came to the festival early and saw it on display at a craft table. I thought of you.'

'*Scarabaeus sacer*,' he said. 'These beetles were dungrollers and considered sacred in ancient Egypt. The ancients noticed the way they rolled a ball of dung over the ground and it gave them the notion of a monster beetle rolling the sun across the heavens.'

'Don't spoil it. I just thought it was a cute little beetle.'

'It is. Thanks, Jool!' He pocketed it gratefully. Julia wasn't so hostile to ancient Egypt after all, he thought, softening his earlier judgment.

They reached the museum and went up some steps. Julia threw a parting glance at the festivities in the park before accompanying him into the dim coolness of the museum. 'I'll teach you to appreciate the past,' Phillip said.

'I appreciate the here and now,' she said.

Phillip took her to the Egyptian room. He pressed his nose to the glass of a case that contained the mummified body of a petite Egyptian lady. 'Isn't she fascinating?' he said. His breath made a mist on the glass and it softened his view of the mummy, making him see the figure through a sentimental haze.

'I'll bet she was quite beautiful once. She would have

worn make-up and perfume just like women do today
and she would have shaved her head and worn beautiful
wigs threaded with gold. See her tiny foot sticking out
the end? She painted her toenails. She was probably
quite young. Many ancient Egyptians died when they
were only thirty or so.'

'It looks like an old, dried-up log with the bark peeling
off it,' Julia said, shuddering.

'It? It isn't an *it*! It's a real woman, or at least she
was, thousands of years ago. She was probably a pries-
tess or a noble and had heaps of admirers who wrote
poetry about her.'

'Poor thing.'

'She's survived for millennia and she's still remembered by us today. Why do you say "poor thing"?'

'Because she's not alive, like us, on this beautiful
summer's day. Can we go back to the park now, Phillip?
It's creepy in here.'

Phillip tore himself away from the case. Julia, his
mother and father — they were all the same. People who
lived for the here and now missed so much of life, he
thought, shaking his head. Couldn't they bear a little
mystery and shadow in their lives?

On the way out of the Egyptian section, he slowed to
look at a sculptured bas-relief from a tomb. It showed a
boat sailing on the river, a curved funerary barque. A
flower-strewn sarcophagus of a dead man lay under a
canopy on the foredeck and surrounding it like a ring of
withering petals were women mourners with ash-strewn
hair who knelt and wailed, their arms upraised in the
Egyptian way.

Light from a window threw dramatic shadows on the
relief, giving it shape and form. Life was like that bas-
relief, he thought. Shadow gave life its oustanding
features. It would be pretty flat without it. Without the

shadow there would be no form, just dazzling, unrelieved light that made you blink.

They left the museum and went out into the bright summer's afternoon. 'Who'd be that Egyptian mummy on a day like this?' Julia said, breathing in deeply as if she'd been afraid to breathe in the museum.

It was a beautiful day, he thought. Julia was right about that. He remembered a few lines of an ancient Egyptian poem that his Uncle William had read to him:

> No life can be prolonged in the land of Egypt; there is
> no-one who will not go to the other world; the period of
> time on earth is only as long as a dream.

The next day, Phillip heard the news about Uncle William. He had died of a heart attack in Egypt while excavating a burial site. They planned to bring his body back from Egypt for the funeral.

Dogstar howled when they read out the last will and testament of William Flanders before the funeral. They were gathered in a reception room in his uncle's country house — members of the family, museum authorities and colleagues of Uncle William, including one young man near the front, dressed in khaki gear, who had the look of an archaeological adventurer himself. They sat in a semicircle of antique chairs in front of a lawyer who had a small briefcase balanced on his knees.

'Quiet, 'Star boy,' Phillip said. He gave a comforting pat to the dog who sat on the black-and-white marble floor beside his chair. The family turned frowns in Phillip's direction, yet it was his dead uncle's specific instruction that they all be present. Phillip had brought Dogstar along because it was a precious link with his uncle.

The room went quiet. Tall antique clocks, like stately attendants, served out the moments with a deliberate click like teaspoons and cups being set out for morning tea. Uncle William lay in state in an ebony box on a small platform.

He looked quite calm, Phillip thought.

The lawyer, a thin, balding man in a grey suit, cleared his throat and continued to read aloud from the document in his hand, Uncle William's last will and testament:

I have, as you all know, given my life to the field of Egyptology and I have decided to follow a custom of ancient Egypt dear to my heart. I wish to be buried with my most precious possession beside me, sealed in my coffin – specifically, a papyrus scroll of the Egyptian Book of the Dead, a document which you will find locked in my wall safe. To ensure that my wishes are carried out to the letter, I stipulate that the said scroll be placed in my coffin in the presence of family witnesses and I further desire that my coffin be sealed immediately, before the rest of my will is read out.

At a signal from the lawyer, a legal assistant went to a wall and swung aside a gold-painted Egyptian hawk's head to reveal a combination lock behind it. The assistant consulted a scrap of paper in his hand, then twiddled the knob this way and that, the mechanism making a soft, ratcheting sound like a clock being wound.

The metal safe door swung open on silent hinges, and the assistant dipped into the hole in the wall, carefully removing an object, a glass cylinder containing a mustard-coloured roll of papyrus. As he moved, the glass cylinder flared like a neon tube in light from a French window.

The assistant dutifully carried it to where Uncle William rested, held it up with the air of a magician about to do a trick, then placed the sacred *Book of the Dead* inside the box beside Uncle William's scuffed, size twelve khaki desert boots. Uncle William looked dressed to go on another expedition. Two parlour attendants, men in black suits, detached themselves like shadows from the curtains and closed the lid on Uncle William and sealed the coffin shut.

It was even quieter now, Phillip thought. All he could hear was the faint squeak of screws going in as they closed the lid tight in accordance with Uncle William's instructions. Uncle William wouldn't have liked leaving with barely a squeak. He would have preferred a noisy send-off conducted in the ancient Egyptian style.

The ancients of the Nile used to hire professional mourners for funerals, women who wailed in the tremulous Eastern way, filling the air with sorrow and at the same time emptying it of all hope as they beat their breasts and threw ash on their heads in a most satisfying manner.

Smoothly, as if this remarkable event had been no more than a punctuation mark in a sentence, the lawyer continued to read out Uncle William's instructions: 'The remainder of my collection of antiquities I bequeath to the nation to be displayed in a list of museums specified hereinafter. . .'

The family shifted expectantly in their chairs. Forget the dusty relics, Phillip could hear them thinking. Now came the interesting part for them. The money. What was the old boy planning to do with the money?

Personally, the money didn't interest Phillip and he stopped listening. They could count themselves lucky if Uncle William hadn't found a way to take his wealth with him as the ancient Egyptians used to do, he thought.

He remembered good times he had enjoyed with his uncle in this house, especially late at night when his uncle's study was as quiet as a tomb and the old adventurer would translate ancient scrolls for Phillip's delight and wonder. He did not much like the idea of shadows in his life at that moment. He wanted Uncle William back. He would have traded a museum full of treasures from the past just to have his uncle with him in the here and now, to see the humorous gleam in his eyes again and to hear his voice fondly reading out some text. Phillip swallowed hard and his eyes stung.

He supposed he should say a prayer for Uncle William, but what prayer could he say for the dead? That his uncle's soul be allowed to enter heaven? Could a prayer from him open a door for his uncle? Uncle William had never been a man of beliefs — a cheerful pagan he had called himself.

His mother gave a sob on the way home in the car. They were a bit upset about Uncle William's death and in particular about the way the old man had decided to distribute his estate. Why were parents so materialistic? They completely overlooked the cultural treasure Uncle William had already given them.

Couldn't they take cheer from a four-thousand-year-old mummified ibis bird?

2

The night visitor

PHILLIP TOOK THE MUMMIFIED IBIS BIRD to school with him the next day.

He hadn't counted on the light fingers of Barry Coomber, a boy known as the school heavy. He should have expected it though. Thievery ran in Coomber's family. His brother Terry was serving a sentence in a youth detention centre for stealing cars and car parts.

Their history period was scheduled to take place after the lunch break, but Phillip had not been able to keep the secret of the ibis bird to himself. He had dropped certain hints to friends during the morning. It was a mistake.

During lunch in the school cafeteria, when he was sitting at a table eating a sausage roll and washing it down with some fruit juice, he saw his ibis bird travelling 'on the wing' once again. It was out of its case. Kids were passing the mummy bird around the cafeteria. It went in a series of hops from lunch tray to lunch tray. Coomber sat smirking at a distant table. 'Here comes Phillip's school lunch,' he called.

Phillip pushed himself away from the table. Barry Coomber saw him coming and slid his weight off his chair to beat him to the bird. A henchman blocked

Phillip's way. Coomber went around a table and joined an even bulkier, slow-moving boy named Hershey who was ferrying a tray loaded with food to a corner. Hershey was known as the school stomach. He always sat alone, undisturbed, to 'pig out' as the kids described it.

'Hi, Hershey,' Barry Coomber said. 'Got something for you. Like some chicken?'

'Love chicken,' Hershey said.

'Well, it's your lucky day, 'cause I don't. Here, have it. It's a new dish on the school menu.' He dropped the mummy bird onto Hershey's plate. 'It's called chicken-in-a-basket.'

'Thanks, Coomber, you're a friend.'

Hershey took his food tray to a corner. Barry Coomber blocked Phillip's way when he tried to stop Hershey. They wrestled. Phillip saw Hershey pick up his knife and fork and saw the implements flash as they converged on the precious ibis bird. Phillip dropped to the floor and scuttled through Coomber's parted legs. He dived on Hershey and grabbed his wrist just as his fork was about to spear the wrappings.

'No, Hershey.'

'Mine,' Hershey said, a piggy sheen in his eyes. 'Coomber gave it to me. Eat your own.'

'You can't eat it; it's a dead bird.'

'Course it's a dead bird; I don't eat live ones.'

'This is a very dead bird, a mummified one.'

Hershey picked it over with his fork. 'Not a chicken in a basket?'

'Not in a thousand years.'

Barry Coomber bent over double laughing, but Phillip had his bird back.

'Pity,' Hershey said. 'I like chicken.'

Just as well it wasn't chicken-in-a-basket, Phillip thought. Hershey would have eaten it, basket and all.

Phillip told the class about the ibis bird and also about his uncle's strange request that a copy of the *Book of the Dead* be buried with him. He was right about Miss Harrison being intrigued by the mummified ibis bird, but not about Julia. He had hoped to impress her. Instead, she wrinkled her nose at the sight of the bandaged bird.

When he had finished his presentation, his history teacher thanked him.

'That was a rare treat. Thankyou very much, Phillip.' She turned to the class. 'I wonder how many of you know about ancient Egyptian beliefs in the afterlife and about the role of the *Book of the Dead*?'

Barry Coomber put up his hand. 'The ancient Egyptians were pretty dumb. They believed in trying to preserve their bodies when they died and so they mummified them and bandaged them up like hospital casualty cases.'

'Do you know why they took a copy of the *Book of the Dead* with them into the next world?'

Coomber shrugged. 'Something to read on the way.'

'That's not far from the truth,' the teacher said. 'The *Book of the Dead* was a collection of magical formulae and passwords used to guide the dead soul through the gateways and guardians of the Egyptian netherworld. The ancient Egyptians had a copy of the book buried with them in their tombs to act as a sort of passport through the underworld.'

'Passport!' Coomber seized on this information gleefully. 'You could get a bad shock travelling on a passport like that. I'll bet Phillip's stupid uncle has travelled straight down to hell!' Barry Coomber sent a recruiting leer around the classroom to draw others into his joke.

Barry Coomber was a red-faced boy with shiny eyes and a manner that was alternately sidling and then bullying. If he had lived a hundred years earlier, he would have been a mutineer below decks on an old-time sailing ship.

'. . .his stupid uncle has travelled straight down to hell!' The words hit Phillip like an elbow in the stomach. He felt his insides go light and hollow and dry as the ibis bird in his hand. The teacher saw his look of shock. Coomber knew he had scored a hit and smiled at Phillip. Julia threw a retaliatory glare at Coomber.

'That's enough, Barry,' the teacher said; then, in an aside to Phillip, she added: 'You know better than to listen to nonsense like that, don't you? Thankyou very much for sharing that piece of history with us, Phillip. You can sit down now.'

Phillip went mechanically back to his desk. He was startled by Coomber's mischievous idea. Was it possible? Had his uncle, with his obsession for ancient Egyptian mystery and magic, unwittingly condemned himself to an eternity spent in a pagan hell in the Egyptian Land of Shades from where none may return? Why hadn't Phillip seen this possibility? Why hadn't Uncle William?

Phillip did not hear the rest of the history lesson. The idea that Coomber had planted in his mind fed on his fears and grew. What had happened to poor Uncle William?

After class, in the schoolyard, Barry Coomber continued to jab at Phillip's fears. 'Tough about your uncle — he's gone to hell.'

'Go there yourself, Coomber.'

Julia fell into step beside Phillip, throwing a glare over her shoulder at Coomber.

'That was a pretty dumb move your uncle made,' Coomber said. 'Now look where he's ended up. I reckon you'll end up there too with your sicko mummy birds and ideas.'

Phillip flared. He stopped and turned to face Barry Coomber. 'At least my uncle's not in prison, like some members of your family.'

'Are you trying to say my brother's in prison?'

'What else do you call a youth detention centre? Don't worry, you'll find out about it when you end up in one yourself.'

'Are you trying to say I'm going to go to prison?'

'I'm not trying. Watch my lips. I'm saying it.'

Barry Coomber's shiny eyes flashed and he dived at Phillip, head first, knocking him to a patch of grass outside a classroom. They wrestled with the grim desperation of boys, an intensity that made professional fighters seem playful by comparison. Coomber was bigger, stronger and had powerful leverage in his arms, but Phillip was slippery and quicker.

'Stop it,' Julia yelled, offering them both a considerable kick in the sides with her shoe. 'Teacher's coming!'

They untangled themselves and got up. Their shirt-tails were pulled out of their trousers. Phillip had lost a few buttons. Julia grabbed Phillip by his shirt sleeve and dragged him around the corner of a building, where he straightened his clothes and brushed grass off himself.

'What a stupid couple of kids!' she said fiercely.

Phillip went to collect his things from his locker and Julia walked with him. On the way home, he morosely kicked a bottle top along the pavement.

Julia tried to cheer him up. 'You don't believe what Coomber said, do you? That *Book of the Dead* stuff is just a lot of silliness. There's only one Book of power and you know what that is. You shouldn't let your mind play on dark and creepy things.'

Julia was a practical girl and she had a girl's impatience with nonsense. 'Do you want to come to my house and play a board game?' she said. 'We don't have to play chess; we can play another board game.'

'No thanks,' he said quickly. He knew what happened to people who played board games against Julia. He was depressed enough without taking a beating from the bright-faced girl. 'What if it's true about my uncle, though?' he said. He went on worrying. 'My uncle may have gone somewhere he never meant to go. Maybe he's trapped there and can't escape. I have a bad feeling about him. What can I do to help him?'

'Nothing. You should read the real Book of power and you'd know.'

'Poor Uncle William.'

'At least you knew him and loved him and he loved you. You're one of the lucky ones. You even have parents who love you, not like me.' Julia was being envious again.

'Perhaps you're right. I need to do some reading,' he said. He went to the city library where he borrowed a copy of the Egyptian *Book of the Dead* — not quite what Julia had in mind. It only deepened his fears. The *Book of the Dead* was a ticket to ride in the Egyptian underworld, it seemed to Phillip — a passport to a place haunted by animal-headed gods, demons, shades and monster guardians.

His mother and father went out to dinner that night. They left him a frozen chicken casserole in the microwave. Phillip couldn't quite face chicken after the incident with the bird in the school cafeteria. He went to his bedroom to read the *Book of the Dead*.

It began to rain; a heavy summer shower. He paged through the *Book of the Dead*. It was an illustrated book showing colour plates of papyrus scrolls unrolled. Columns of hieroglyphic characters crawled like marching insects over the mustard-coloured papyrus. In between the columns of symbols were illustrations, fine colour vignettes that were beautifully drawn with figures in proper proportion, not like clumsy drawings of the Middle Ages. The subjects of the illustrations were fantastic. Phillip saw human figures with the heads of apes, dogs, snakes and crocodiles. He saw monster serpents and gods, including Osiris, the god of the dead, seated on a throne in his pylon in the Hall of Judgment.

One of the largest illustrations showed a ceremony called 'the weighing of the heart' where the heart of a dead man was weighed in measuring scales against a single feather of truth. The scales were operated by Anubis, a dog-headed man-god, who looked a lot like Dogstar with his pointy face and ears, and the verdict of the weighing was recorded by a human figure with the head of an ibis bird whose name was Thoth, the god of wisdom.

Standing by, ready to pounce should the dead man's heart fail to pass the test of innocence, was a monster called the Devourer, a beast with the head of a crocodile, body of a lion and the hindquarters of a hippopotamus.

The chapter headings themselves sent a chill through Phillip:

The Ferryman
Gates of the Other World
The Tablet of Destiny
Repulsing the Slaughtering Knives
The Ladder to Heaven
The Block of Slaughter
The Chamber of Torture
The Pylons and their Doorkeepers
The Lady of Tremblings
The Pylon of Osiris
The Great Judgment
The Ravisher of Souls

Night of the Great Battle
The Field of Offerings

He stopped reading and took the ibis bird out of its glass case on the bookshelf. It was his last link with Uncle William. If only it really had powers of magic, he thought; if only this lump of decaying fibre could spread its wings again and fly to Uncle William and lead him out. He twisted it around in the bowl of light from a desk lamp. There was nothing magical about the way the bird looked now. It was only a long-dead bird.

Dogstar growled, reminding him of its presence. The dog lay near the door watching him. Phillip put the bird back on the bookshelf and he went back to reading his book. He came to a chapter entitled 'The Book of the Opening of the Mouth'. He had seen movies where just by the utterance of certain magical spells, a mummy had sat up in its sarcophagus and gone out to stalk the night. Rain like a scattering of small stones hit his bedroom window.

Daringly he read some words aloud. 'Thy mouth was closed, but I have set in order for thee thy mouth and thy teeth. I open for thee thy mouth and thy teeth. I open for thee thy mouth. I open for thee thy two eyes. I have opened for thee thy mouth with the instrument of Anubis. . .'

Phillip flicked a glance at the ibis bird. Nothing happened. What did he expect? It lay there like a stuffed sock. He went back to the book. 'Horus open the mouth, Horus open the mouth. . .' There was a squeak. He checked on the bird. The bird was still imitating a stuffed sock.

Was it something at the window? He twisted to check. He saw a branch of the peach tree move in the wind like a beckoning hand. It squeaked against a pane.

A shower of rain threw itself against the glass, washing the image away. He rose and went to the window to check. Rain spangled against the glass.

This wasn't helping Uncle William. He couldn't help him by reading a book. Maybe he should say a prayer for him – despite what Julia said. He wondered how to go about it. He felt awkward about the idea. He wasn't used to praying. Should he say it standing, or kneel at the foot of his bed? Standing up didn't seem right and kneeling wouldn't work. Dogstar would run over and lick his face if he went down on his knees. His bedroom didn't seem the right place to pray for Uncle William. It felt too far away.

Maybe he should go to Uncle William's house in the country. No, that wouldn't help. Uncle William wasn't there any more. It would be better to go to Uncle William's resting place, where a prayer wouldn't have to travel so far. Now? It was raining and it was dark. He resisted the idea. Wait for a cheerful sunny day instead, he told himself. But could he wait? A cold, nagging dread prodded him to do something. Did darkness and a bit of rain matter? Would he let that stop him from helping his favourite uncle?

He opened a cupboard in his bedroom and took out a denim coat. He put it on and pulled on a crackling yellow raincoat over the top of it. It smelled of last year's storms. Next he took a bicycle headlamp from a shelf. 'Are you coming, 'Star boy?' he said to the dog that was already on its feet, wagging its tail.

He went downstairs, with the dog bounding excitedly beside him. He pulled a bicycle helmet over his wiry fair hair and wheeled his racing bike out of the garage, swung himself onto the seat and pedalled swiftly down the street. The bicycle had ten gears and even at top speed Dogstar stayed with him, not in the street but on the pavement running level with its master.

He was bound for a place called Ravenwood cemetery. It was a five kilometre ride. The way was still fresh in his mind. He had been there only the day before when he had attended Uncle William's funeral service. The rain slackened off as he rode and he cheered as a breeze scrubbed his face. His bicycle light cut a hopeful wedge in the road ahead.

Glancing to one side, he saw Dogstar running in the sinewy, body-stretching action of a greyhound. Phillip could hear the *tick tick* sound of its claws on the pavement. Dogstar had no difficulty keeping up and could outstrip the bicycle if it chose.

Phillip turned at some red brick gates that reared at an entrance to the park and Dogstar turned in beside him. They went along an avenue. Phillip could hear the *tick tick tick* of Dogstar's paws more loudly on the bitumen and even his panting breath. They met a path and turned.

When they reached the darkened city of stones, he climbed off his bike, chaining it to a park bench, and he unclipped his bicycle headlamp to use as a torchlight.

He was glad of Dogstar's company. The long-legged pharaoh hound stood as high as his hip and Phillip could hold it by the collar as he walked. Phillip's bicycle lamp swept over the headstones as they walked. He probed the night in search of a landmark, a stand of spire-topped cypress trees that he remembered seeing near Uncle William's grave. There they were. He guided Dogstar towards them.

Phillip walked past his uncle's resting place without finding it. He went by it a second time. Had he been mistaken? Normally he had a good sense of direction. He was looking for Uncle William's monument, a small pink marble obelisk that looked like a miniature

Cleopatra's needle.

Phillip had missed it because it was lying flat on the grass, overturned. His first thought was that vandals had gone on a rampage through the cemetery. It had happened before. He had read about it in the local newspaper. But if these were vandals, they were very selective ones. The only grave they had touched was Uncle William's. They had turned it over as violently as if they had taken a bulldozer to it.

He shone his light over the rubble and earth. Did he dare go closer and look in the hole? He was frightened, but not at what he might see in the hole. He was scared of what he *wouldn't* see. Yet he had to do it. His fingers tightened around Dogstar's collar. 'C'mon, 'Star boy, we've got to take a look.' They went gingerly to the edge and Phillip spilled a splash of light into the hole.

It was empty. Someone or something had swallowed up Uncle William.

Dogstar barked as a hand from the shadow of the cypress trees came out and grabbed Phillip's shoulder. The dog tugged on his arm, almost wrenching itself free. Phillip twisted, flashing his torchlight on the figure of a man. He lifted the beam to the man's face. He had first seen this man at the funeral.

'What do you want? Leave me alone or I'll set my dog on you,' he said shakily.

The man blinked, raised his hand defensively to shield himself. 'Don't do that.'

Phillip didn't know if the man meant the light or the dog, but he kept the bicycle light staring in his face. Then he felt Dogstar's wagging tail slap against the side of his leg. According to Dogstar, the man was friendly. That was a relief. He eased out a nervy sigh of relief. He turned the light away a fraction, but still left enough light to reveal the man's face.

It was a rugged face with broad, calm, green eyes beneath a battered hat. He wore a khaki safari jacket, trousers and desert boots. He dressed a lot like Uncle William.

'They've taken him,' the man said. 'I'm Willard Chase, a colleague of your uncle's. He told me about you.'

Phillip jumped at the news. Perhaps this man could explain the fears that were crowding his mind like moths around a pool of lamplight. 'You mean you're an Egyptologist like him?'

'Not exactly. I'm an investigator, a sort of archaeological detective. Real archaeologists dig up antiquities from under the ground. I don't. I dig them up from criminals who steal them and take them underground a second time. It's harder than the first kind of archaeology. I sift through layers of conspiracy, treachery and greed.'

'My uncle's gone. And the papyrus with him,' Phillip said in a dead voice.

'I'm afraid the underworld has got them both,' the man said obliquely. He spoke with an educated American accent.

'What can I do?'

'Go home, kid; this is my job now. I think I know where to look.'

'Can I come with you? He's my uncle, or at least he was.'

'No, go home, before you get wet through to the skin.'

'Aren't you going to call the police?'

'Pointless. They can't go where I have to go. . .'

'Will you tell me if you find him?'

'Sure, now go home.'

Phillip shrugged. 'C'mon Dogstar, let's go. Good night,' he said to the man.

'Night. Take care, son.'

It was anything but a good night and it wasn't over yet.

On the ride home he felt the shadows closing in like a valley around his beam of light. He felt alone and powerless, even though he could hear the comforting tick of Dogstar's paws on the pavement beside him. Phillip couldn't handle this himself. He had to speak to someone.

He rode the bicycle back into the garage at home, took off the helmet and peeled off his yellow raincoat. He unclipped the bicycle lamp and put it into the pocket of his denim jacket.

His parents were still out at dinner, he found to his disappointment. He looked up his history teacher's number in the telephone book. He dialled the number.

'This is Violet Harrison. I'm out right now. Please leave your message after the tone. . .'

He wondered about trying to fill the empty silence that followed, but he had only his own empty fears to put there. He dropped the receiver. He looked at his wristwatch. It was 9.30. Not too late to try Julia.

At least she was at home.

'Phillip! You, this time of night?'

He pictured the clean-faced girl and the surprised smile at the other end. He imagined her twiddling a plait. 'I'm a bit scared, Julia. In fact, I'm pretty shaken up. Strange things have been happening. It's my uncle.'

'What have you been doing? Tell me. Did you read the book I told you to read?'

'No, I read the other one. The Egyptian *Book of the Dead*.'

'No wonder you're upset.'

'It isn't just the book that's upset me. I've just been to visit my uncle's grave.'

'Alone?'

'With Dogstar.'

'In the dark? Are you sure you didn't dream it, Phillip?'

'Julia, I don't know what's happening. My parents are out and there's no-one else I can talk to.'

'You're serious. You *are* a weird boy. Listen, stay there and stay calm. You obviously need a good talking to. I'll try to come over to see you. I should be able to sneak away. Nobody would think to check on me. Oh, and while I'm trying to get there, do what I told you to do. Read the other book. *Do it.*'

'Don't come here, Julia. It's wet and I don't want you to upset your mum and dad.'

'They're not my mum and dad.'

'You know what I mean.'

'Stay there. I'll bring a board game over and we'll play a game.' She put down the phone.

Phillip sat at his desk. The *Book of the Dead* was still open at the place where he had left it. He looked at an illustration of the ibis-headed god Thoth. The pagan god looked sinister with its small bird head, thin reptilian neck and broad, muscular shoulders.

Phillip checked that the mummified ibis bird still rested safely on the shelf. Calm down, he said to his fears. Others were helping. The stranger was helping to look for Uncle William. But where would he look? Didn't he know what Phillip knew? There was nowhere on earth to look for Uncle William.

Coomber was right. Uncle William had travelled straight to hell and the earth had convulsed and swallowed him up. Yet the stranger had managed to spread a certain calm and confidence to Phillip. I think I know where to look,' he had said.

Phillip heard a squeak. Dogstar bristled and gave a

growl deep in its throat, but its tail thumped against the floor. Phillip turned to the window, expecting to see the peach tree branch moving in the wind, but instead glimpsed a grinning face covered in winding cloth.

'Who's that?' He didn't have to ask. He recognised the shiny, bullying eyes of Barry Coomber between the bandages. He went to the window and pulled it up. Someone slid down the peach tree and fell heavily to the ground.

'Is that you, Coomber? Don't be a goof!' Coomber was pulling a stunt to frighten him. Phillip tried to sound brave and angry, but a shake in his voice betrayed the strain he was feeling. 'All I need is some stupid kid like you fooling around. Go home!'

The garden below glistened wetly in a light from across the street. Coomber was hiding. 'Do you hear? I'm not even going to bother to come down and look for you, so you might as well go home.' He slammed the window shut.

He tried to look at the *Book of the Dead* again, but the pictures of monsters and gods unnerved him. He turned on a television set that sat on a shelf. A grisly scene of a vampire flickered onto the screen, Count Dracula swinging open the lid of his coffin.

Phillip switched channels. A commercial for Kentucky Fried Chicken bounced onto the screen. It reminded him of Hershey trying to eat his ibis bird. He tried another channel. This time he found a re-run of *Indiana Jones and the Temple of Doom*. He switched off the set. He enjoyed Indiana Jones movies, but not tonight.

Phillip looked around for a distraction. His glance ran along a line of books that crowded the shelves. It settled on a small, black, battered volume given to him by his grandmother. It was that other Book of power. It had sat in his bookcase unopened for years. He took it down now. Feeling the texture of its leathery cover in his fingers reminded him of the soft, wrinkly touch of his grandmother's hands. He shivered. It was as if she had just given it to him. He remembered how she used to read to him on the back porch of their house in a comforting, creaky voice like the chair she used to rock in.

Phillip took the Book to his bed and stretched out on his back. He paged through it. The Book, once well-used, opened with a will of its own at certain favourite places, especially the Psalms. He read some pieces at first silently, then out loud.

The words had a calming effect like cool water on a hot forehead. He put the book down and closed his eyes to think. The rain began to fall again. He hoped Julia wouldn't try to come over after all. She would only get wet. He was all right now. One good thing, though. The rain would chase Barry Coomber away.

Perhaps his fears were groundless and he was imagining things. There was some other explanation for what had happened. Perhaps Uncle William had been buried in the wrong cemetery plot by mistake and they'd had to move him.

Time seemed to hang in stillness.

There was a flash of lightning and blue-green light spurted like a broken power cable cracking around his room. He opened his eyes and found that he was not alone any more. A phosphorescent glow lit a corner of the room and in its centre stood a beautiful white bird with feathers that dazzled.

It was a sacred white ibis bird.

'I have come to thank you for saving me from the jaws of your dog and later from the jaws of the piggish boy who would have devoured my precious remains for his lunch.' It spoke without moving its beak and Phillip heard the voice in his mind.

'Who are you?'

'I am Thoth, the magical ibis.'

Phillip recovered quickly from the shock. Uncle William had given him the bird. Did he know? He remembered Uncle William's note. . . 'These sacred ibis birds are rich in magical significance. The ibis, you will remember, symbolised the bird-headed god Thoth. He was the god of wisdom, magic and writing and was also the author of Egypt's *Book of the Dead*.' Was this a chance to help Uncle William? It was too good an opportunity to let pass.

Perhaps the holy bird might show its gratitude in some useful way. 'If you're really grateful,' he said to the bird, 'there's one small thing you can grant me in return.'

'What do you have in mind?' the bird said, taken aback.

'A wish, Wise One,' Phillip said, 'but only a small one. I'd like a trip.'

The sacred bird thought about it, shifting from one leg to the other. 'Very well, Phillip, that's not too hard and I'm feeling generous. I'll grant you your wish.'

'May I go anywhere I want to go?'

'Why not?'

'Anywhere?'

'Anywhere. Even California if you want to see Disneyland.'

'Further than that. How about a visit to your realm?'

The bird tilted its head and balanced thoughtfully on one leg, fixing Phillip with a single unblinking eye as hard as a diorite bead. It seemed to relent, dipping its beak in a nod.

'Egypt, my homeland? Fine. Anywhere you like; I said so.'

'So you did. Thankyou, Lord Thoth. Now everyone knows that sacred ibis birds don't go back on their word. Especially you, the bird who weighs men's souls in the scales of truth in the underworld, the bird who sets down verdicts in the heavenly scroll. You are the most honest of all the holy ones in the Egyptian heaven and you always stick to your word.'

'True,' Thoth agreed, arching its long black neck to preen its bright white chest feathers, for it was a vain bird. 'So exactly where in Egypt do you want to go?' it said. 'Do you fancy a cruise on the Nile? Just name it and it's yours. Sheraton cruise? Hilton?'

'I'd like to journey into the Land of the Dead so that I can try to rescue my uncle who has made a terrible mistake,' Phillip announced.

All of a sudden, a single leg was not enough to support the bird. It needed both legs to stand on. 'You've tricked me!'

'Too late! You've agreed! You said *anywhere*.'

'You're a pretty devious boy, even in your dreams,' the bird remarked, a wicked gleam in its eye.

'Thankyou, Wise One.' Coming from the bird of wisdom, this was high praise. What other boy had ever succeeded in tricking Thoth, the symbol of wisdom?

'All the same, you are right. It doesn't do for a god to go back on his word,' it said. 'I'll grant you your wish, but there are catches. I can dish out surprises, too.'

'Name them,' Phillip said obligingly, grateful that Thoth hadn't blasted him into nothingness.

'I will show you where to find your uncle, but for your impudence I will not show you a way out. That will be up to you. If you fail, you too will be lost forever.'

'Fair enough.'

'That's not all. Do you happen to know an ancient Egyptian tale about a prince and a doom dog?'

'Yes, I do,' he said. 'My uncle read it to me when he gave me Dogstar as a puppy. It's a story about a boy whose fate was predicted at birth by the Seven Hathors. The Fates said that he would meet his doom through a snake, a crocodile or a dog. To protect him from these dangers, his family kept him at home. He grew very lonely until one day, feeling sorry for him, someone gave him a puppy as a present. Except. . .'

'Yes?'

'The papyrus that tells the story is unfinished. Only a fragment remains. Scholars have never learnt the truth. Does the boy meet his end through a crocodile, a snake or the dog? Or does he somehow elude all three fates?'

'You may find out sooner than you think. For your impertinence I now pronounce the same fate on you. If you journey into the land of the dead, you may meet your end through a crocodile, a serpent or a dog.'

'A dog? You don't mean — not Dogstar! My own dog wouldn't turn on me, would he?'

The bird shrugged its wings. 'Who knows? Dogstar may turn out to be your doom dog. And note this well, if you do perish in the Egyptian underworld, you will never reach heaven. You will fall into the pit of everlasting nothingness where the Ravisher of Souls will devour you.'

Phillip gulped.

'Do you still want to go?' the bird said, giving a squawking laugh like a parrot.

'Yes,' he said, 'to find my uncle.'

'Then you must face what happens, presumptuous boy.'

3

The ferryman

PHILLIP WAS NO LONGER IN HIS BED, but on sand under moonlight and stars. He was no longer alone. Dogstar, Coomber and Julia lay sprawled in a semicircle around him as if they had been flung down to earth.

'That's nice, Phillip,' Julia said peevishly, sitting up, 'knocking me flying just as I reach your front door. Did you set a booby trap or something?'

'I'd like to know how you threw me out of the tree like that,' Barry Coomber said, brushing sand off himself.

Phillip looked around. If it was a trap, he had fallen into it himself. There was no sign of the house, of streetlights or of the neighbourhood. He felt for the lawn under his fingers and came up with a handful of sand. Sand? He was a very long way from home.

'Sorry,' he said. 'I fell asleep. I must have been sleep-walking.' He stood up. Sand trickled down the back of his legs. He brushed it off. 'Did you two lead me here?' Phillip said. 'Which way is home?'

'Don't be silly, Phillip; we're asking you. What are we doing here? Did you call me over just to play a trick on me?' Julia said.

'And me?'

'I didn't call you over, Coomber. You came to frighten me and if you've been frightened yourself, it serves you right.'

'How would you like a punch?' he said.

'Don't fight again, you two. I want to go home.'

They all got up, including Dogstar. The dog rubbed itself against Phillip's leg. Phillip took hold of its collar. 'Home, boy.'

Dogstar whined and sat down again. 'Home, 'Star boy, do you hear me?' To encourage it, Phillip took a step in one direction.

'Is this home, Dogstar?' It dug its paws in the sand, resisting. 'This way, then?' It pulled again. 'No? Then this way.'

Still the dog pulled back. 'So it has to be this way.' Not according to Dogstar. Phillip had run out of directions. 'Not any of these ways?' Dogstar sat stolidly, resisting tugs on its collar. It gave a whine. It wanted to go home, too.

'Oh no.'

'What do you mean "oh no"?' Julia said. 'I don't like "oh no".'

'I think I understand,' Phillip said.

'What?'

'We can't go home from here. I'm afraid we have a bit of a journey ahead of us,' he said. 'It's my fault. I asked for it.'

'You're asking for it now. Stop fooling around and tell us where we are,' Coomber said in an ugly voice that was nevertheless edged with panic.

'Come to think of it, it's your fault, Coomber. *You* put the idea in my head,' Phillip said, remembering.

'This isn't my fault. I just climbed up your peach tree to give you a fright. Can't you take a joke?'

'Is that why you've got that bandage around your

neck like a casualty case?' Julia said. 'You look like a mummy who's coming apart.'

In the moonlight they could see the folds of white crepe bandage glowing around Barry Coomber's head. He unwound it, leaving it around his neck like a scarf.

'It was the bird,' Phillip said. 'It's no ordinary bird. Something weird happened because of it.'

'Something weird happened all right,' Coomber agreed. 'I'm remembering now. There was a lightning flash just before I fell out of the tree.'

'Yes, I saw a flash, too,' Julia said. 'It blinded me as I walked up to the front door. I thought somebody snapped on a front light.'

'The bird has done this,' Phillip said. 'I was visited tonight by the ibis bird, only it wasn't the mummy bird. It was a real bird and it glowed. It told me things.' Julia and Coomber stared at him in disbelief.

'Real birds don't speak.'

'This one did. It came to thank me for saving the mummy bird from Dogstar and Hershey. It said I could make a wish, any wish I liked. I wished that I could travel to the underworld and try to rescue my uncle. That's why I'm here. I've been allowed to come here to look for him.'

'Don't say creepy things,' Julia said. 'Your uncle's dead; you can't go looking for him. Tell us where we are, Phillip.'

'Coomber knows. We've gone where he said my uncle went.'

'Garbage,' Coomber said.

'I told you not to say things like that, Phillip,' Julia said, agreeing with Coomber for once. 'This is the world. There's sand under my feet and I can hear water lapping.'

'The river,' Phillip said, thinking quickly. 'We'd be near the river. We're going to have to cross it.'

'Stop right there,' Coomber said. 'You don't have to carry on being a jerk. You've had your revenge. I'm sorry, okay? I want to go home. I got wet climbing in the tree and now I need to change my clothes.'

'You'll soon dry off in the desert air,' Phillip told him. 'If my guess is right, we're in the desert at the edge of a great river, the greatest river in history. We have to cross it to the western side.'

'Phillip, please don't talk like that. I'm getting very scared. I don't think I deserve a scaring, do I? I only came over to help you.' The pleading note in her voice made him feel like putting an arm around her shoulders. He didn't though. Not in front of Coomber.

He touched her arm instead to calm her. 'I'm not scaring you any more than I'm scaring myself, but something has happened. I don't know exactly what, although I have ideas. It shouldn't have happened and certainly not to you two and Dogstar. I don't know how you were dragged into it. It must have been because you were at my house just at the critical moment.'

'I'm not going to play along with this. I'm going to stay right here until someone points the way home,' Coomber said. He flopped down on the sand. 'You can all shove off if you like.'

Phillip shrugged. 'Come on, Julia, we can't stay here. We must find a way over.'

He took her arm and walked her towards the sound of lapping water.

'Hey, where do you lot think you're going?' Coomber said. 'You're not leaving me here.'

Phillip turned and said to him soberly, 'You don't understand what's happening to us, Coomber. I'm not sure I do, but if you ever want to get home again you're going to have to stick with me. I have a journey to make and for some reason you're tagging along. That's bad luck for me as much as for you.'

'Garbage.'

'Then stay.'

'We should stick together.'

'Then come.'

Barry Coomber got up, reluctantly. They walked, Dogstar's collar pulling keenly in Phillip's grip. The dog trembled with excitement and energy. They walked for about fifty metres.

They reached a reed-lined edge of a great stretch of fallen moonlight on water, a river that stretched as far as the eye could see. A low moon lay on the surface, its silvery trail splintered by gentle waves.

'You really mean this,' Julia whispered beside him.

'Somebody really means this. Somebody or something,' he said. 'Just think of it as a game. You like games.'

'Some games. I don't like this one. I don't like things that I can't make any sense of.'

'Don't think about it. Just be with me on this journey and stay with me — there and back if we can make it. We can only go forward because, until we have been there, there's no back to return to.'

They walked along the riverbank.

'It's the sea,' Coomber said.

'It's a river,' Phillip said, firmly.

'Why do you think we have to cross it?' Julia said.

'To get to the other side.'

'Don't be smart, Phillip.'

'No, I mean the *other* side. . . the nether region. The west.' He pointed. 'It's over there somewhere.'

'How do you know it's there if we're lost?'

'Because I've read about it. The place we have to reach lies in the west, across the river.'

'Are you looking for a bridge or something?' Coomber

said.

'There's no bridge here. We'll need a boat to get across. We must look for the boatman.'

'What boatman? Stop being mysterious,' Julia said.

'Not just any boatman. *The* boatman. You'll know him by his face. He's the ferryman whose face is turned backwards.'

'Turned backwards? How would he know where he's going?' Coomber said scornfully.

'He knows,' Phillip said. 'He faces backwards so he can watch his ferry and make sure that only the right souls come aboard.'

Dogstar's collar shook in Phillip's hand. The dog growled softly. Coomber, who had sharper eyes than the others, saw it before the rest of them. 'There's something tied up at the edge of the river. Looks like a boat.'

The shape of a sailing vessel separated from the darkness and gathered form as they drew nearer.

'Keep your heads below the reeds,' Phillip whispered to the others. They ducked and went closer, bent at the waist. He signalled the others to stop. They parted the reeds to look. They saw a large wooden ferry boat, in papyriform shape — swept up at stem and stern like an archer's bow. It had a mast, a painted deckhouse amidships and a single, long rudder.

'It's like a boat out of a history book,' Julia whispered.

A gangplank ran from the stern to the riverbank. Phillip knew what had to be done. The boat was their only way across.

'There's somebody on board.'

A bare-chested man dressed in a white linen kilt appeared in a pool of light from a torch flame, coiling some rope, but he wasn't watching what he was doing. His head was turned towards them. So was his back. His head was twisted at an impossible angle.

It was the ferryman from the *Book of the Dead*. The ferryman's name was Herhaf, the ferryman whose face is turned around. Phillip was certain about it. Now he knew that his wish had been granted. He was being given a chance to go to Uncle William across a gulf that no living person had ever crossed before. He hoped it didn't mean that he was dead himself. He bit the inside of his cheek to feel if it hurt. It hurt. He was alive.

'He's seen us; he's watching us,' Julia said.

'No, he isn't.'

'Look at him. What kind of weirdo is that? His head's screwed on the wrong way,' Coomber said.

'Like yours,' Phillip snapped at him. 'Get down lower. If he sees us, we may never get on his boat.'

'I don't want to go on a boat with a guy who isn't looking where he's going. He'll probably run us into something.'

'We're *going*,' Phillip said.

'Are we?' Julia said. 'Aren't we getting in deeper by going on the boat? Shouldn't we stay here until it all changes back again and we wake up in the morning and it's time for school?'

'There's no school tomorrow; it's Saturday,' Coomber informed her.

'We have to go on — at least I have to, to find out about my uncle. I've brought us here and I have a feeling that I am the only one who can lead us out again.'

'Did you love your uncle that much?'

'Yes,' he said, 'and I believe he loved me.'

'I envy you,' she said with a shake in her voice. 'Nobody ever loved me that much!'

As she spoke, there was a startling rustle in the reeds as if something heavy dragged itself towards her. Julia stiffened. 'What was that?'

'Just a crocodile,' Phillip said in a matter-of-fact voice.

He pulled her to a safe distance from the sound. Coomber followed with a new willingness.

'Crocodile?' Julia said. 'Did you say "just a crocodile"? You don't have to sound so calm about it as if you were expecting one.'

'It's just that I know the sorts of things to expect here. We must climb on the boat and the only way we can do that is to go around towards the prow where the ferryman can't see. He only looks behind. We'll need a diversion. I'll go and talk to him and keep him occupied while you and Coomber jump on the boat near the prow. We can't all rush on at once.'

'You're going to talk to that creature?' Julia said. 'What do you talk about to a man whose head is turned backwards?'

'Memories, of course,' Phillip said.

'Sorry I asked.'

They crept past the dark bulk of the ferryboat. Phillip went to the stern.

'Evening, Ferryman,' he said, 'can you ever remember a night as grey as this one?'

'Looking back, I can remember plenty,' he said in a defensive voice. 'Who are you?'

'Someone you wouldn't remember.'

'Looking back, I can't say I do.'

'You must have lots of memories, always looking back.'

The Man Whose Face Is Turned Around nodded. 'I do, and I look back on them all the time, but it isn't as congenial as you might think.' He gave a sigh.

'You mean the benefit of hindsight isn't such a benefit after all?' Phillip said conversationally.

The ferryman's eyes were dark and painted dramatically in the ancient Egyptian manner, the rims outlined in black like the shapes of fish, with tails at the sides.

They looked thoughtfully back as he considered Phillip's question. 'It's a curse always looking back,' he said. He began to chant a repetitive piece, more of a grumble than a song, as he coiled the length of rope.

'It's not much fun always looking over your shoulder. My wife says to me: "Look ahead, Herhaf, look ahead. Think of the future." You can't see where you're going when you're always facing backwards. It's not much fun eating your dinner with dinner guests looking at the back of your head. I see only the sorrow of what is behind, the disappointment of what has been, never the hope of what is to come. Only the past, never the future. It's not much fun always looking over your shoulder. . .'

'Sorry, I didn't mean to dwell upon the past.'

'Come a little nearer, boy, into my torchlight,' he said. 'Let me take a look at you. Don't be scared.' Phillip went further into the light of the ferryman's torch, almost to the edge of the gangplank. 'You're not a shade,' the ferryman said.

'No.'

'I suppose you're too young to be a ferryman?'

'I'm not a ferryman.'

'It's just that your head's turned around like mine,' he said, 'though not quite as much.'

'My head's screwed on perfectly straight.'

'No, it isn't,' the ferryman said with an emphatic shake of his head. 'You're backward looking, like me. You love to look back to the past, to the very far past. Your thoughts are always filled with the long ago and the far away. You are a boy who is in love with the past.'

Phillip couldn't deny it. 'Well, yes, I do happen to like the past,' he confessed. 'I've always thought it would be the very best place to live.' As he spoke the words, Dogstar suddenly bared its teeth. Phillip tried to pat it to calm it, but surprisingly it nipped his hand.

'What's the matter, 'Star boy? Don't be afraid.'

'It's not afraid. It's angry. With you. Put yourself in its place. It dogs your footsteps every day. How do you think it feels having a master who doesn't enjoy living in the present? Be warned: looking back isn't such a wise thing to do. One day you'll look back on my words and agree. Before too long, I'd say. Take care that you are not lost in the past — forever.'

The ferryman's face was turned towards Phillip, but his bare back faced him. Phillip stole a glance over the ferryman's shoulder to see how the others were doing.

Coomber made his way to the boat first. Trust him to leave Julia on her own in the reeds, Phillip thought. Coomber ran like a football forward making a tackle and threw himself on board with such force that Phillip saw the boat rock.

Where was Julia? Coomber gave her a wave from the boat. The reeds parted and a pale arm gave a response above the reeds. She was following, almost at the edge, when a dark, lethal length of crocodile charged at her with a startling rush like a powerboat. Coomber hung over the edge, holding out his arms to her. She leapt straight onto Coomber, knocking him to the deck. They were both safely on board.

'What was that?' the ferryman said.

'Just a crocodile or a hippo,' Phillip said. 'Tell me, don't you enjoy your memories?' he said, trying to hold the ferryman's attention.

'Frankly, no, looking back. But I can't stand here talking about the past. There are passengers coming. If you turn your head around and look over your shoulder you'll see them coming.' Phillip twisted his head, although not quite as far as the ferryman's. He couldn't see anybody coming, but he could hear low singing and he saw reeds parting like hair as an invisible procession progressed through them towards the gangplank at the stern of the boat.

'I'll see you again,' Phillip said.

'I won't forget you,' the ferryman said.

The ferryman waved to something behind Phillip. Phillip drew back into the reeds. He heard them coming, but couldn't see them. He heard the swish of grass, feet on the gangplank, the creak from their weight. The ferryman came forward to meet them. A current of fear found a gap behind Phillip's collar and trickled down his spine. Were these unseen passengers souls going on board for the journey to the other side?

'C'mon, Dogstar,' he whispered. He went with the dog towards the prow of the boat. He wished that a cloud would come over the moon. It was as bright as dusk. Proceeding carefully, he parted the reeds and crept to the prow, holding Dogstar's collar. 'You next. On you go, 'Star boy.' Dogstar made a run and leapt easily onto the prow. Phillip ran next and vaulted on board, landing in some ropes, nets and covers that smelled of fish.

Julia and Coomber were squatting in shadows. 'You took your time,' Coomber said.

'Sh-sh.'

Phillip went around the deckhouse to check that he hadn't been seen climbing on board. The walls of the deckhouse were painted in a chequered pattern of orange, white and blue and there was a small grille-like window on one side. Phillip peered around a corner. The ferryman's body was facing him, but his head wasn't. Phillip allowed himself a sigh of relief. They had smuggled themselves on board unseen. He rejoined the others.

'This boat smells fishy,' Julia said. 'It reminds me of a bait box my father uses when he goes fishing — my stepfather, that is,' she corrected herself.

'What now?' Coomber said. 'There's nobody else on board. Why will the ferryman set off across the river with an empty boat?'

'Listen,' Phillip said.

They heard a low singing and the drum of feet on the deck. They also heard a jingling sound like pieces of metal dropping onto the deck.

'People are coming on board!'

Dogstar rumbled in the dark next to Phillip. 'Not people, not any more, although they were people once. You can't see them. They're shades. They mustn't see us, either. We must hide under these covers.'

'What are shades?' Coomber said.

'They're not sunglasses if that's what you're thinking. They're shades of the departed.'

'This is getting horrible, Phillip. Do you mean they're souls?'

The singing grew fuller and the boat gave a dip with new weight coming on board.

'Yes; get under the covers quickly.'

Coomber was the first under, like a frightened kid diving under the bedclothes. If he couldn't see the shades, he certainly didn't want them to see him. They lay listening to each other's bottled breathing under the covers.

'Goodnight folks,' Coomber said. 'Wake me up when it's over.'

Dogstar began to pant. 'It's stuffy in here,' Julia said.

Phillip folded back one corner of the cover, allowing in some air and a view of the mast and the stars above.

A rumble came from the stern. They were raising the gangplank. They heard the rasp and squeak of ropes and saw a large rectangular sail with a vertical zigzag pattern slowly being hoisted above the boat by unseen hands. It bellied and flapped in a breeze before it was sheeted securely. The boat moved away from the riverbank.

They scudded upstream, moving at an angle away from the eastern bank towards the west. The west was lit by a red glow like a dying sunset, even though the moon was shining. He rested and closed his eyes. He did not know how long they journeyed.

A hot glow on his face made him open his eyes. Sunset? How could it be? He lifted more of the cover, raising himself on one elbow. Great flames stood on the water around their boat, but the flames did not touch them, even though the lower yard of the sail almost dipped into the tongues of fire.

The others threw off the covers to look. 'We're on fire,' Barry Coomber said. 'What did I tell you? That guy's too busy looking over his shoulder to see what's happening.'

'What do we do, jump overboard?' Julia said.

'The fire isn't on board,' Phillip said. 'Take a look. The flames are on the water.'

It was true. 'Must be an oil spill.'

'It's a lake of fire.'

Julia gave Phillip an exasperated shove. 'You told us we were going to the other side of the river, not into a lake of fire.'

'We must go through the lake of fire before we can reach the other side.'

'We'll cook,' Coomber said.

'The ferryman hasn't cooked. He makes the trip every night,' Phillip reasoned, reassuring them. He did not add that the ferryman was immortal and they weren't. The flames felt awfully hot. He expected them to fly on board at any moment and flutter like red parrots through the sail and rigging. Miraculously, they sailed on unharmed.

The boat creaked. The shades on board began to sing loudly and beat their bare feet on the deck.

They were passing through the fire. He patted Dogstar, who panted like a steam engine. 'It's okay, boy, we'll get through it.' The deck had grown hot beneath them. Phillip lost sight of the stars. They seemed to have entered a hollow, but the breeze still blew, taking them on. The flames roared. They saw the sides of a rocky hollow close in around the vessel.

Rock shelves reared around them. There were creatures on the rocks. Coomber pointed them out. Apes. They sat on ledges, watching the ferryboat pass, their close-set eyes sweeping the boat from stem to stern. They were the sacred apes on the lake of fire, Phillip thought.

'Don't let them see us,' Phillip said. 'They may warn the ferryman. We're nearly there, I think.'

In the light of the flames, Coomber made another discovery. There were small shiny ingots lying all over the deck. Suddenly it explained the jingling sound that they had heard earlier. These were *deben* pieces used to pay the ferryman for the journey. Ancient Egyptian money.

'It's money the shades have paid to the ferryman,' Phillip explained.

Coomber stuffed a handful of ingots into his pocket. 'You mustn't take them,' Phillip said. 'They belong to the ferryman.'

'You shouldn't steal other people's things,' Julia said.

'Who cares? The ferryman won't know. He's busy looking the other way. You do the same.'

They berthed at a stone quay. They waited until the gangplank was lowered and they heard the drumming of feet running down it before they jumped over the side onto the stone quay, hiding in the shadow of the ferry.

Dogstar gave a pull on Phillip's arm. Dogstar seemed to know the way. 'Come on,' Phillip said. 'Dogstar wants us to follow.'

They ran into a breeze-filled tunnel. Phillip thought it might be the entrance to a cave, but it was only an arch of rock and it opened out into fresh air. They found themselves in a sandy desert again. It was lit with a twilight glow.

The desert stretched out to meet a line of far-off cliffs. 'We're on the road to the netherworld and must find the gateway,' Phillip said.

There were dunes around them, shifting as if disturbed by a breeze, forming and reforming themselves in wavy lines. A growing hiss made them put on a spurt. The wavy lines were snakes. Julia screamed softly, a muffled sound with the back of her hand over her mouth.

'The road to the gateway is infested with snakes,' Phillip told them. 'Just keep moving.'

'Horrible!' Julia shuddered.

One shiny, dark snake came slithering into their path and Dogstar broke free. The dog snapped the reptile between sharp teeth and shook it, cracking it like a whip and throwing it distastefully aside. Another came and another. They ran.

Coomber turned to see if the ferryman was following. He discovered much worse behind them. 'Don't look at what's coming after us!'

Phillip twisted to look as they ran. He saw a snake as wide as a path slithering behind them. Its head was squat and diamond-shaped and its eyes shone like headlights.

'What can we do? It's catching us.'

Julia screamed.

'Throw something at it.'

'What?'

They hunted for stones in the sand as they ran, but there were none, only wavy patterned sand where snakes had left their wriggled signatures on its surface. Coomber dug into his pocket and came out holding a few shining ingots of copper and silver and gold, the money from the ferryman's boat.

He stopped and threw them at the snake, like a load of buckshot. The serpent's mouth opened like a wet trap, swallowing the scraps whole; it didn't hurt the creature, but it stopped it. It curled up in a circle and raised its head to watch them go.

They came to some pink-coloured cliffs. The moon had paled. Darkness was settling. It was very quiet here. This was the realm of the goddess Merseger, the lover of silence, Phillip guessed.

Dogstar slowed. They toiled up a path that led up the cliff face. 'What are we looking for?'

'I don't know,' Phillip said. 'Somewhere there's a gateway. I don't know what it looks like.'

They saw torches shining in the dark and Phillip knew that others had found the gateway ahead of them. He signalled the others to drop under cover behind some rocks. They saw two white men dressed in khaki and three dark men of the desert wrapped in Arab galabias and with strips of cloth around their heads.

'We're not alone.'

'They can show us the way.'

'They're not here to show us the way,' Phillip said. 'We're in trouble if they see us.' He saw the glow of a torch splash on a mustard yellow surface – a roll of papyrus in one of the men's hands. . . Uncle William's papyrus. These were the thieves, the ones who had raided his grave at Ravenwood. They were consulting the scroll not as a book of magic, but as if it were a map, pointing to it and then at a rocky ledge near an overhang of rock.

The new arrivals settled back in the cooling desert air

to watch the strangers. Phillip told Coomber then about his uncle's grave and how his uncle and the papyrus had disappeared. Also about the stranger Willard Chase who had gone to look for him.

'Couldn't you have left him to find your uncle,' Coomber said, grumbling, 'instead of dragging us into this?'

Phillip ignored him. 'We've got to follow them. I have an idea that Uncle's scroll was not just a normal *Book of the Dead*; it's some kind of map.'

But where would it lead?

When it was safe they would follow, he decided — but carefully, in case the men had posted a guard at the entrance.

4

Anubis

THE REST GAVE PHILLIP TIME to collect his thoughts. Events had tumbled one upon the other with speed and shocking unexpectedness.

'I'm getting cold,' Julia said, shivering.

Archaeology was a patient science, where toothbrushes and sieves were more respectable implements than bulldozers and shovels. The people on the cliff weren't archaeologists. They set into the rock on the ledge with picks that made sparks fly off. Was it bare rock they were chipping through? Or a filled entranceway?

The ring of their biting picks set a jackal howling in the valley below. Dogstar whined.

There were crumbling sounds and the ringing stopped. They heard one of the men give an excited shout. There were more blows with the picks and the sound of rubble falling hollowly into a gap behind.

They watched as the group widened the hole they had made and then they saw their torches swallowed up by the hole. They waited until they could no longer hear them, then approached the entrance cautiously. Had they left a guard?

A pile of stone lay crumbled at the entrance. Had it

been an inscribed door or a bare door disguised to look like virgin rock?

The gap yawned blackly. 'We can't go in without a light,' Julia said sensibly.

That's when Phillip tapped his denim pocket and discovered his bicycle headlamp. He switched it on. 'You knew we were doing this. You even packed a torch,' Coomber said, aggrieved.

'I used it when I rode to the cemetery,' he said. 'Let's follow before they get too far ahead.'

They went along a tunnel, the bicycle lamp throwing a fan of light. It wasn't a man-made tunnel; it was more like a bedding plane in a natural limestone cave. As they went further along, the quietness gave way to the drip of water. It was everywhere; some drops falling with musical plinking sounds, others making clicking sounds like geckoes on a summer's night, other drops ringing throatily in hollows like the sound of frogs.

The air was laden with moisture like a cool breath. It played on Phillip's body, cooling him still more after his run through the desert.

The passage gradually throttled, making them bend double to clear a jagged, saw-toothed roof. It brought them down to the water, an underground stream that scoured noisily over limestone. Here the air was swollen with moisture and it ached with cold. The rushing stream carried an invisible second stream of icy air on its back.

Phillip wondered how they were going to cross the stream, but the lamp showed him a way. Beside a cluster of freakish helictites, pointed like a hand, they found a place to cross. They saw a row of stepping stones tearing little streaks in the surface of the stream. They crossed on them gingerly, careful not to slip on the soapy-textured stone.

Once across the stream, they followed Phillip's beam

of torchlight along a gallery beside the water. It was flanked by a wall draped with formations of fragile, flowstone curtains stained with minerals. He stubbed his sneaker on a flake of rock as he walked and the fractured limestone gave off a pungent, gun-powder fragrance.

The passage they followed again narrowed. They had to bend. It took them into another section. They straightened to find themselves in a haughty chamber. Phillip felt as if they had entered the ice-palace innards of a monster. Wet stalactites, stalagmites, crazy helictites that defied gravity, flowstone, oozing moonmilk and rimstone pools — they all gave the impression of a giant stomach at work digesting something. He hoped it wasn't them.

He remembered the story of Jonah swallowed by a whale. It was a story in the Book that his grandmother had read to him, the Book with the soft, leathery cover like the touch of his grandmother's hands.

The ceiling and the rear of the chamber receded in darkness. They looked around wonderingly. The most striking feature of the cave was a natural limestone formation near a wall. 'Hey, that looks like a throne,' Coomber said. 'I wonder if anybody's ever sat on it? I'm going to be first.'

'Be careful—'

He jumped into the cradle of stone. 'Okay peasants, I'm in command.' He banged the arm of the chair with his fist. It turned the world upside down. The limestone floor suddenly gave way. The throne tipped Coomber out and they all slid like laundry in a laundry chute down a smooth tunnel of rock.

'Phillip!' Julia reached for Phillip's hand and he grabbed hers. They slid hand-in-hand into a void. He still held the torch in the other hand, its wobbly beam wildly searching the darkness. He had impressions of the rock sliding past his eyes in a blur before they levelled out, skidding over a smooth, flat floor of stone.

They sat up.

'Is everybody okay?'

Phillip ran his torch over the frightened faces of Julia and Coomber and Dogstar who came and licked his face to reassure him. They were in a chamber deeper down, yet it was pierced by a dim fall of starlight that did not light the whole chamber, but gave form to a tall tablet of stone in its centre.

They went closer. Phillip's bicycle lamp flickered and went out. He shook it, tapping it against his leg. Perhaps the batteries had jumped out of their sockets. He flicked it once or twice, but nothing happened.

'Let's take a look at that stone,' he said. There was light enough to see it. It looked like a monument rather than a natural formation. It was smooth and had a chiselled edge.

They went closer. It was like the shock of discovering your own name written on a gravestone. He heard Julia's sharp intake of breath.

Three names and symbols were written there, dimly lit by starlight.

Carved in stone was the name 'Phillip Simpson' and beside it a hieroglyph of a dog or a jackal. Below it was 'Julia Smith' and beside it the symbol of a crocodile. Then 'Barry Coomber' and beside it the sign of a serpent.

'How can this be?' Julia said. 'It isn't possible. Who knew we were coming? It's all written here as if someone knew.'

'It's the Tablet of Destiny,' Phillip said.

'*Our* destiny? But what does it mean? Is it a prophecy?' Julia said.

Phillip shrugged. 'It's a warning, at least. I must be careful of a dog or a jackal. You, Coomber, must watch out for a serpent and you, Julia, look out for a crocodile.'

'I've already had a scare from a crocodile,' Julia said. 'In the reeds.'

'And I've already been frightened out of my wits by a snake, the one I threw the money at. But what about the dog next to your name?'

Phillip didn't tell them that the ibis bird had warned him about a doom dog. Dogstar nudged Phillip and he patted its head. 'We'll see,' he said swallowing.

'It looks like that dog of yours.'

'Don't be dumb, Coomber,' he said.

Phillip was still fiddling with his bicycle headlamp when they heard a regular *tap tap tapping* sound followed by approaching footsteps. He felt Dogstar's fur bristle against his jeans. Its growl rumbled deep in its throat. They peered into the twilight of the chamber.

A man came with a stick, tapping the floor in front of himself, like an insect with its feeler. He was an old, bald man with a shiny dome head and a spotted animal skin wrapped around him.

Phillip fiddled more urgently with the batteries and his bicycle lamp jumped into life. He shone it in the stranger's eyes, but the old man didn't blink. The milky scars of blindness lay over his eyes. 'I am the blind servant,' he said. 'I will lead you into purification. Come with me, helpless ones.'

'We're not helpless and we're not going with you until you tell us where you're taking us,' Julia said firmly.

'This is the only way beyond. You must be pure to go to the next stage. You must go through purification.'

'I could do with a freshening up,' Coomber said.

They gathered to confer. 'What do we do?' they asked Phillip.

'I don't know,' he said. 'I don't like the look of him and neither does Dogstar, but if it's the only way ahead. . .'

'What's a creepy old guy like this doing down here, anyway? And what does purification mean? I don't like the sound of it.'

'Sounds like some kind of decontamination chamber.'

They didn't know what else to do: they were a bit shaken by the revelation of the tablet and overcome by a feeling that they had lost control and passed into the power of other forces. They reluctantly followed the blind man.

It was a mistake.

They were led into a dimly lit chamber where a gang of bald-headed dwarves pounced on them. Julia screamed and Coomber and Phillip wrestled a few of them to the ground. Dogstar flew at one of them, but was immediately snared in a net by two more, while others swiftly ran lengths of binding material like bandages around the dog, immobilising it.

'The dead must be purified,' the blind servant said. 'It serves no purpose struggling.'

They were dragged to marble blocks. 'We're not dead, you horrible old man,' Julia shouted at him. 'Let us go. Phillip, can't you do something? What's happening to us?'

Phillip was as powerless and baffled as the rest of them. Though small, the malignant dwarves were muscular and moved with silent power. Mutes. They held each of them down on the marble blocks while their legs and arms were secured with ropes.

A broad-shouldered man wearing a black jackal mask came into the room and the old man bowed. 'I am Anubis, the Lord of the Westerners,' the jackal-headed one said, in a voice muffled by the mask. 'I am the god of the wrappings. I will prepare you for wrapping, helpless ones. But first we must remove your heart for the Weighing of the Heart in the Pylons of Osiris that is to follow.'

They're just trying to frighten us, Phillip thought.

'Get away!' Julia screamed as they came at her with knives and pincers. But they didn't touch her with the instruments. They pretended to cut her open and to pull living organs from her body, yet there was nothing to see. An attendant held out a jar and the dwarves dropped unseen things into the bottom, things that landed in the jar with wet slaps.

It was a clever trick. They did it to each of them. It was quite realistic, Phillip thought.

'They're not going to mummify us, are they?' Coomber said. 'I don't want to end up like a casualty case.' One of the mutes had discovered the length of crepe bandage that was still wrapped around Coomber's neck and he unwound it, stretching it interestedly between his stubby fingers as if amazed at its stretch quality.

'You must wait for the next stage of purification, where you will soak in a bath of dry natron. You will be purified for seventy days before you can go further,' the jackal-headed one said.

'Seventy days!' Coomber said in a high, indignant voice.

Then the chilling creatures withdrew, taking torches with them and leaving them alone in the gloom of the chamber. 'We're lucky,' Phillip said to cheer them all up. 'If we were royalty, we'd be purified for 120 days.'

'That's not a lot of a comfort,' Julia said. 'We're stuck and nobody can help us, not even Dogstar.'

Was the man in the jackal mask the dog of doom? Phillip wondered. Was it going to end in failure so early? Phillip tasted despair.

With the cold stone pressing on their backs, they lay in the darkness, talking, trying to keep the fears away from their minds.

'I wonder what my mother will be saying? She always checks on me late at night before she goes to bed,' Phillip said, 'although she hasn't done it lately. She won't come into my room on account of the bird.'

'Mine doesn't,' Julia said. 'Mine probably wouldn't notice if I never came back. That's what happens when you don't have your own parents.'

Phillip twisted his head so that he could see her. 'Why do you always say things like that, Julia? Your new parents care a lot about you.'

'No, they don't. It's never the same as having your real parents.'

'What happened to your real parents?' Phillip knew, but he wanted her to talk, to take their minds off their situation.

'They gave me away.'

'I heard they were killed in a car crash.'

'Same thing. They left me,' she said.

Seventy days. It was a funny place for it to end. The ropes were tight. Even Dogstar was bound up tight.

'Bedtime, kids? Want me to tuck you in?' Willard Chase, the archaeological detective, crept into the chamber and flashed a torchlight into Phillip's face.

'Don't do that,' Phillip said.

'What, shine the torch?'

'Make jokes. Get us out of here, quickly.'

They ran along a passageway decorated like a tomb with processions of sunburnt men carrying offerings of food and wine, fowls and loaves of bread. Up above them the ceiling was painted with a myriad of stars. They reached a fork in the passageway. They stopped. 'Right or left?' Phillip asked the stranger.

'Um. . .' Willard Chase scratched his chin. 'I don't really know.'

'You don't know? I thought you were an expert on the

underworld!'

'Not this underworld, the criminal underworld, and I'm afraid my sense of direction lets me down occasionally.'

Having a bad sense of direction would be quite a handicap for a man who crawled around pyramids and tombs, Phillip thought. 'All I know is that we must keep heading west,' the archaeological detective said. He gave a shrug. 'I guess we'll try this way. Follow me.'

Dogstar pulled back and wouldn't follow. 'You're going the wrong way,' Phillip said. Dogstar made a dive in the opposite direction, jerking Phillip towards the other passage. 'My dog knows the way. We'll follow his nose.'

'Handy,' Willard Chase said. 'A dog with a magnetic nose!'

They followed Dogstar's lead. When they were sure that we weren't being followed, they slowed. 'How did you kids get here?' Willard Chase asked them as they walked. Willard Chase's flashlight was brighter than Phillip's bicycle lamp. Phillip pocketed his lamp to save the batteries.

'We stowed away.'

'On a jet aircraft?'

'On a boat.'

'You couldn't have got here on a boat. I only saw you a short while ago. You must have flown. Wealthy parents, huh?'

'My uncle gave me something before he died,' Phillip said, referring to the bird.

'Ah, an inheritance.' Willard nodded understandingly. 'And you decided to start a search of your own. I told you to leave it to me.'

'Just as well I didn't if you can't find your way around down here. Maybe we can help each other. We're both looking for my uncle.'

Willard shook his head. 'Let's get something straight. I'm not looking for your uncle. He's dead. I'm looking for that copy of the *Book of the Dead*. It's a very valuable document. It isn't what it seems and it shouldn't be in the wrong hands. Those grave robbers could use it to let a great deal of evil into the world.'

'Let me guess,' Phillip said. 'It's more than a collection of magical spells; it's an ancient map. Am I right?'

'You're pretty smart, kid. That's right. It's a map leading to the real treasures of Egypt hidden in the underworld and guarded, according to legend, by the guardians of the underworld.'

'You mean those loonies who captured us?'

'No, they were probably just some harmless crazies living among the ruins. You mustn't believe in such things as animal-headed gods, demons and guardians. They don't exist except in people's minds. I've spent years and years chasing around places like this and I've never yet seen a mummy sit up in a sarcophagus or a demon stalk down a corridor.'

'It's good to have a grown-up along,' Julia said, reassured by Willard's calming influence. 'I was getting very frightened with just us three kids running around down here on our own. We were seeing things — snakes and crocodiles and people with their heads on backwards.'

The passage opened up into a chamber. They walked into the chamber of slaughter, a storm of swinging knives with blades that shone like lightning flashes.

5

The hall of knives

THEY STOOD IN A HALL OF KNIVES, each knife attached
to a pendulum pole and swinging from the ceiling in
long, scything strokes. The slaughtering knives of the
Book of the Dead.

It was like being inside the Grim Reaper's grandfather
clock. Buzzz. A knife made a long swishing run in front
of them. They turned around to go back. Another knife
swung behind them, and another, sealing their exit. Julia
screamed and jumped onto Willard's back.

'What do we do, Willard?' Phillip yelled.

'This isn't good,' Willard said.

Phillip saw a beam above their heads. 'Haven't you
got a whip or something you can use to grab onto that
beam?' Phillip said.

The archaeological detective screwed up his face in
disbelief. 'Whips aren't exactly standard equipment in
archaeology!'

Willard had clearly never watched an *Indiana Jones*
movie. 'Never mind.' Phillip had seen an escape.
Through the swinging forest of blades, he saw a ladder
rising out of the chamber. 'There's a ladder in the middle
of the chamber,' he shouted. 'We must try to get to it!

Grab a pole when it swings by and ride it to the ladder, only watch out for the blades.' What about Dogstar? He'd be quick enough and agile enough to dodge the blades, Phillip decided. 'Go to the ladder, boy,' Phillip said. Dogstar knew about ladders and how to climb them.

'You expect me to catch one of those whizzing blades?' Coomber said, shrinking as a blade swished close enough to shave his arm.

'You're crazy,' Willard said to Phillip.

'If we don't try it, we're going to end up like sliced salami!'

Phillip waited until a deadly pendulum arced past, then he sprang up, catching the pole high enough to avoid the gleaming metal blade at its base. It must have had some weighted mechanism. It wasn't just swinging with its own weight. It sucked Phillip away, taking him at exhilarating speed to the back of the chamber.

'Get ready, Julia!' he shouted. He held out an arm to grab her, using his sneaker to shield the cutting edge of the blade as it swished by on the return. Julia let go of Willard Chase and leaned out to meet him. Phillip swept her up in one arm. She managed to get one hand to the pendulum and the other to Phillip's ear. He pulled her close and she let go of his ear and took the pole and they swung away, their cheeks pressed together.

Encouraged by their trapeze work, Willard and Coomber tried it next. Soon they were all swinging like mice in a grandfather clock.

'Jump off at the ladder!' Phillip shouted to the others. Phillip and Julia were lucky. Their pendulum blade took them close to the ladder. 'Make a grab for it as we go by,' he said to Julia, who had screwed her eyes shut in terror. She opened her eyes to look. The ladder rushed to meet them. She gave a squeal and Phillip let go of her.

She jumped and landed firmly on the ladder. 'Good girl!'

He climbed a bit higher up the pole and waited for it to swing back to the ladder. The pole reached the end of its swing, paused, then rushed back. He saw Dogstar dart nimbly between the blades to reach the ladder safely.

Phillip leapt. He landed on the ladder above Julia. Willard landed on the floor not far from the base of the ladder where Dogstar now crouched, its head held low to stay clear of the passing blades. Coomber hit the ladder with a force that would have shaken it if it wasn't made of bronze and he ended up with his legs sticking through the rungs.

They climbed — the Ladder to Heaven. Phillip remembered the chapter headings in the *Book of the Dead*.

They climbed into a misty light, with the air growing thick and perfumed. Phillip reached the top first and stepped onto a stone floor. The others followed. He bent at the ladder and looked down the hole at Dogstar.

Dogstar, still crouching at the base of the ladder, lifted its pointy face to look up. It gave a shrill bark. 'Come on, 'Star boy. Up! You can make it.' He whistled through fingers jammed in the corners of his mouth. Dogstar shot up the ladder like a whippet after a hare.

'Some dog!' Willard said, impressed. 'And you're some kid. That was quick thinking down there, Phillip,' Willard Chase congratulated him. 'Amazing. Obviously you've done this sort of thing before.'

'You mean you haven't? I thought you were in the archaeology business? Indiana Jones does things like that in his sleep.'

'Not me. I do most of my investigations on my knees with a magnifying glass.'

They had climbed to another level inside a structure. The walls were made of huge slabs of stone. They decided to press on. Guided by Dogstar, they followed a passageway.

The tomb robbers must have heard them coming and set a trap for them. They entered what looked like a burial chamber. As they went through a stone archway, great blocks suddenly rumbled like thunder behind them, throwing dust and stone chips in a shower over their heads. The force alone helped propel them to the other exit, but only Willard and Dogstar made it through. An avalanche of heavy slabs thundered down in front of the remaining three, blocking their way and shutting off the light of Willard's torch.

They threw themselves onto the floor and covered their heads while bits of stone and dust rained around them. When the noise stopped, they sat up, coughing.

'Where's Dogstar?'

'He made it through with Willard.'

'Well, at least somebody got through. We're not all stuck in here. Somebody can help dig us out.' Phillip found his bicycle headlamp and switched it on, playing the cone of light on the pile of rubble in front of them.

'Are you kidding?' Coomber said. 'Look at that pile. It looks like a mountain's fallen down. It'd take an army to get us out of here.'

'Why did Willard have to go ahead of us? We're on our own again and we don't even have Dogstar to help,' Julia said fretfully. 'Willard's not going to save us this time.'

'He didn't save us last time,' Phillip said drily.

He got up and went to look around the room. It had been a burial chamber once, but there were no treasures left now. Like so many tombs, it had been plundered in antiquity. The only things left were rows of stumpy figurines collected in boxes.

'You wanted an army — well, we've got one,' he said, going to the boxes.

Julia joined him. 'Little clay men. What are they?'

'They're servant statues. They're called *ushabtis*.'

'What do they do?'

'They do work for people in the next life. Thousands of these little figurines were buried in tombs. They were labour-saving devices for souls in the other world. In ancient times, the Egyptians were liable to be recruited for public work and so they dreaded the same thing happening in the next life. These statues were called "Answerers" by the Egyptians. If their souls were called upon to do work in the next life, these substitute figurines would answer in their place, saying "Here am I".'

Phillip ran his light over the rows of stumpy, mummiform figurines. They stood with their arms crossed, holding hoes in each hand and a basket on their backs. They wore pleasant expressions on their faces.

'They're cute,' Julia said, 'like the seven dwarves.'

'Seven hundred dwarves, would be more like it. There's an army of them here.'

'Great. We need an army to dig us out,' Coomber said, cynically. 'Why don't we put them to work?'

Phillip shone his light on Coomber. 'What did you say?'

'I said we need an army to dig us out. Stop shining that light in my eyes.'

An idea surfaced like an unexpected life raft in Phillip's mind. It was a mad hope, but then this was a mad night. 'Maybe we can put them to work for us,' he said. 'Take them out of their boxes, all of them. Stand them in rows on the floor. I have an idea.'

'This is no time to play with garden gnomes, Phillip.'

'They're not garden gnomes. They're labourers, magical labourers dedicated to serve. Let's see if they can do some work for us. Let's see if they really do obey.'

Phillip took the small men glazed with blue faïence

and set them on the floor. It was a bigger job than Phillip had expected. It was a labour force of hundreds.

'This is the dumbest thing I ever heard. It's mindless,' Coomber said.

'I don't know what we're doing or why,' Julia said, 'but we might as well be mindless since anything's possible tonight. I suppose it's better than sitting around waiting for the air to run out.'

Coomber reluctantly joined in. They worked rapidly in the torchlight. Soon a host of figurines stood like an army on parade.

Phillip chose one of the dumpy figures, a larger one than the rest — possibly an overseer, he guessed. The *ushabti* was a genial-looking fellow with bulbous features, ears pushed out by a bulky wig and a helpful smile on his face. A false beard hung from his chin. Hieroglyphic writing ran around his mummiform base.

'What does the writing say?'

'I can't read hieroglyphics, but I do happen to know what it says, almost word for word. My Uncle William had lots of *ushabtis* in his collection and he translated the inscriptions for me. I'm going to say it out loud. Stand back.' They fell in behind him as he squatted on the floor, the blue *ushabti* in his hands.

'O Ushabti! If Phillip is required for labour in the Hereafter, say thou "Here am I".'

'O Ushabti! If Julia is required for labour in the Hereafter, say thou "Here am I".'

'O Ushabti! If Coomber is required for labour in the Hereafter, say thou "Here am I".'

'I *thought* this was mindless,' Coomber said.

The army of small men remained motionless. One on a rickety base fell over and splintered with a sound that made them jump.

'You shouldn't put your faith in magic, Phillip,' Julia

said, sternly disapproving.

Nothing's going to happen, Phillip thought, his shoulders drooping. He was wrong. Something did happen. The connection in his torch broke again. The torch flickered then went out. Darkness swarmed in front of his eyes. 'Hang on folks, I'll soon have it working again.'

He felt for the small, grooved edge that slid back to open the battery housing. He found it with his thumb but, as he pulled on it, one of the pencil torchlight batteries sprang out like a stone from a catapult and rattled across the floor. He reached out for it and a small warm foot stepped on his hand in the dark. 'Stay where you are, Julia.'

'I'm not moving.'

'You too, Coomber.'

'I'm not moving.'

The chamber was filled with the sound of scuttling feet.

'I've lost a battery. It's rolled over the floor somewhere. Hang on a minute; can't be far.' Another small foot stepped on Phillip's outstretched hand. Something bumped his arm and moved it aside.

'Are there rats in here?' Julia said in a shivery voice. 'What's all that scurrying?' The chamber was rustling with the sound of shuffling figures. There was a clinking sound and a small spark flew off some stone. Then there were more ringing sounds of metal hitting stone.

'Somebody's trying to dig us out.'

'Good old Willard.'

It sounded like a vast working party, Phillip thought.

'They must be getting close. Sounds as if they're right here with us.'

The chipping and banging reached a ringing clangour. Bits of rocks crumbled onto the floor. In the confined space of the chamber, it sounded like machine-gun fire. Phillip went on hands and knees looking for the missing battery. How far could it have rolled? He found it just as the rescue party broke through and Willard's torch dashed light into the room. There was a small stampede and things rushed from the searching yellow glare of Willard's lamp.

Rats?

'You guys okay?'

'We're fine,' Julia said gratefully. Phillip stuffed the battery along with the bicycle headlamp into a pocket.

'You guys must have been pretty keen to get out of here. What did you use, jackhammers?' Willard said. 'How did you break through so fast?'

They looked at each other. Then they looked at the *ushabtis.*

The army of figurines stood immobile, frozen to attention on parade. 'Got company, I see,' Willard grinned. 'Come on. I discovered it was the tomb robbers who tried to stop us, but they've moved on.'

Phillip was the last to leave the chamber. 'Thanks, men,' he whispered to the assembled figures in the darkened chamber. 'Great work.'

Perhaps it was the squeal of his rubber-soled sneakers on the stone floor as he turned, but Phillip thought he heard a chuckle behind him.

They pressed along a coldly sweating stone passage that stretched endlessly ahead of them. They no longer needed their torches here, for the walls were lit by a series of wall-mounted torches with rasping flames.

'Perpetual fire,' Willard explained. The torches threw their moving silhouettes on the walls like a running frieze of soul-shades — a boy holding a shadow dog with a sharp, jackal face and pointed ears like spear tips, a man in a hat, leaning forward as he made big strides along the passage, a girl with flying plaits of hair and bringing up the rear, a bulky boy.

They reached a 'T' junction in the passage. Dogstar hesitated, momentarily unsure. He sniffed the air exploratively, his pointy snout swivelling around like a gun barrel.

'West will be this way, I'd say,' Willard Chase said, pointing one way. Dogstar immediately took off in the opposite direction. 'So I was a hundred per cent wrong,' the man of archaeology said sheepishly.

Willard was turning out to be dead reliable when it came to choosing directions, Phillip decided. The man was consistently wrong.

'Whoa!'

The line of running figures collapsed into each other like a telescope folding when Phillip brought them to a halt, holding out his arms to prevent them running on.

'What is it?'

They moved around Phillip to see, blinking in wonder. The stone passage suddenly widened to present a towering stone pylon. Its top was lost in darkness. Twin entrances cut black squares in the stone and out of each of these squares stepped a glittering creature with a feather on its head and a feather-shaped sword swinging in its hand.

It spoke. Or at least they both did at once in a silvery harmony like a stream chattering over stones. 'We are the two sides of Maat, the Lady of Tremblings, the goddess of truth. One of us is truth, the other falsehood.

'Before you may pass our gateway, you must solve a mystery. One of us can only tell the truth and one of us can only lie. The real entrance lies behind the sister of truth and death lies behind the sister of lies. You may ask one question of either of us, one question only to determine who guards the door of truth. If you are right, you may pass; if you are wrong, you will be slain.'

As if to underline this threat, the sisters took a step nearer and swung their feather-shaped blades, making the air whistle. They were identical; very beautiful in a glittery-eyed way, dressed in gauzy pleated dresses, like the paintings of goddesses in tomb frescoes. Their eyes were dramatically painted in the Egyptian style — and swept up at the corners — and their mounds of long dark hair were threaded with gold. They looked like a couple of very lovely and deadly bookends, Phillip thought.

They must have picked up his thoughts. 'You,' they said, pointing at him, 'the one who is not afraid. You may ask the question.'

He shrank from their pointed fingers. 'Why me?'

'This is your journey of truth. You must face the first challenge.'

Phillip swallowed.

'Are you frightened of a couple of girls?' Coomber said derisively. 'They're just holograms anyway. Watch.'

He went closer. It was like walking into spinning propellor blades. The ladies swung their swords in a blur of whistling metal.

'Watch where you swing those things!' Coomber said, backing hastily away, examining a nick in his shirt sleeve. 'You could cut somebody.'

'I don't think they're holograms,' Willard said.

'Ask the question!' they said imperiously.

'Maybe we should run for it,' Willard Chase said.

The sisters of the sword smiled and pointed behind Willard. A huge block of stone rumbled and fell into place with a ground-jarring crash, sealing off their escape. 'I'll do it, I'll ask the question,' Julia said, quickly. 'I'm good at puzzles. Let me.'

'*He* must ask it!' the twin goddesses said, pointing to

Phillip, and the silvery stream of the harmony of their voices took on a cold, rattling edge as if slivers of ice had entered it. Dogstar gave an excited bark and sank to the floor, making itself comfortable as if settling to watch a show.

At least Dogstar was confident, Phillip thought.

He stepped closer to the two glittering ladies. They stood immobile, their swords raised above their heads in a threatening pose. He examined them in turn. As he paced thoughtfully in front of them, their eyes followed him, sliding like gleaming dark fish in their beautiful, painted faces.

'How long have I got?' Phillip said to them.

'Take care!' they said, quivering. 'That is a question in itself!'

'Sorry. But that's not my real question. . . and there's one more. . .' The ladies tottered a bit as if they were going to set on him with their swords. 'No. No,' he said hastily, drawing back a bit. 'Just a question about the rules. . .'

'Do not attempt to trick us.'

'No, it's an honest question, really.'

'Speak.'

'Can my question be about anything?' It was important to know this. If he were permitted a question about anything, he could simply ask one of them if his name really was Phillip. If the lady was the liar, she'd say no; if the truthful one, yes.

The glittering sisters weren't stupid. 'Only a question about the right doorway or guardian is permitted. We shall merely answer "Yes" or "No".'

Phillip shrugged. 'Not that easy, hm? Well, it was worth a try.'

Phillip inspected the first one. She reminded him of an old-time pop singer called Cher. So did the other one.

Which one was the liar? How did liars look? Did they look any different from other people? Liars were supposed to avoid looking you in the eye, weren't they? He tried staring them out in turn: their stares made him tremble inside. Their unblinking, dark eyes were as mysterious as night.

He wished Julia were facing this test. Julia could see through them. She knew about puzzles and games. She could figure it out. Somewhere at the back of his mind, Phillip had a memory of this puzzle. It was a very ancient puzzle. If only he had taken the trouble to find out the answer. It just proved that no knowledge was truly wasted and even a piece of trivia could save your skin. You never knew when it would come in handy.

Now it was an examination question with very deadly results if he failed. The grim sisters would use their blades deftly, he had no doubt.

Truth. Which one was the lady of truth?

His eyes went up to the top of one of the guardian's heads where a tall feather, an ostrich plume, stood, the ancient Egyptian symbol of truth, the feather that was weighed against a man's heart in the scales of truth in the Hall of Judgment. This was his journey of truth, the ladies had said.

He groped for ideas. What question could he ask just one of them that would reveal the truth? 'Have you ever told a lie?' Would that reveal the answer? Everyone has told a lie. No, these were goddesses: things were different for them.

'Ask your question, youth!' they said and they laughed in a silvery way.

6

The great ape

PHILLIP GLANCED AT THE OTHERS.   They stood in a
semicircle, watching.   'Go very, very carefully,' Julia's
look said.   'It's a game, so think of the rules and how
you can use them.'

'Good luck, kid,' Willard Chase's expression said.
'You're pretty smart; let's see what you've got this time.'
'Serves you right,' Barry Coomber's eyes said, shining
maliciously.

Dogstar lay panting, its tongue lolling from its mouth
and the mouth itself half-smiling as if it were thoroughly
enjoying Phillip's predicament.   Its ears twitched expectantly like radar dishes as if waiting to catch Phillip's
response.

Phillip turned back to the guardians of the double
gateway.

Like a climber on a sheer cliff face, his mind hunted
for a crack of hope, a tiny foothold that would provide
some purchase.   What were the facts?   One lady could
only lie.   One lady could only tell the truth.   Yet there
was one more fact they had revealed.   The doorway, the
escape, lay behind the lady who told the truth.   Somehow
that narrowed the possibilities.   These were the only

cracks in the wall.

He jammed some tiny mental pitons into these cracks and raised himself on their logic. A positive lady and a negative lady. A plus and a minus. If only he had paid more attention in algebra class. There was probably a mathematical solution to this puzzle if he could think of it. Plus times minus was a. . .

Forget algebra — he was confusing himself. He must think of a single, revealing question to ask.

He must calm down. It was like answering exam questions — he could never answer them in a panic. He must still his mind. There were ripples in his mind. He willed the ripples to steady. With an effort of will, he pictured his mind as a calm surface like a lake and now he began to cast questions on it like a fly fisherman, but none of his hook-like questions had the power to catch the truth he wanted.

One question to one lady. It couldn't produce the right answer. He was casting in the wrong direction. There was no single question he could ask just one lady about herself and her doorway that would reveal the answer he needed. That, too, was a fact. He raised himself a little bit higher on that fact.

The new view it afforded him allowed him to see another fact. If there wasn't a question he could put to a lady about herself and her doorway that would give him the answer, there must be another question that wasn't about the lady he addressed or her doorway.

It would need to be a question put to one lady about the other. Yes. That was the key to the riddle.

A large gap appeared in the cliff face. It was big enough to jam a sneaker into. He was starting to feel more secure on the cliff face. He saw a flicker of a frown appear in one of the guardian's foreheads.

Now he had to formulate a question that would attract

a 'Yes' or 'No' answer. But it had to be a question that would attract a different answer from each of them. One would have to say 'Yes' and the other 'No'.

Does your sister guard the exit? No, that wouldn't help. If she said 'Yes' or 'No', he still wouldn't know. The answer lay in the way they would be constrained to answer by their natures. Use the *rules*.

'I have my question,' he said, calmly.

'Then ask it.'

He picked one of the guardians at random and went close to her. He could smell the perfume of mysterious unguents surrounding her. The sword in the hands above her head swayed warningly.

'My question is this. . .'

He heard Julia catch her breath. She made a strangling noise like a student in class who is bursting to give an answer to a teacher's question, but who has not been asked. Julia had worked it out. Trust Julia. Dogstar closed its mouth with a snap and gulped. Willard shifted uneasily behind him. 'He's bluffing,' Coomber murmured.

'Ask it.' The sword quivered.

'Here is my one question: If I asked your sister if she was the one guarding the exit, would her answer be "Yes"?'

A spark leapt into the eyes of the goddess.

Phillip's question left only two possibilities. If he'd asked the truthful sister if her lying sister would answer 'Yes', she would have to say 'Yes' on behalf of her sister — she would know that her sister would tell a lie. On the other hand, if he'd asked the lying sister if her truthful sister would answer 'Yes', she would say 'No' — she had to twist the truth and lie.

Therefore, the sister who answered 'Yes' was the one telling the truth and the one who guarded the right doorway, and the one answering 'No' was the liar.

'You've heard my question. What is your answer?' Phillip said, emboldened.

'My answer is No! Curse you, boy!' the false goddess screamed. She exploded like a collapsing star in front of Phillip's eyes. A single feather floated down to the stone floor where she had stood.

Julia gave a cheer. Dogstar barked shrilly. 'Well done,' Willard Chase said.

'I knew the answer all along,' Barry Coomber said, yet a reluctant note of respect had crept into his tone.

The remaining guardian, the real lady of truth, smiled at Phillip and lowered her sword. 'You asked rightly, youth who loves the past. You may come through my gateway and I will meet you later to lead you into the Hall of Judgment, but only if you can pass more tests. . .' She stepped into the square of darkness of the entrance and disappeared.

'Clever Phillip!' Julia squeezed his arm. 'I thought I was good at games, but you hit on the answer before I did.' From Julia, it was high praise.

Willard Chase patted him on the back. 'Brilliant, but I suggest we get out of here quickly before the lady with the sword comes back and makes us all sit a written examination.'

They went through a dark entranceway that opened up into another torch-lit passageway. 'We've lost contact with the tomb robbers,' Willard said. 'They obviously have an easier way through the system. We must hurry.' They broke into a run.

Bright light and heat exploded around them, stabbing their eyes.

Phillip narrowed his eyes against the glare. They were out-of-doors in sunlight. How was it possible? They had left the darkness of the passage and come out blinking into dazzling midday. Ahead towered another mighty pylon of stone and in front of the gateway lay an ornamental garden with sycamores and date palms and a reed-fringed pool.

The air quivered with the heat. Phillip sucked some air into his lungs. It was fresher than the air in the passage, but so hot that it scalded. It was noon and shadows had crawled to the feet of the trees like hounds.

They were not alone in the garden. 'Look what's waiting for us this time,' Coomber said.

A giant dog-faced baboon sat in a pool of shade under a tree. They approached it cautiously. 'Careful,' Willard said. 'Baboons can inflict a nasty bite.'

It sat behind a gaming board at a trestle table and an empty chair stood across from it. It sat perched on its back legs in a high-backed inlaid chair and it was attended by a wrinkled old man. It waved a dark, rubbery paw at the new arrivals. 'Who will face the next challenge?' it said.

'What now?'

'To pass through the next gateway you must first defeat me, the great ape, in a game of senet.' The baboon pointed to a gaming board spread out on the table in front of it.

Julia pushed her way to the front. 'I'll play.'

'Anybody can beat a monkey,' Coomber said scornfully.

'That's no ordinary monkey; that's the god of wisdom,' Phillip said. 'It's Thoth the ibis bird in another form. He takes the shape of an ibis bird or an ape.'

'He's mine!' Julia said with relish. She went eagerly forward. 'I'll take him on.'

'A girl!' The ape laughed. 'You're going to challenge the victor of a thousand senet matches, you — a slip of a girl?'

Julia stitched a sweet smile on her face that the baboon

would have been wise to fear. 'I'll play with you.'

Willard Chase went to stop her. 'Maybe I should handle this one,' he said. 'I'm pretty good at chess.'

Phillip blocked his way. 'Julia isn't just pretty good; she's deadly. That big ape's in for a headache,' he said in a low voice.

Julia climbed happily into the chair. Phillip was starting to feel sorry for the baboon already. 'What are the rules and how do we play?' Julia asked. The old man went to her side and murmured in her ear.

Julia nodded as he spoke. Phillip studied the great ape. For an animal, the ape's gaze was disturbingly intelligent, Phillip thought. It had deep-set eyes that provoked. The eyes had the look of being startled by some sudden, brilliant insight. The ape had a long dog-like muzzle and big, savage teeth. Phillip noticed that its body was never at rest. It was as if its body were twisted by an energy inside itself trying to work itself out. It shifted in its chair, fiddled with the arm of it, scratched itself with long, useful fingers.

Julia nodded, following the old man's instructions about the game. 'Got it,' she said.

The old man went to the ape. 'May I set up the pieces now, Sacred Ape?'

The ape leaned forward, eager to begin. 'Theban rules?'

'Suits me,' Julia said. Julia had changed. The clean, sweet face of the girl had turned as cold and bright as a diamond.

The ape chose black and Julia white. The white and black pieces were set up on the board. The old man, who was acting as referee, handed the ape a leather cup. The ape rattled the contents; then, with a turn of its hairy wrist, spilled the dice in the form of three knucklebones onto the gaming board.

There was a murmur of disappointment from the baboon. It was a poor throw, it seemed, and did not qualify it to begin. The cup was given to Julia. She rattled the knucklebones before tipping them onto the board.

'White begins,' the referee intoned. The bones agreed, showing a perfect score. Julia looked pleased. It meant that she could begin to impose her pattern on the game. Julia never liked losing time. She opened her attack at the centre.

Phillip, Coomber and Willard Chase drew closer, into the shade of the tree. Dogstar went to sleep. The ape threw again. It was a better result this time, but still the bones did not agree.

Willard Chase murmured in Phillip's ear. 'It's a bit like chess, I seem to recall, except that the dice are used to open games and if necessary settle a draw. The object of the game is to penetrate the opponent's lines and capture his men, so it's a good thing that she's started early.'

Julia, looking calm, pressed her attack in the centre. The ape threw again, a little roughly this time so that one of the knucklebones tumbled off the edge of the board. Quick-fingered Barry Coomber caught it in midair, holding it in a clenched fist.

He held the ape's breath in his hand, for the remaining knucklebones on the board agreed and the ape's fate lay with Coomber. Since the knucklebone had not hit the floor, it was technically still in play. Coomber had only to place it on the board palm down. Barry Coomber hesitated.

Phillip guessed what he was doing. He was exploring the ridges of the knucklebone with tiny pressures of his palm. The ape looked spellbound. The referee coughed. Coomber put his hand down, still covering the knucklebone and, in doing so, gave it an almost imperceptible twist.

The ape cried out and the referee stiffened.

'Are you going to accept it or not?' Coomber said, smirking.

He was cheating, but at least he was trying to help Julia and that was something, Phillip thought.

The ape's eyes burnt into Coomber's. 'I accept it.'

Coomber lifted his hand. The bone agreed with the others on the table. Barry Coomber had helped the ape.

'You traitor!' Phillip said, giving him a shove. 'Whose side are you on, Coomber?'

'You two think you're so smart, so let's make a game of it. I hope he makes a monkey out of her!'

The ape licked its lips and opened its game, meeting Julia's attack. It recovered swiftly. In three moves it had blocked Julia's thrust, turning her thoughts back to defence.

The ape was quick and deadly.

Julia altered her style of play. She used one of her favourite tricks, closing her eyes between moves and studying the board in the serenity of her mind. It seemed to help. In five moves she regained firm enough ground to consider her next attack, but now the ape was taunting her with another line of attack.

The novelty of Julia's play went at first unnoticed by the baboon. It took it for a sign of concentration, but when her play began to slow and she spent long periods with her bright eyes closed, the ape leaned forward, directing a current of resentment across the board.

'Why does she sit with her eyes closed?' the ape growled. 'Does she think because I am a monkey that she can beat me in her sleep?'

Julia's head nodded like the heavy umbel of a papyrus plant in a breeze. A bee came to dream in the air around her head, but Phillip knew that there would be no dreams

going on in Julia's mind, even though she appeared to be
asleep. She would see clearly, as though lit by a shaft of
sunlight, an ivory board with thirty squares and black-
and-white patterns slowly forming on it.

'I wonder if this will wake her up?' the ape said in a
loud voice. Julia must have heard the firm click of an
ivory piece being placed on the board. Without looking,
she knew that the ape had placed the piece to provoke
her. It would be a bold move, daring her to seize an
opportunity.

A bee buzzed near Phillip's head, a drowsy sound.

The referee spoke. 'Your move, young mistress.'

'Wake up; it will be lights out for you soon enough!'
the ape said.

Julia opened her eyes and gave a small nod to herself,
confirming that its move was the one she expected.
Ignoring the offering, Julia opened a new line of attack
instead. It cost her one of her men. The ape sent her
reeling back.

It was just as well that Julia had decided to play in the
darkness of her mind. It helped her forget that she was
playing against a monkey. Looking at the creature, she
ran the risk of underestimating it. With her eyes closed,
she was better able to take its measure.

Even so it seemed that she was discovering the
presence of a vast mind and will, an intellect so broad
and deep that she could not get past it. It was always
there like an unending wall, blocking her way. Julia
fought back. The baboon closed in.

Julia's shoulders slumped a fraction. In the first few
moves she would have seen the depth of the ape's play.
Had she realised that in straight play she had little hope
of winning?

Her best chance lay in trying to defeat not the player,
but the animal. Julia held her ground, narrowly avoiding

the loss of another man. The ape sent one of its men in pursuit.

Julia closed her eyes, considering her next move in trance-like silence. She could probably sense the ape's frustration. It kicked the table, jarring the pieces on the board. The referee coughed gently and the ape stopped. Julia opened her eyes and placed the ape's pursuing man in danger.

The ape looked surprised.

The novelty of her playing style had given Julia some advantage, it appeared, but it was critical that she maintain it.

In the garden of the ape's mind she had planted a weed of uncertainty and now she would have to tend it so that it grew, feeding on the ape's powers of concentration. At that moment, the weed both fascinated and irritated it. How could she make it assume even greater importance in its mind?

The ape slipped out of danger. Julia made a move.

'I think that's a mistake,' Willard murmured to Phillip.

It was at this stage of the game that Julia had a bold idea and a change of tactic. Did she dare make the next move without opening her eyes? The ape shifted its piece, putting it down with a sharp click on the ivory board. Without opening her eyes, Julia tried to guess the move it had made.

'It's your turn to move, young mistress,' the old man said at a prompting glare from the ape.

Julia allowed her head to drop further, holding it in her hands so that she had no possibility of seeing. 'A request, referee. After my next move, I'd like all moves to be called out by yourself. I also request that you move my pieces for me.'

There was a pause as the old man considered this unusual request.

'Your answer, old man!' The ape snapped its teeth warningly.

The referee shrugged. 'As I see it, there is no unfair advantage to be gained from it. It is therefore within the rules and allowable.'

The ape fumed. Julia called out her next move with her head down and eyes shut. 'White on square nine to square eleven,' she said firmly. The referee carried out the instruction.

'How is it possible?' the ape said in a voice that struggled for understanding. 'Is she a magician that she can play in a trance?'

'You must play, Sire.'

'See, she has put me in grave danger, all without opening an eye!'

Julia waited with her head in her hands, her plaits hanging across the backs of her fingers. It was beginning to work. The weed in the ape's mind deepened its roots and spread, taking a firmer hold of the creature's concentration. Very soon, with luck, it would grow to become a tangle of confusion. The ape placed its next piece softly, surreptitiously.

'Black from square twenty-one to seventeen,' the referee called jarringly.

The garden held its breath, not a leaf stirring. 'White from eleven to fourteen,' Julia threw back swiftly.

The ape let out a hiss as the referee played out the move for the girl. 'I'll teach you to open your eyes, girl!'

The ape shifted its attention to another part of the board. Julia countered. It switched again to a new attack from a different quarter; the game grew richer, more complex.

Julia saw the ape's strategy. It was testing her memory, hoping by opening as many fronts as possible to confuse her. It did not know that in chess displays

Julia could play three games at the same time and win.
It did not know how clearly the pattern of the play lay
in the stillness of her mind. She was able to counter each
move successfully.

Julia's shoulders lifted. Strength flowed into her. She
took it from the ape.

'This is not allowed. You are distracting me with your
antics, girl,' the ape said in a voice that pleaded for support.
The referee replied with deference, but firmness, too. The
girl's tactics were quite within the rules and, if anything,
gave the ape an advantage, he pointed out. Was there a
moistening of glee in the old man's dry voice?

'She will not defeat me in her sleep!' The weed had
wrapped itself around the ape's mind and now it was
frightened, trying to find a way out. It made a sudden
thrust to one side of the board that appeared to place Julia
in danger, but there was no depth to the move.

The referee called out the ape's move. Julia took the
sword out of the ape's hand and turned the point on it.

'White captures,' the referee announced, taking one of
the ape's pieces off the board.

'She has bewitched me!' the ape said, jumping up and
down in its chair in its agitation. 'You have all seen it.
Don't let her do this to me!' Nobody intervened. 'Very
well,' it said petulantly, 'if nobody else will stop her, I
will.' Too quickly the ape made its next move.

Julia replied at once, closing in on it.

'Open your eyes!' the ape shrilled, clapping its long
hands. 'I command it.' There was an edge to its voice.
Its nerve and its self-control teetered on that edge. Julia
played on, moves apparently suggesting themselves to
her without effort. In two more moves she placed the
ape in a crisis.

The ape hated her perfectly at that moment. It hunted
for some way of escape and found it. 'We will break for

refreshments,' the ape announced in as calm a voice as it could muster.

'Can he do this?' Phillip blurted out.

'It is within the rights of each player to call a break,' the referee said.

The ape relaxed in its chair. This would give it time to regain its balance. 'We shall break, girl, and you will not think about the game. I forbid it! You must sing a song or do something else.'

Julia opened her eyes. She saw an ape whose close-set eyes were stung to anger.

'I give you my word, Sacred Ape. Even better, I'll give you my next and final move.' She called over the referee and whispered in his ear. He nodded.

With that, she gave the ape a wave and climbed out of her chair. 'Let's go for a stroll, Phillip; I'm getting sticky sitting here.'

He joined her. The ape, the old man and Willard watched the two of them walk away. They did not try to leave the garden. Julia dragged Phillip into a grove to watch.

The ape looked at the referee speculatively. A gleam of interest had enlivened the old man's eyes. 'If she has abandoned the game, then it is over and I have won,' the ape said.

The old man shook his head. 'I'm afraid not, Sire. Technically, your opponent is still here — at least until her final move is played out. Only then can the game be considered abandoned.'

The ape turned its attention to the board again. It flicked a glance at the referee as if hoping to read his mind, to see the final move that was stored there.

'Quit monkeying around and play,' Willard suggested. 'Can't you even win against an empty chair?'

A breeze came up. It was hot and made the leaves in the trees clash.

Which piece had the girl planned to move?

The ape reached out to grab a piece, but its hairy fingers refused to close around it. It paused in midair. It selected another piece, slamming it into an adjoining square. There. It was a move that suited the ape's mood. It was a bold move that suited the anger it felt. It wanted to smash the girl's chances.

'White nineteen to twenty.' The old man called out the girl's final move and executed it promptly. He bent over the board following the move, examining the state of play. 'Ah yes. As I feared, it is the end of the game, Holy Ape. She holds you. See, there is no move that you can make without placing one of your pieces in danger. It is over.'

'Nonsense, decrepit old fool! There must be a way! First she plays me in her sleep, now she plays me in her absence. No girl can beat me that easily. I am the sacred ape. I am Thoth.' The ape leaned over the board, bending to the task of solving the problem.

Julia gave a chuckle beside Phillip. 'I've got him!' she said.

The ape gave a cry of rage and, raising both feet, it kicked out at the board, sending pieces tumbling to the ground. Then it ran away screaming like a hit animal into the shadows of a grove. 'You may all pass through the gateway,' the old man said to them with a grave bow.

'He was a monkey to play against you, Julia,' Phillip said. 'He never really had a chance.'

'Thankyou, Phillip. You were pretty good yourself today.'

They joined the others and together they passed through the pylon of the second gateway. They worked their way deeper into the land of the dead.

Phillip had never admired Julia more than at that moment.

7

Seti

THEY RAN THROUGH THE PYLON gateway and on into dark passages lit by torchlight. Phillip felt as if he were running into the heart of a great pyramid. In places the passage was level while in others it climbed into galleries with great voids on either side.

He wondered who would face the next challenge. He hoped it would be Coomber. He was still angry about Barry Coomber's act of treachery. Coomber had actually helped the ape against Julia.

'Why did you do it?' he said. 'Don't you know what'll happen if any one of us fails in a test?'

'I'm not afraid of failing tests. I do it every week at school.'

'If we fail a test here we're stuck — for all time. We'll never find our way out again. Do you hate Julia — and me — so much that you'd spite yourself for all eternity?'

'She came through, didn't she? What are you griping about? I knew she would.'

'She came through, but no thanks to you.'

The next challenge came sooner than any of them expected. They ran into a large hall that looked like a workshop or factory. There were charcoal fires burning in forges with bellows and rows of worktables and craftsmen's tools on the tables.

Willard Chase made a swift inspection of the tables. 'It looks like a royal workshop. Jewellers, I'd guess. See those shiny bits on the tables? Glass. Faïence. Gemstones. Strips of gold wire. All the signs.'

Barry Coomber reached out to grab a handful. Julia slapped his hand, venting some of the resentment she felt at his earlier betrayal. 'No sticky fingers.'

It was as well that she stopped his thieving. A giant of a man, a sunburnt, bare-chested overseer carrying a leather whip, lumbered into the room. He looked like an extra out of a Hercules epic.

'I am the royal overseer, Seti,' he announced in the rumbling voice of a giant. 'Your next challenge is a mystery — a great theft of a royal treasure in these workshops and you must solve it.'

'Theft — that sounds like you, Coomber. You're good at thieving.'

'Leave me out of this.'

The overseer pointed at Barry Coomber. 'You have chosen yourself. Step forward.'

When he refused, the giant cracked his whip, not with force, but with deadly accuracy, curling the forked tails of the whip around Barry Coomber's waist and dragging him into a clearing between the workbenches.

Coomber struggled, but soon gave up. The giant leaned over him like a tower. 'Here is the mystery. If you fail, you will roast in the forges.'

He clapped hands that were the size of cymbals. A moment later, twelve dwarves filed into the workshop. Phillip looked at the group in disbelief. They had the peculiar bulging features common to dwarves and stood like twelve stunted *ushabti* figures – the little carved servant statues they had seen earlier.

After the shock had receded, Phillip noticed certain things about them. They had evidently taken a beating, for they carried red and blue welts on their bodies and one's tiny arm was bandaged like a mummy.

'Here are the suspects,' the overseer said to Barry Coomber.

'Did they escape from a circus? I've never seen such a bunch.'

'They are all royal craftsmen, goldsmiths and jewellers from the royal workshop. Dwarves are favoured for this profession, naturally.'

'Why naturally?'

'You will need to have sharper wits than this to survive your challenge. Dwarves are favoured because of security. If they should decide to steal any valuables and succeeded in escaping from the heavily guarded royal workshops, their appearance would make hunting them down a lot easier. It's easier finding a dwarf than a man of average description.'

It was a piece of quaint yet practical Egyptian logic, Phillip thought.

'Listen well,' the giant overseer said to Barry Coomber. 'Here are the facts of the mystery. It is called the riddle of the missing emeralds.'

The dwarves stood blinking at him, their bulging eyes staring like those of men being strangled, their faces pale and forlorn as the overseer went on. 'A consignment of rare emeralds, a gift from the king of Mitanni, arrived in the workshop to be inlaid in the hilt of a ceremonial dagger. They disappeared without trace. Since the workshop is heavily guarded by a company of Medjai police, Nubian soldiers who are as cruel and dedicated as insects and who cannot speak the language of the workmen, the thief could not have gained entry from the outside; therefore, the guilty one is certainly one of these craftsmen.'

The overseer studied Coomber. 'I think you have already heard enough, judging by your bored expression. You know which one is the crooked one, I suppose?'

'They all look crooked to me,' he said, eyeing their misshapen forms.

'Ask them any questions you wish,' he said, folding his oiled, muscle-bound arms.

Barry Coomber approached a foreman among the dwarves, a strapping little man with a chest like a cask. He carried a staff of office. The boy leaned bullyingly over the man. 'Did you beat them black-and-blue?' Coomber asked.

'No, master, it was the Medjai police.'

'They went to town it seems. Why is this one's arm in bandages?'

'He broke his arm himself, master. An accident. His own doing entirely.'

'Not the Medjai. He did it himself? Are you sure?'

The foreman nodded. 'He fell while working the forge.'

'Did anyone see it happen?' Coomber asked.

'No, young master, nobody saw.'

Barry Coomber swaggered along the line of stumpy craftsmen, feeling himself to be six feet tall. He stopped in front of the dwarf with the bandaged arm. 'Casualty case, huh?' The dwarf shifted uncomfortably under the stare of Barry Coomber's shiny eyes. The little man looked down at his feet.

The feet, surprisingly, were the size of a normal man's. At least this one had been spared a beating by the Medjai police, Phillip thought. They probably considered him to be in a bad enough state already after the accident.

'Who treated your arm?'

The dwarf's arm had been set in splints and then immobilised in bandages, the bent arm supported in a sling around his neck. It was a professional job. Ancient Egyptian medicine was highly advanced.

'It was a physician of the royal factories, master,' the dwarf said in a manly voice.

'Are you hurting?'

'Not now, young master.'

Phillip could guess what Coomber was thinking as he eyed the dwarf's bandaged arm. They all could. 'Don't you think that would be a bit obvious?' Julia said.

Coomber shrugged and went back along the line of dwarves, stopping in front of the foreman. 'What sort of security do you have here?'

'It's a fortified village, master. The royal factories are guarded, in particular the royal workshop of the jewellers and goldsmiths, for this is a fort within a fort.'

'Well guarded?'

The foreman shifted uncomfortably; he seemed eager to speak his mind, but feared the overseer.

'Speak freely,' the giant with the whip said.

'We are virtually prisoners here. The Royal Jewellers Workshop is surrounded by guards with orders to kill escapees. The jewellers and goldsmiths work apart from the rest of the royal factories and only go to the village between shifts.'

Coomber had an idea. 'Couldn't the culprit have swallowed the emeralds?'

'Master, we work a ten-day shift. At the end of this period, the workshop physician supplies the men with a powerful purgative to clear their stomachs. Only when a workman is cleared' — he made a graphic, downwards sweep across his stomach — 'can he leave.'

'Does this doc stay in the royal workshops?'

'Doc?'

'Physician.'

'Yes sir. He is an old man and does not trouble to go

to the village. He is employed mainly for the task of checking the men and attending to minor ailments. He claims to have mined more precious stones from men's stomachs than the royal miners have dug up from the mines of the southern desert.'

Julia made a face.

This was going to take time. Phillip, Julia and Willard sat on the workbenches to watch and Dogstar curled up on the floor. Conflicting impulses wrestled inside Phillip. He found himself hoping that Coomber would fall flat on his face, but he knew what would happen if he did. He should wish Coomber success.

'Tell me about the missing emeralds,' Coomber said. 'Who first noticed that they had disappeared?'

'I did, master,' the foreman said.

'Did you know how long they had been missing?'

'Only for one day. I saw the emeralds myself in the morning.'

'What were they like?'

'Beautiful master, like shining drops from the Great Green.' The Great Green was the Egyptian name for the ocean, Phillip recalled. Barry Coomber licked his lips as if he could taste the precious emeralds. 'What did you do when you saw they were gone?'

'I notified the overseer and the Medjai. More soldiers were placed around the workshops so nobody could escape with the emeralds. Then the workshops were searched. The overseer supervised personally. All the workmen were present: none has escaped.'

Coomber jerked a thumb towards the dwarf with the arm in bandages. 'When did he break his arm?'

'On the morning the jewels went missing.'

'The dwarf says his arm was treated by a physician from the royal factories, not by the doc from the workshop. You allowed him to visit a doc on the outside?'

'We had to, sir, but not on the outside entirely; still within the royal factories. As I said, it is a fort within a fort. When the dwarf broke his arm, the old medic tried to fix it. The man refused to let the old fellow touch him, however, and quite rightly demanded that he be allowed to see his own doctor in the village. His doctor fixed him up. It was while he was away that I discovered the emeralds were missing. I sent guards to bring him back here, even though I knew he couldn't escape to the outside world. There is another wall around the entire complex.'

'What happened next?'

'The man protested about being dragged back to the workshop. He demanded sick leave and freedom to leave the complex entirely to visit his family in Thebes in order to rest, something allowed the men every five years.' The foreman looked at the man. 'Naturally I was suspicious. "First we'll search your arm," says I.

'"Oh no you won't," says he. "Don't you dare lay a finger on me."

'"Very well," says I, for being a little person myself I know how delicate little people can be regarding their health, "I won't touch you. I'll get the medic to look at you; after all I'm no barbarian, you know."

'"What?" says he. "Let that old quack touch my arm? If he makes a mistake I'll lose the use of my arm and never be able to work again. I am one of the best jewellers in Egypt and deserve to have my own doctor."

'"No, you don't," says I. "It's no good making a fuss; we want to see what you've got in that bandage."

'"A broken arm," says he. "What else?"

'Well, we won in the end, but what a fight it was! We took off the bandages and looked.'

Coomber smiled in a cynical way. 'And let me guess. The emeralds weren't there. But tell me, was his arm really broken?'

'It certainly was, master; it dangled quite uselessly like the neck of a wrung goose and the man cried out in pain. "I'll fix it! I'll reset it for you!" says the old medic, rushing to bring his first aid kit, keen to prove that he could do more than dispense medicine.

'At this the injured man began to jump up and down, heedless of his twisted arm. He threatened to sue me and the medic for damages if we so much as touched his arm again. He was not a slave, he said, but a free and honest workman who knew his rights. He demanded his own doctor be fetched to reset the arm.' The foreman shrugged his shoulders. 'So we gave in and called his own doctor.'

'Then the rest is obvious,' Coomber said. 'I can see a shifty one being pulled a mile away. You're talking to an expert. The doctor had the emeralds.'

'No sir, he was searched this time on the way out and he protested a great deal about a professional man being subjected to irrigation of his insides.'

'He didn't have them on the way out. He brought them in. You'll find them in the wrappings of that man. He and the doctor were both in the scheme together.' Barry Coomber pointed to the guilty dwarf.

The dwarf with the broken arm looked as if his bulging face would burst. He backed away. The overseer caught hold of him. With the foreman's assistance they unwound the bandages. The dwarf ceased his struggling. They removed the splints and were unwinding the last of the bandages when a small hide pouch fell to the floor.

The dwarf fainted clean away with fright. Barry Coomber opened the strings of the pouch and spilled some glittering green droplets into the cupped palm of his hand. 'Here are your missing emeralds.' He tipped a stream of droplets back into the pouch, tied it again and tossed it to the overseer who caught it.

'The dwarf broke his arm on purpose,' Coomber said. 'Amazing you may say, but the emeralds are no doubt worth a king's ransom — each one of them. He broke his arm, then of course went to see his physician in the village. At that point he had no doubt hidden the emeralds about his person — swallowed them, no doubt. Because he was an emergency case and in obvious suffering, he was able to avoid the castor oil treatment. He then gave the emeralds to the doc in the village who kept them.

'When the emeralds were discovered missing, the injured man was searched and, not surprisingly, there was no sign of the emeralds. . . since he had passed them on to the doc. The doc was sent for after the arm needed resetting the second time. Who would think of searching the doctor on the way into the place?'

'What reason could he have for bringing them back here into the royal workshop?'

'Obvious. Getting the emeralds out of the workshop was one thing. But they still had to get them beyond the outer fortified village. Only by putting the emeralds on a man who had already been searched and was considered clean could they hope to get the emeralds out of the complex and onto the market. The injured workman had requested leave, remember. It was a pretty crafty plan. The injured man had been cleared where his arm was concerned. He could even be sure of passing the castor oil test before going out.'

'Why did the physician not try to get the emeralds out?'

Barry Coomber shrugged. 'He was a professional man who couldn't risk being caught with them. Besides, it was probably the dwarf's plan all along and, being a jeweller, he would be the best one to sell them, having contacts in the jewellery market and knowing the emeralds' true value. No, it had to be the dwarf who went through with it.'

At this the dwarf, lying on the floor, opened his eyes to glare redly at Coomber. 'Got you,' Coomber smiled, shaking a finger at him. The taunt had a more dramatic effect than Coomber guessed. The dwarf exploded in a shower of sparks like a malfunctioning robot.

Barry Coomber turned smugly to the giant overseer. 'Pretty smart of me, huh?' he said.

Phillip cringed for him, but he was grateful, too.

'You may pass,' the giant overseer said. 'You have solved the mystery of the missing emeralds.'

The tomb travellers went on, penetrating deeper and deeper into the Land of Shades.

8

The great beetle

THE PASSAGE THEY WERE FOLLOWING widened at the entrance to a massive tomb labyrinth cut in the stone.

'What now?' Coomber said, looking at the maze of entrances. 'How many times do I have to come to the rescue?'

Another barrier. Who would be the guardian of this gateway? Phillip wondered. He listened. There came from far away a scouring, hollow roar like that of an approaching train in a tunnel. It reminded Phillip of being in the railway underground.

'A train down here?' Julia said.

A rush of air began to blow on them. It came not from the tunnel directly ahead, but from a branch of the maze to their left. It had a foul smell of waste.

They drew back into the passage to a place where it narrowed, flattening themselves against the walls, their heads turned to face the advancing threat. Through the soles of their shoes they felt the rumble of something heavy rolling towards them. They heard a hissing, clanking noise like the labour of an engine and a sound like a cockroach scuttling in the pantry in the middle of the night, but magnified a thousandfold.

What would emerge? Phillip expected a bright light to dazzle his eyes and a locomotive to come pouring out of the darkened opening. Not being able to see it was the worst part. The tunnel took the echoes and twisted them out of shape.

'It's getting very close, whatever it is,' Julia said. Her plaits swung around her face and her fringe fluttered on her forehead in an ugly breeze that blew on them.

'This isn't good,' Willard Chase said. His nostrils flared with the smell of the breeze.

Phillip swallowed hard.

The noise rose to a gargling roar like a cistern flushing through a giant piece of plumbing. A blast of fetid odour hit them like a wave as the creature came into view. . . It thundered out of the tunnel, rolling a huge brown ball of earth in front of it and it pulled up with a metallic screech in front of the travellers. They shrank against the wall of the passage.

'A beetle!'

It wasn't just any beetle. It was a scarab beetle the size of a locomotive and it rolled a dark ball like a dead planet in its widely spaced legs. The ball was so big that the beetle was almost standing upright to see over it. The beetle had a shell of armoured, horny plate the colour of anthracite and its eyes bulged like plexiglass canopies on a fighter jet, shedding a green glow as it glared down at the tomb travellers.

'It's the great beetle,' Phillip whispered in awe.

'I am Khepera, the guardian of the labyrinth!' it said in a crackling, electric-sounding voice. 'If you cannot pass my test, I will crush you under my earthen sun that I roll across the passages of the sky of night.'

'What a gross, smelly bug!' Julia shuddered, wrinkling her nose.

'That's a ball of dung it's rolling ahead of itself,' Phillip whispered. 'In ancient Egyptian mythology, a scarab beetle rolled the sun from east to west across the heavens.'

The obscene orb, weighing tonnes, bulked so large that it stood higher than the beetle and it was smooth and packed hard from rolling. There were grim memories on its surface where it had overtaken victims, gathering them up in its mass. Phillip saw the soles of grass sandals stuck on the outside. Julia made a choking noise as if she were going to be sick.

'One of you miserable souls — and one only — must find your way through the maze and then, having found the way, must come back to lead the others through it. You have only a short time.' Blue lightning arced between its feelers like sparks between electrodes. 'Then I shall enter the labyrinth and roll my dead sun after you, crushing you.'

The dead sun did not shed light, but a stench of doom that prickled in Phillip's nostrils.

'You have little time!' it said again. 'Choose which one of you will go!' The beetle withdrew, taking its ball of dread back into its tunnel in a rapid blurry movement like a spider clutching prey into a hole.

The tomb travellers exchanged bleak looks. It was going to be the most dangerous test yet. Finding a way through a maze would be challenging enough. Remembering the way back would be just about impossible, especially knowing that at any moment the mad insect could come thundering along a passage to squash them.

Willard Chase took off his hat and ran his fingers agitatedly through his brown hair. 'Why did it have to be a labyrinth when it's my turn!' He groaned. 'You guys may not have noticed, but I don't actually have the world's best sense of direction. Even if I blundered through the maze, I'd never find my way back to fetch you, not unless I could leave a trail of string or something behind me.' He swept them with a hopeful glance. 'I don't suppose one of you happens to be carrying a ball a string?'

They shook their heads and his eyes dulled over again. 'No. Thought not.' He put the hat resignedly back on his head, pulling the brim low over his forehead as if to shield himself from the challenge ahead. 'Well, here goes, but frankly I don't like my chances. I've been in a tomb labyrinth before. If I hadn't gone with a good guide to show me the way back, I'd still be in there. . .'

'Wait, I'll go.' Phillip stepped forward.

'You've had your turn, kid.'

'This won't really be my turn. It'll be Dogstar's. The beetle said one soul could go. Dogstar doesn't count as a soul. We'll go together.'

'Stop trying to be a hero all the time. It doesn't impress anybody,' Coomber said irritably.

Phillip ignored him. Julia protested. 'Even if you could find a way through, Phillip, how would you find your way back to us in time? Who knows how long that disgusting insect will give you before it comes rolling its filthy ball after you?'

'With that ball rolling behind me, I'd get through the maze in a flash,' Coomber said, but it was only a boast and he made no effort to step forward.

'I'll need your clothes,' Phillip said. 'Yours Willard and yours Coomber. Just your shirts. I need to lay a trail.'

'Our shirts won't stretch all the way through a maze.'

'What's on your mind, kid?' Willard said.

'I'm going to lay an invisible trail for Dogstar. If we tie our shirts together by the sleeves and let them drag on the ground behind Dogstar's collar, they should lay a broad enough trail of scent for him to follow back.'

'Clever Phillip,' Julia said approvingly.

'Not bad but, if that's the plan, I can do it as well as you can. Let me go with Dogstar,' Willard Chase said.

Phillip shook his head. 'Dogstar won't go with you. It'll have to be me. You wait here.'

'It's very brave of you, Phillip,' Julia said uneasily.

'Your shirts, please,' Phillip said, pulling off his own. He put his denim jacket back on over his bare skin. Willard removed his shirt and, reluctantly, Coomber did the same. Phillip knotted the shirts together at the sleeves to make a lengthened train of material which he then attached to Dogstar's collar.

Coomber, typically, thought of an objection. 'What if the bug comes rolling its smelly dungball after you? It'll cover the scent for sure and you'll never get back. You'll be stuck on one side of the maze and we'll be on the other.'

Phillip paled. He hated Coomber for bringing it up, but Coomber was right. He would have to take some extra precaution, but what? How could he record every bend and twist of a maze? Bend and twist. That gave him an idea. Perhaps it could work. He kept it to himself though and said, 'I'll just have to be quick.'

'Which entrance will you choose?' Julia said. 'There are dozens of tunnels!' It was quiet now and yet the silence had a stretched, sustained quality like a note of tension. She looked around at each tunnel in turn, her bright eyes narrowing in a look of loathing when they came to the beetle's hole.

'It doesn't matter where I go in,' he said. 'Entering a maze is easy enough. It's designed that way, to lure you in. Getting out's the hard part.'

'But you could walk into a dead end.'

'Unlikely,' Phillip said. 'If it was a dead end I'd be safe from the beetle. You can be sure that all these entrances meet up pretty soon. I can pick any tunnel I like.'

'Then why not pick that one over there?' Barry Coomber said in a cynical tone. He pointed to the tunnel where the giant beetle had gone. 'You could start a beetle collection.'

'Very funny!' Julia said angrily. Coomber smiled and tried to draw Willard into his joke. Willard gave the boy a tired look.

Phillip's face darkened, but he ignored the remark. 'We'll take the tunnel right ahead of us.' He patted Dogstar. 'Let's go, 'Star boy. Find a way through!'

Julia stood stiffly anxious, pale with concern for Phillip. Willard Chase looked helpless, trapped by his own limitations. 'Good luck, kid. Glad you came along.' Coomber slid down the wall and sat on the floor, turning his head disinterestedly away. Phillip took out his bicycle lamp, fiddled in the battery housing, and switched it on. He gave a wave before he and Dogstar went into the maze.

Surprisingly, he did not need the light after the first turn in the passage. The maze was lit by some overhead light source which at times threw bright light and at others hard shadows, depending on the angle of the passage they followed. He put the lamp away.

He expected the maze to smell like a farmyard since the beetle rolled its foul ball through it, but it was clean-smelling and so was the floor. Perhaps it was flushed after each trial or renewed itself magically to avoid leaving clues for souls to follow and so present a fresh obstacle for each soul trying to penetrate its mystery.

There was nothing claustrophobic about the labyrinth. It was a maze made for a giant; huge, intersecting passages allowed the overgrown beetle that guarded it to charge along its length even where it veered at sharp angles. Phillip let Dogstar run free. It was easy following the train of knotted shirts sliding along behind the dog. Phillip tried to remain calm and to project a confident air to the dog.

He walked at a steady pace behind Dogstar, his hands thrust in his pockets, but he fiddled nervously with a comb in his pocket as he went. Dogstar threaded through the maze like a needle, the trail of shirts, brushing the floor behind it, marking the way back. The trail slid out of Phillip's view around a corner. Phillip quickened his step, rounding the corner. Relief. Dogstar was there.

The animal reached a junction of three passages, sniffing the air. He remembered another time, not so long ago, when he had followed Dogstar. The animal had stolen the ibis bird from his bedroom and fled with it in its mouth and he had followed it from room to room. The bird was behind all this, Phillip thought. The words of the sacred ibis came back to him now. . . 'Note this well, if you do perish in the Egyptian underworld you will never reach heaven. You will fall into the pit of everlasting nothingness where the Ravisher of Souls will devour you.'

Phillip gulped.

'Do you still want to go?' the bird had said, giving a squawking laugh like a parrot.

'Yes,' he had said. 'To find my uncle.'

'Then you must face what happens, presumptuous boy.'

Dogstar cut and wheeled, running this way and that. It ran into a blind alley and wheeled again, its lean body moving like fluid trying to find a course to follow. 'Good boy, keep going. . .'

Another dead end, another doubling back. Phillip listened for the scouring sound that would signal the rush of the scarab beetle. He heard nothing but the accentuated *tick tick tick* of Dogstar's paws on the stone and the pharaoh hound's sniffing as it plucked at the air questingly with its sharp nose. It was hunting for the smell of fresh air, he thought, for the slightest current of air that would reveal a path through the maze. Dogstar gave a yelp of frustration. They ran into a blank wall, a dead end. It turned and doubled back on its track.

'You're going well, 'Star boy. Keep at it,' Phillip said encouragingly. They seemed to be making progress. If only he knew how much time the great beetle would give them!

They came to a branch in the passage. Which way? Dogstar sniffed, then turned left. Phillip went after it. They had penetrated the heart of the maze. How far did it extend? What if it were endless like this nightmare he was living through? He looked at the twisting, darting dog and wondered if Dogstar could be the prophesied doom dog, leading him to disaster. Perhaps it would abandon him here to wander the maze for all eternity. It was a horrible thought. So was the idea of being rolled up in the beetle's ball of dung.

The disgusting brown ball loomed in Phillip's memory. He remembered seeing the soles of grass sandals stuck in the side and pictured his own sneakers sticking out. Would the bottoms of his Reeboks be his only memorial? He was crazy thinking he could dare the gateways and guardians of the Egyptian underworld and survive. Even if he did get through, even if he found his uncle, could he ever find a way back?

He pushed the thought from his mind. He missed the sun, the feel of its warmth on his skin.

He would hate to wander here for all eternity like poor Uncle William. Phillip wondered if he would ever see his uncle's kindly, mischievous face again. How much further did he have to go to find his uncle? How many more gateways and fearful guardians must they pass through before they reached their destination — and where was that? He presumed it would be a place called the Field of Offerings, the Egyptian heaven.

He thought of the others waiting behind at the entrance to the maze, counting on him, and he walked more purposefully.

Dogstar froze in arrested step and growled, twisting its ears like radar dishes. It had heard something. Phillip stopped to listen, careful not to step on the trail of shirts.

Phillip felt a hollowness in the bones of his legs. The scouring sound he had dreaded hearing floated out of a passage to greet his unwilling ears. It was a long way off, no louder than the soft scrubbing sound of somebody cleaning their teeth behind the closed door of a bathroom. Khepera the great beetle was on the move through its labyrinth.

'Quickly, Dogstar, the bug's on the loose!' Phillip heard the scouring sound grow, echoed around the wide corridors of the maze. He pictured it scuttling metallically, rolling its ball of doom along, hardly able to see. Maybe it did not have to see. Maybe it could smell. Unlikely, Phillip thought. The scent of its evil cargo would blunt its smell receptors. It was more likely that it charged around blindly like a locomotive out of control, flattening whatever lay in its path.

Dogstar, sensing a new urgency, pulled away. Phillip broke into a run after it. He felt as if they were running in an oversize pinball game, except that the pinball chasing them was not a shiny ball, but a loathsome mound propelled not by a spring release but by a demented beetle.

Dogstar made a final burst down an interminably long section of corridor that led to an exit and they were out of the maze and back in the safety of a narrow corridor.

Phillip patted Dogstar. 'We made it!' He hastily undid the shirts and left them on the ground. They would only slow the dog on the way back. He took hold of Dogstar's collar. 'Okay Dogstar, back to the others. As fast as you can go and I don't care if you drag my feet off the ground! Go, boy!'

Dogstar shivered and gave a cry of dismay. It heard the turmoil of the beetle's approach and knew it was near. Phillip felt a rush of foul air blow against his damp forehead. Dogstar launched itself back into the maze along the stretch of corridor, jerking Phillip after it. Phillip struggled to keep his footing. It was no easy matter keeping up with a pharaoh hound. Phillip could not help admiring its rapid, scribbling flow of movement.

Dogstar took the maze with far more confidence than the first time, but the way back was only slightly easier. Locked onto the trail of scent they had laid, Dogstar had to follow every twist and turn they had made before — even running into the dead ends, backtracking, running into more dead ends, turning again, running in new directions — yet they were able to cover ground more speedily than the first time when they had been hunting for the right path.

Where was the armour-plated beetle? It was hard to hear over the rasp of his own breathing and the pounding of the blood in his ears. Was that a draught he could feel at the back of his neck, a rush of air propelled by the advancing scarab beetle and its dungball?

'You could have brought my shirt back with you,' Coomber said as Phillip and Dogstar spilled out of the maze to rejoin the others.

'The beetle's on the prowl,' Phillip said, 'but we've marked a path. Come on, hurry!'

Phillip's lungs were on fire and he would have liked nothing more than to slide down to the floor and rest, to suck air back into the hurting spaces inside him, but there was no time now. They followed Dogstar and Phillip into the maze.

'I thought you'd found a way!' Coomber grumbled as they ran into a dead end, bumped into each other and had to double back on their tracks.

'Stop grumbling and keep following.'

They followed Dogstar's erratic, invisible trail, the sounds of their running feet echoing in the maze. They ran towards a 'T' junction at the end of a passage.

The great beetle cut across their path with the unexpectedness of a speeding freight train at a blind level-crossing and without the benefit of warning lights. Powered by shiny, insect-leg pistons, it rolled a mountain of stinking freight across their path. Only the quick reactions of Dogstar and Phillip saved them. The line of running travellers collapsed in a sprawl of bodies and tangled limbs. The speed of the beetle's passing created a vacuum that sucked at their hair.

'I think he had the right of way,' Willard Chase said drily, untangling himself from the heap. Julia gave a shaky sigh and climbed off Phillip's back. Coomber's leg held him down. He pushed it off, freeing himself. They climbed to their feet. Phillip took hold of Dogstar's collar again. 'Come on, boy, it'll be back.' They approached the junction cautiously. Dogstar stopped, looked left and right, sniffed the air, whined, then sat down.

'Oh no,' Julia said, 'Dogstar's lost the scent.'

'The beetle's gone and fouled the passageway,' Coomber said.

'That thing's obviously not house-trained,' Willard Chase said, pointing to the smelly brown smudge on the stone floor.

Dogstar shivered with distress and looked helplessly up at Phillip.

'Just great!' Coomber said. 'Then we're lost. There's no way to find a path now. Nobody could remember the way through this.' Julia began to sob.

'Don't worry, Julia,' Phillip said. 'I was afraid this might happen so I took an extra precaution. I made a coded record of our path through the maze.'

'Rot, you couldn't have,' Coomber said.

Phillip slipped a hand in a pocket and took out a black plastic haircomb with rather badly twisted teeth.

'It's no time to worry about your messed-up hair,' Julia said, her voice tightening with urgency. 'We're in big trouble.'

'Yeah, even a girl wouldn't worry about her hair now!' Coomber said acidly.

'This,' Phillip said, holding up the comb, 'is my map. I used it to record the way through the maze. It's polythene and unbreakable according to the maker and so the teeth bend. See, here's a tooth bent to the left. That represents a turn of a passage to the left; here's a tooth turned to the right, that's a turn to the right. If we passed a passage without turning, I skipped a tooth and left it straight. Get it?'

'Pretty useful, kid,' Willard Chase said dubiously. 'That might have helped us if we were just starting out, but we're already somewhere in the middle. Where is our present position on your comb?'

Phillip lost some of his enthusiasm and squinted closely at his comb.

'I don't believe this!' Coomber said. 'It's not your comb but your brain that's twisted, Phillip. Whoever heard of following a comb?'

'At least it's something,' Julia said, grasping at this hope. 'It's worth a try.'

Phillip pointed at his comb. 'We've just made four right-hand turns in a row. . . that means we're here! See these four bent teeth?'

'Then what's the next turn, Phillip? Left or right? Oh hurry, Phillip, I can hear that thing coming back!'

'Left.'

Phillip gave Dogstar's collar a tug and guided him left and then left again and then right. Dogstar should have picked up the scent again by now. Judging by the clean look of the floor, the beetle had not yet been over this section of the system. Dogstar barked shrilly with excitement. It had hit the invisible trail of scent. They ran on. Between them they were finding a way through.

Phillip felt a breath of success and relief blowing on the back of his neck, cooling the perspiration. At least he thought it was that.

Julia turned and screamed.

The pinball beetle was hurtling along the passageway, its mound of manure reeling in the distance between them. They hit a straight section of passageway. They passed two passages. Dogstar stopped again, confused. 'Not now, boy, keep going!'

'He doesn't know the way.'

A glance at the stone floor explained why. The beetle had been over the section, leaving a filthy brown smudge.

'Look at your comb!'

'I am, I am!' Phillip was already doing just that and blinking in horror. The wind from the rush of the beetle was fluttering his hair like a gale.

'This isn't good,' Willard said in a small voice.

'If you don't do something, Phillip, that running compost heap is going to smear us all over the passageway.'

Phillip stared at a gap in his comb. 'One of the teeth is missing. . . It's supposed to be unbreakable!'

'This is no time to ask for your money back,' Coomber yelled. 'We're going to be in the poo any second!'

There were three choices open to them here: straight

ahead, left or right. 'I don't know which way to go!' Phillip said in a voice that cracked with strain.

They had been so close to success, now this!

'Let's go left!' Willard Chase said, taking charge.

That decided Phillip. If Willard chose left, then the correct way would be diametrically opposite — right. Willard's sense of direction was unerringly faulty. 'Right!' Phillip said with certainty.

They turned right. So did the beetle, but at least they were on track again. Dogstar barked in relief and stretched its body in a run.

'Faster!' Phillip yelled to the others over his shoulder. 'Dogstar's on the right trail again.' The awful rush of foul air behind them told them that the beetle was rapidly closing.

They sprinted the last long straight out of the maze like finalists in the Olympic hundred metres dash and threw themselves headlong onto the floor of the passageway in a part too narrow for the beetle to follow.

They had made it. Phillip twisted. An icy hand grabbed his insides. Julia wasn't there. 'Where's Julia?' he said in a dead voice.

'Phillip!' Phillip heard a hollow, ringing scream trail out of the labyrinth. Julia had somehow become separated from them in the last dash to the exit of the maze. Perhaps she had fallen. Why hadn't he kept a watch on her?

Dogstar acted before any of them. It ran bravely back along the stretch of corridor that led to the maze. Phillip jumped up and ran after it, his legs shaking underneath him.

'Julia, this way!' he shouted, cupping his hands around his mouth.

'Phillip, I'm here!' Julia appeared at the end of the corridor and began to run. Dogstar extended its sinewy body in an elastic, pouring run. It did not stop when it came level with Julia, but flicked past. It had seen what had turned the corner.

The beetle was hastily clawing its ball around the bend, getting it lined up like a bowler taking aim at the last pin, the frozen figure of Julia who had turned to see Dogstar flash past her and now saw the terrible beetle lining her up for a score. The pharaoh hound accelerated and sprang up and over the curved mound of the black sun to snap at the beetle's head. The metallic planes of the creature's palpus mouth ground the air like great shears.

'Run, Julia!' Phillip shouted. His shout gave power back to Julia's legs. She broke into a shaky run. Dogstar danced out of the reach of the beetle's way, barking shrilly. The creature made a horrifying clicking sound. Julia kept running. Phillip held out his hand to her to grab her hand and drag her the last few yards to safety.

Dogstar knew that it could not survive the flashing, grinding planes of the beetle's jaws for long. Once applied, the jaws could snap its body in two. Dogstar jumped back over the black, foul sun of the dungball and made a bolt for freedom.

The beetle roared after it, building speed like a train going down a gradient, sucked along by its deadweight of rolling stock.

It would take more than a loaded train to catch Dogstar from a standing start.

Phillip felt his heart go out to the dog as it hit speed in a dashing, scribbling flight. Dogstar at full stretch was a sight to see. He loved the dog and its Maker at that moment, loved its bravery and its perfection and its beauty in motion. It was a living, warm-blooded creature of the real world.

Phillip, Julia and Dogstar hit the narrow passageway

at almost the same time. The beetle met the wall like a derailed train hitting stanchions, sending a shower of sparks, stone chips and foul mud. . .

The beetle exploded, blowing bits of flaming shell around like a tank taking a direct hit from a missile. The walls of the labyrinth toppled like dominoes. A blast of foul air rolled over their heads, then it was quiet.

'I'll never like beetles again!' Julia said, her face still hidden in her hands. 'Not even ladybirds!'

9

The last gateway

THE TRAVELLERS RESTED. They sat on the floor of the passage with their backs against the wall. Phillip patted Dogstar and rubbed its back and it enjoyed Phillip's appreciation, wagging its tail. 'You saved us, boy,' he murmured. 'And I thought you might be my doom dog.'

'You weren't bad yourself, kid,' Willard Chase congratulated him. 'Ever thought of becoming an archaeological detective? I could do with an assistant.'

'It isn't over yet,' Coomber reminded them unpleasantly.

'You and Dogstar were both wonderful,' Julia said. 'Don't listen to him. What's wrong with you, Barry Coomber? Would you choke rather than give anybody credit?'

'Nobody gave me credit for solving the mystery of the missing emeralds,' he said. 'I noticed that.'

Phillip surprised him. 'I'll give you credit,' he said. 'I think you were pretty smart. And if it hadn't been for you, Coomber, we'd still be stuck in the maze. You're the one who warned what would happen if the beetle went over the trail of scent. That's what made me take precautions and mark the route on the teeth of my comb.'

'Do you mean that?' Coomber said. 'Nah, you're just trying to get around me. You're a crawler like that beetle!'

'I worry about you, Barry Coomber!' Julia said.

'You boys were great,' Willard Chase said. 'And so were you, Julia. That game of senet you played against the great ape ranked with the matches of Kasparov or any chess master,' he said to her. She smiled happily.

They sat silent for a while.

'Willard,' Phillip said, 'do you remember when you rescued us from the mutes and the embalmers?'

'Vividly.'

'You said they were probably just some harmless crazies. You said you didn't believe in animal-headed gods and demons and guardians. They didn't exist, you said, except in people's imaginations. Well, what do you say now? You've seen a hall full of slaughtering knives, a sword-swinging goddess of truth, a game-playing ape, a giant overseer of ancient royal factories, and a great scarab beetle in a labyrinth. You've been very quiet about all of this.'

'We each have our own private nightmares,' Willard said.

'But you do admit that what has happened has happened.'

'Once in Africa I studied the Bushmen. They have a saying. Somewhere there is a dream dreaming us.'

'Somewhere there is a *nightmare* dreaming us would be more like it,' Coomber said.

'Perhaps. Yet who am I to say that this nightmare isn't real?'

'You mean you really have seen a mummy sit up in a box or a demon stalk a corridor?' Coomber said.

'There are demons enough stalking our minds.'

'Why are you here?' Julia asked Willard. 'Is it really

because of the scroll? I know why Phillip is here — to find his uncle. I'm not sure why Coomber and I are here though. I think we were swept up in it accidentally.'

'I'm here to retrieve an artefact, the scroll that was stolen,' Willard said.

'My uncle's *Book of the Dead*,' Phillip said.

'Yes.'

'Do you think the tomb robbers who came ahead of us have been through the same trials as us?' Julia said.

'No,' Willard said. 'The scroll shows a way to avoid the gateways and guardians. It shows an easy way to the underworld and its riches. It is a very dangerous document which I must take out of their hands. They could use it to let great harm into the world.'

'Wouldn't they have made copies of it?'

'They wouldn't have dared. It's far too precious to have copies floating around. That will be the only scroll on earth — or under it. I must get it out of their hands.'

'What will you do with it?' Coomber said.

'That's up to my uncle,' Phillip said. 'It belongs to him.'

'You still believe you're going to find your uncle?' Julia said, giving a sad shake of her head.

They did not run now, but set off along the corridor at a purposeful pace. How many more challenges could lie ahead of them? Phillip thought. They had each faced a task — except Willard Chase. Would he avoid having to face a task now that Phillip and Dogstar had taken his place?

Phillip went ahead of the others, leading the way with Dogstar. A series of doors had slammed shut on them after passing through each challenge. Coming back this way would be unthinkable. There was only one solution. They would have to recover the *Book of the Dead* from the tomb robbers. It was the quick way out. But first they had to find his uncle.

Did Uncle William know that they were drawing near? Did gleams of hope ever reach those in the Land of Shades? He wondered what the Field of Offerings, the Egyptian heaven, would be like and if they would ever reach it. The Egyptians believed it was like the valley of the Nile where they had lived, a place where people went about their normal business, planting crops and harvesting them and enjoying a life like the one that they had left.

They believed that.

What did he believe? He remembered his grandmother's worn hands and the soft leathery cover of the Book of power she had given him. Did he believe in another life? He heard the footsteps of the others behind him as they settled into an easy rhythm, travelling Indian file along a stone corridor lit by the lamps of perpetual fire.

If he did believe in another life, it wouldn't be a dark place like this one. It would be a place where a sun shone, a personal sun like a presence that you wanted to draw near to. That sun was still vague to Phillip, like a morning sun that was still behind the hills, but he believed that this sun and a knowledge of it would rise for him. It was there behind his thoughts, limning the horizon with its promise. Uncle William had no beliefs. He had not stopped to believe. He had always been lost in the past and now *that* was literally true. He was lost in the Egyptian eternity.

Phillip remembered the ferryman's words: 'Your head's like mine; turned around.'

'My head's screwed on perfectly straight.'

'No, it isn't,' he had said with an emphatic shake of his head. 'You're backward-looking like me. You love to look back to the past, to the very far past. Your thoughts are always filled with the long ago and the far away. You are a boy who is in love with the past.'

Phillip had not been able to deny it. 'Well yes, I do happen to like the past,' he had confessed. 'I've always thought it would be the very best place to live.' As he had spoken the words, Dogstar had suddenly bared its teeth. Phillip had tried to pat it to calm it and, surprisingly, it had nipped his hand. 'What's the matter 'Star boy? Don't be afraid.'

'It's not afraid. It's angry. With you. Put yourself in its place. It dogs your footsteps every day. How do you think it feels having a master who doesn't enjoy living in the present? Be warned. Looking back isn't such a wise thing to do. One day you'll look back on my words and agree. Before too long, I'd say. Take care that you are not lost in the past — forever,' the ferryman had said.

Phillip patted Dogstar absently as he walked. What had the ferryman meant? His head wasn't turned around, was it?

They turned a bend in a passageway and walked into a painted tomb and into the brandished spears of a row of Nubian guards. Cowering in the corner was a group of grimy-looking men covered in stone dust and plaster. A pile of picks, hoes and baskets lay at their feet.

A couple of dignitaries in white robes bowed to the new arrivals. 'Welcome,' one said. He was a large fat man with a devil's beard. 'This is your last gateway. It is the mystery of the robbed tomb. I am the overseer of the royal necropolis. You must decide who has robbed the tomb, who of those present is the guilty party. If you do not point the finger of guilt correctly — and prove your assertion — you will be put to the spear. All of you. Who will face this challenge?'

'I'll handle this one,' Willard said confidently. In an

aside to the others he said: 'At last, my speciality. Tomb robbery. I'm a lot better at this than mazes.' He seemed to grow taller beside Phillip. His broad, green eyes looked calm and assured, like the time when Phillip met him in the graveyard at Ravenwood.

Phillip patted his shoulder. 'Good luck, Willard.'

The dignitary bowed again. 'Then I present the mystery of the robbed tomb,' he announced like a television host introducing a crime movie.

'May I look around?'

'Naturally.'

'And ask a few questions?'

'Anything you like, except the answer to the mystery.'

Willard Chase strolled around the ancient Egyptian tomb with the air of an art connoisseur in a gallery. He craned to look up at the ceiling that was painted in midnight blue and decorated with a myriad of stars. He looked measuringly at the walls, evaluating the painted scenes that enlivened them — scenes of harvests and animals and fishes and flowers, of papyrus reeds and hunters on skiffs throwing fowling sticks at birds. He frowned when he observed that in many places the pastoral beauty had been shattered.

Some angry hand had taken a pick or a chisel to the surface. The face of one personage, depicted in many poses and in many places in the tomb — evidently the tomb owner — was consistently obliterated. The chisel had also been taken to columns of hieroglyphic characters.

This was clearly a royal tomb, judging by its size and the refinement of its decoration, yet it was stripped of the usual tomb furnishings and treasures which kings traditionally took with them into the afterlife; the tomb was empty except for a plain wooden sarcophagus. Even the lid of this had been lifted and flung to one side. Willard

Chase went closer and looked inside. Evidently it was empty for he did not pause long.

'What can you tell me?' Willard asked the fat official.

'We at the royal necropolis learnt of a break-in taking place. It was reported by this man Senenmut, a former architect of the royal family.' He pointed to a tall, wily-faced individual with a wispy beard and dark, slow-moving eyes.

'As a result I came here with Lord Senenmut and a body of necropolis guards and caught a band of tomb robbers red-handed — those wretches who cower in the corner.' He pointed an accusing finger at the sullen group on the floor.

'*He* told us about this tomb — he set us up to rob it!' one amongst the tomb robbers protested, pointing at the clever-faced architect.

The fat official aimed a kick at the tomb robber, making him scuttle like a crab out of reach. 'You dare to point a finger at Lord Senenmut — a builder of tombs?'

'May I ask a question?' Willard Chase said, turning to the tall man named Senenmut. 'You are the architect of this tomb?'

'Yes.'

'Who does the tomb belong to?'

The dark eyes slid slowly away from Willard's gaze. 'I am sworn to secrecy.' He shrugged. 'My lips are sealed for eternity.'

'How did you learn that it was to be robbed?'

'As an architect, I work with labourers and artisans all day long. Many labourers, regrettably, are tomb robbers. I have my spies among them.'

Willard now made another circuit of the tomb. He took a magnifying glass out of a pocket and began to study the hieroglyphic characters marching along a wall, paying particular attention to the parts that had been hacked out of the plaster.

'Can you read hieroglyphics?' Phillip whispered in admiration when Willard followed the marching hieroglyphic columns of images along a wall and drew near to him.

'Not easily, it's never easy, but yes, I can. The written ancient Egyptian language was by no means precise. They had no vowels, for instance.' He ran his magnifying glass over a particular section and his lips moved silently as he translated the words to himself.

When he thought he had the gist of it, he read it out for Phillip's benefit:

'Before this child was born, the Seven Hathors predicted its fate:

This royal child, though not a prince, shall wear the double crown and beard, yet shall bear a child, and shall take. . . or assume. . . the role. . . or place. . . of a king for all eternity.'

'That doesn't make much sense,' Phillip said. 'What is meant by have a beard and bear a child?'

'This tomb didn't belong to a man.'

'But it says he wore the double crown and a beard.'

'A false beard — a ceremonial beard. All pharaohs wore those. And it didn't say he. No, this tomb belongs to a woman, a woman who assumed the role of pharoah, even wearing the royal kilt and beard and the double crown. Her name was Hatshepsut. Her architect and favourite was Senenmut, the man standing over there. She was hated by succeeding kings who expunged her name and image from all monuments in Egypt.'

'Then you know who this tomb belongs to?'

'Yes, but it still doesn't tell me who robbed it.'

Willard went to the group of bedraggled men on the

floor. 'Where are the articles from this tomb? You are going to be punished for your crime whatever you say, so you might as well tell the truth.'

'There was nothing here when we broke in tonight, Lord; it was just as you see it.'

He turned to the overseer of the necropolis. 'Were there ever reports of this tomb being broken into earlier?'

The overseer looked awkward. 'To be honest, we did not know of its existence. We thought this tomb belonged to a long forgotten Old Kingdom king and that it had been robbed in antiquity.'

'There must be something I've missed in the translation,' Willard Chase said in a frustrated voice. 'Think, Chase, think.' He went back to the inscription. 'There must be another clue here.' He read it out loud again: 'This royal child, though not a prince, shall wear the double crown and beard, yet shall bear a child, and shall take. . . assume. . . the role of a king for all eternity.'

'You said "place" before,' Phillip corrected him. 'You said, "and shall take or assume the role or place of a king for all eternity".'

Willard shrugged. 'Role, place, it doesn't matter. . . or does it?' He wheeled to throw a questioning look at the architect. 'Hatshepsut took the place of a king in her life. Maybe she did the same in *death* — not just the role, but the place. . . Yes, that would make sense of the bit about "for all eternity". You can't assume a role for all eternity, but you can take a place, if that place is a tomb!'

He turned to the overseer of the necropolis. 'I think I have found the robbers of this tomb. . . It was the owner of this tomb, Hatshepsut, and her architect Senenmut. . . They robbed it in the sense that they never put anything here in the first place. They also robbed it from the king who owned it before her. Egyptian monarchs had a habit of doing that. They probably even defaced it to save her nephew the bother in case he came here, a double precaution. If my guess is right, Hatshepsut's body and her tomb treasures lie very close. . .'

Willard Chase bent and took the handle of one of the tomb robber's picks lying on the floor. He raised the pick head while the assembled group held its breath, and swung it at the wall. Chips of plaster and paint flew off. He stripped away a section of a fowling scene that showed flying birds and throwing-sticks in the air. Behind it, disappointingly, lay solid stone, but Willard kept chipping away.

'Stop, you desecrator of tombs!' the man called Senenmut howled like a jackal. 'This is a royal tomb you are destroying!'

Willard's pick, striking sparks off stone behind the plaster, now revealed the edge of a block. The tomb was not solid stone, not carved out of virgin rock as it had first appeared. Senenmut moved to stop Willard, but the official and two Nubian guards blocked his path.

The fat man clicked his fingers and some Nubian guards picked up other implements and joined Willard in his labours and the tomb rang with the clangour and bite of digging tools. They cleared the edges of a block of stone. Two Nubians put their shoulders to the block and pushed. It grated back and fell with a hollow thud into a space behind what was obviously a false wall.

The fat official brought a torch to the hole they had made. He and Willard peered into the space behind. Phillip crept nearer so that he, too, could see. Their eyes feasted on the gleam of gold, cups, animal heads, chests and furniture. . . obviously the real tomb and treasures of Hatshepsut!

Willard explained. 'Already, before the end of her reign, Hatshepsut was hated by the priests and by her nephew, the warlike young Thutmosis whom she kept from power for many years. She knew what would happen to her tomb after her death. Her remains, her name and images would be expunged from memory. She had also seen the fate of many of her predecessors, whose tombs had been robbed within years of their deaths, no matter how deeply dug or securely locked in pyramids.

'Senenmut, her beloved architect, devised the perfect scheme to hide his queen for eternity. He caused her tomb to be built inside a larger, existing king's tomb. But that wasn't enough. The queen's grave goods and her body were put behind the false walls of this smaller tomb and this outer tomb was then systematically vandalised. The safest tomb of all is one that has already been robbed, but only if others know that it has been robbed. Senenmut tipped off these tomb robbers deliberately, knowing that once the tomb had been officially entered and was known to be worthless and empty, it would be safe.'

'Then whose tomb was this originally?' Phillip asked.

Willard shrugged. 'The tomb of some forgotten Old Kingdom monarch, robbed long ago no doubt. Senenmut probably discovered it while building monuments and mortuary temples for his sovereign. Am I right, Senenmut?' He turned to question the architect.

Senenmut, the architect, turned to stone. Cracks, like black lightning, ran around his body and head. He gave a cry and split with a loud bang. They blinked as the man crumbled into a heap of dust on the floor of the tomb.

The fat man gave the pile a distasteful kick with his sandal and a small cloud of dust puffed into the air. 'You may pass through the final gateway,' he said.

Even Coomber looked relieved. 'Well done, Willard,' Phillip and Julia said. They went beyond the last of the gateways and guardians.

10

Hall of Judgment

THEY WERE MET IN A PASSAGE by the Lady of Tremblings, Maat, wearing the single ostrich plume of truth on her head. She smiled at Phillip. 'You passed the tests, Boy Whose Face Is Turned Backwards. Now you must enter the pylon of Osiris and be judged in the Hall of Judgment. I am here to usher you inside.'

She took Phillip's hand. The lady's touch was like a flame, yet cold. It sent tingles to his elbow. Julia moved closer to Phillip and gave the lady a hard and cool stare. 'Come, all of you, to face your judgment,' the lady said in a silvery voice. She led Phillip into a huge hypostyle hall with papyriform pillars of crushing size and capitals that were lost in the darkness of the roof. The floor was painted with blue zigzag lines like wavelets and there were painted fish dabbing their mouths on the surface. It was as if the travellers were walking through a marsh created in stone. It was the primordial marsh, the place where the ancient Egyptians believed the world began. Phillip heard a shimmering, musical sound, like that of insects on a summer's night.

'What's that sound?' he asked the Lady of Tremblings.
'You hear the priestesses playing their sistra.'

It was followed by a low, dirge-like chanting. 'We are entering the presence of the king of the dead, Osiris. Your souls must be judged against my single feather of truth and, if you are found wanting, you will fall into the everlasting pit where the Devourer will feed on your souls.'

'What must we say?'

'You must say the words of the negative confession.'

'What words?'

'From the *Book of the Dead*. . . haven't you brought one with you?'

'I have nothing. . .'

The Lady of Tremblings trembled in a sigh. 'Then I fear you shall have to tell the truth. You must make up your own negative confession without the help of the formula. Take care to speak only the truth.'

Shafts of light fell from the darkness of the roof. Phillip saw an amazing tableau of frozen figures gathered in the gloom. He saw a statue of a man with a mummiform white body and a green face. He was seated on a throne under a canopy.

A small ornamental lake glinted underneath his throne. Out of the lake grew a lotus flower. Tiny humanoid figures stood like visiting bees on the open lotus flower. Behind the throne were two women in sheath dresses, goddesses by the look of them, their hands raised in adoration. Phillip couldn't quite tell whether they were real or statues, since they stood in heavy shadow under the canopy.

A set of scales stood in front of the throne, bathed in a shaft of light that fell from the ceiling. Other figures came out of the gloom, a man wearing a black, jackal-head mask and another wearing an ibis head.

The ibis-headed one gave a warning cackle that reminded Phillip of the bird that had visited him in his bedroom. The Lady Maat felt his hand tense and she gave it a squeeze of comfort. The jackal-headed one came to Phillip, holding up his hand to indicate that the others must wait. Maat released Phillip's hand and the jackal-headed one took it and guided him to the set of scales. His touch was cold and reptilian. Maat followed them. In a gracious movement, she plucked the tall ostrich plume from her head and dropped it into the right hand pan of the scale. It floated into the pan. The scales were exceedingly sensitive. The pan dipped under the weight of the feather. The bird-headed one held a pen and palette and a strip of papyrus and stood by like a secretary waiting to record the results.

Drawing closer to the canopied throne, Phillip saw other things. The statue in white was not a statue at all, but a human figure wrapped in a winding sheet. His face was emerald green and his eyes shiny black beads. They burnt into Phillip.

'Make your confession,' the figure cracked like thunder, but without moving his lips. The jackal-headed one released Phillip's hand and placed a small, heart-shaped object in the opposite pan of the scales. The arm of the balance tipped dramatically. The jackal-headed one adjusted the tongue of the balance until the pans were level. The bird-headed one, Thoth, drew nearer, inspecting the balance closely. Phillip looked at the heart-shaped object in the pan of the scales. It represented his heart. It would dip with any lie he told and he would be declared guilty. What was truth to these creatures of Egypt's underworld?

'What must I say?' he asked in sudden panic.

'Say what you have not done,' the jackal-headed one prompted him.

'There's so much I haven't done. How long have you got?'

'All eternity, in theory.'

'I don't know where to begin.'

The jackal-headed one clucked impatiently: 'You must say you have not committed certain sins.'

'Even if I have?'

'Beware of the Devourer,' the jackal said in a warning growl.

'Which sins in particular?'

'That you have not stolen cakes from the gods, not acted wickedly by having cut the banks of the running stream in the fields of irrigation. . . the usual.'

'Of course I haven't done *those* things. . .'

The bird-headed one dipped his beak over the pan looking for the slightest movement. It did not quiver. 'Don't you have a scroll with the magical words?'

'You mean magical words can save one's soul?'

The jackal-headed one gave a sigh of impatience and dug into his kilt, producing a small roll of papyrus. 'Luckily for you I happen to have a spare copy left by another soul or this would take an eternity and frankly I would like to go to lunch. Here, read this.' He handed Phillip the scroll.

'I can't read hieroglyphics,' Phillip said. He took the scroll hesitantly and unrolled it. He found to his surprise that he could read it, even though it was covered with mysterious symbols. He read it aloud:

'I have not committed sins against men. I have not opposed my family and kinsfolk. I have not acted fraudulently in the Seat of Truth. I have not known men who were worthless. I have not wrought evil. I have not defrauded the humble man of property. . .' Phillip trailed off. 'This has nothing to do with me. This isn't my confession.'

The statue beneath the canopy gave a moan.

There was a rumbling sound and a square of stone

grated open in the floor, leaving a square black hole. Blue smoke issued from it.

'Take care,' the jackal-headed one said. 'Beneath your feet is a pit and in it waits the Great Devourer, the monster eater of the dead. It waits with gnashing teeth for its meal of souls. Make your negative confession.'

'You have no right to judge me,' Phillip said spiritedly. 'I will be judged by another and he will judge me not by some formula recited like a multiplication table, but by my faith in him and by the true goodness of my heart.' Phillip wondered how all this came to him almost without thinking, but somehow it did.

'Who is this judge you speak of?'

'The true God and his Son who died and rose from the dead.'

'As did Osiris.'

'But the true God's Son died for our sins.'

'Men die for gods, not the other way around. What kind of god is that? Make your negative confession or be thrown into the pit.'

Phillip swallowed. 'My negative confession? Very well, here goes: I haven't thought enough about others. I haven't forgiven people who are my enemies, like Coomber. I haven't enjoyed each day — been grateful for my blessings. I haven't taken enough opportunities to do good, to think of others who are suffering. I haven't been pleased about the success or gains of others. I haven't judged others lightly. I haven't been patient and kind. . .'

'Cease! What kind of negative confession is that?' the jackal demanded.

'It is the truth. Judge by your own scales. Look at the heart and the feather. They haven't moved the pans. If you judge things by a formula and rules, then you cannot throw me into the pit.'

The pans were level and had not stirred. The jackal-masked man shook his head in puzzlement. 'Next!' he called, like a doctor in a waiting room.

Julia stepped forward and Phillip joined the others. 'Good for you, Phillip,' she said, going to take her turn at the scales.

'Only the truth, Julia — you know, the things you haven't done. . . look into your heart,' Phillip whispered as she passed him.

'Begin your negative confession,' the jackal said.

Julia raised her chin, unafraid of silly creatures. 'I have not been grateful for the kindness and love of others; I have not forgiven my parents for leaving me alone in the world so that I would have to be adopted by strangers. I have not loved my adopted parents as if they were my own. I have not put into practice the things that I truly believe, the things I have read in the one true Book of power.'

'What Book of power is that?'

'It is called the Bible, which means the Book.'

'The *Book of the Dead*?' the jackal-headed one asked.

'The Book of the Living and of those who will live forever.'

The scales remained immobile, although it seemed to Phillip that a draught stirred the feather of truth in its pan.

'Next.'

Phillip gave Coomber a shove. 'For once in your life be straight, Coomber. Lie now and you know what's going to happen? I'm going to be rid of you *once and for all*. You wouldn't like that, would you?'

'Shove off!' He went to the scales. 'Is that supposed to be my heart?' he said, pointing into a pan and sneering.

'It is your heart. Feel your pulse; it is gone. Your

heart is here in the scales.'

Coomber felt for his pulse. He put his hand inside his shirt, flattening it against his chest. He paled. He took it out and held his wrist in his fingers. 'I can't feel anything.'

'Enough delay. Speak your negative confession.'

Barry Coomber gulped. 'I haven't left other people's stuff alone. I haven't kept my hands to myself. I haven't liked a lot of people. I don't like Phillip or his goody-goody girlfriend, Julia, or Willard who couldn't find his way out of a paper bag. I haven't been very honest in my life. I haven't wanted other people to succeed. I couldn't have cared less if Phillip had got lost in the maze or the baboon had beaten Julia at the board game, although I am getting pretty sick of tests. This is almost as bad as the end-of-year exams and I'd like to go home now. . . is that enough?'

All eyes went to the scale. It did not tremble. Willard Chase came forward next.

'State your negative confession.'

'I think I'll keep my private weaknesses to myself,' he said, with a secretive smile. 'Here's my negative confession: I have not plundered the offerings in the temples, I have not defrauded the gods of their cake offerings. I have not carried off the *fenku* cakes offered to the spirits. I have not diminished from the bushel. I have not stolen land from a neighbour and added it to my own acre or encroached upon the fields of others. I have not added to the weights of the scale, nor depressed the pointer of the balance, nor driven the cattle away from their pastures. . .'

'He's quoting the real *Book of the Dead*,' whispered Phillip to Julia. 'He remembers it line-for-line.'

'Now that is what I call a proper confession,' the jackal-headed one said approvingly. He threw a glare at the others. 'Why couldn't you come clean like this man? Pass, soul, you are justified.'

'Pass into the Field of Offerings,' the figure under the canopy boomed.

'Thanks,' Phillip said with a wave.

The Lady of Tremblings came to take Phillip's hand again, but Julia stepped in between. The lady smiled and led them out of the hall into the Field of Offerings.

Their trials were over, Phillip thought in momentary relief. Then he remembered about the tablet of destiny and its warnings about the serpent, the crocodile and the dog of doom. Those trials still lay ahead — for Coomber, for Julia and for himself.

They must find Uncle William.

There was no sun in the Field of Offerings and no life. There were figures in a landscape, farmers behind cattle and ploughs in fields and others in various activities, but they were frozen in action. The Field of Offerings was as static as a tomb painting and lit not by a sun, but by a wintry grey light. It was a treasure-house of abandoned offerings, food on tables, jars of drink, chests of gold and ivory, animal skins — all left lying around for the dead, but the dead could not enjoy them.

The tomb travellers came upon a man standing on a skiff in the marshes. His arm was upraised and he held a curved throwing stick in his hand which he was about to hurl at a flight of waterfowl that a cat had flushed from the reeds. The cat was frozen in mid-leap as were the birds in flight.

This was the Egyptian heaven. They had found their eternity, a frozen eternity as rigid as a bas-relief. The tomb travellers passed a woman in a patterned halter dress. She carried conical loaves of bread balanced in a box on her head and a fowl held by its wings in her free hand. Her painted eyes stared blankly into eternity. Next they came upon a fat vizier who looked like a carved wooden statue and carried a staff of office. Coomber gave him a bump and he fell over like a block of wood and lay with his unblinking, painted eyes staring at the sky.

Phillip felt numb. The ancients had wasted their lives and dreams. How much of their lives had they spent preparing for this, planning and building their tombs, stocking them with treasures, instead of enjoying the real treasure of life in the here and now? This frozen tableau was no exchange for a single, living moment.

The only one excited by what he saw was Coomber who bent to stuff objects into his pockets — gold rings, scarabs, abandoned jewels, hoarded treasures that the Egyptians dreamed of taking with them into eternity, but which of these rigid figures could enjoy them?

Phillip went rigid himself. He saw a figure in the frozen landscape that he recognised and he ran, crying, to greet him. 'Uncle William!'

Uncle William did not respond to Phillip's call. Uncle William, dressed in his khaki expeditionary gear, looked like a statue of an explorer. He shielded his eyes with one hand as if searching the horizon. His giant moustache hid his normally smiling mouth. 'It's me — Phillip. Can't you hear me?'

Uncle William looked pale and waxen. Dogstar crawled to his feet, whining.

The others joined them, standing back in respectful silence, all except for Coomber. 'I knew your uncle had gone to hell,' he said. 'I was right.'

Uncle William's once-humorous blue eyes were glazed and unblinking and their focus seemed to be turned inwards as if contemplating some horror within himself. 'I've come all this way to find you and you're a statue!'

'I'm sorry, Phillip,' Julia said. 'You've gone through so much. . . for this!'

'There's nothing we can do here, son,' Willard Chase said comfortingly, putting an arm on his shoulder. Phillip numbly moved away.

He circled his uncle in disbelief. It was the same Uncle William he had known and loved, but he wasn't there any more. It was like visiting a familiar home where you had once lived long ago. He felt an aching absence.

Dogstar's cries grew into a howling wail. It was a sound that filled the air with sorrow and at the same time emptied it of all hope. It reminded Phillip of the day that they had read out Uncle William's will.

The metal safe door had swung open on silent hinges, the assistant had dipped into the hole in the wall and carefully removed an object, a glass cylinder containing a mustard-coloured roll of papyrus. As he had moved, the glass cylinder had flared like a neon tube in light from a French window.

The assistant had dutifully carried it to where Uncle William rested, held it up with the air of a magician about to do a trick, then placed the sacred *Book of the Dead* inside the box beside Uncle William's scuffed, size twelve khaki desert boots. Uncle William had looked dressed to go on another expedition.

Two parlour attendants, men in black suits, had detached themselves like shadows from the curtains and closed the lid on Uncle William and sealed it shut.

All Phillip had been able to hear had been the faint squeak of screws going in as they closed the lid tight in accordance with Uncle William's instructions. Uncle William wouldn't have liked leaving with barely a squeak. He would have preferred a noisy send-off conducted in the ancient Egyptian style. The ancients of the Nile used to hire professional mourners for funerals, women who wailed in the tremulous Eastern way, filling the air with sorrow and at the same time emptying it of all hope. . .

Phillip threw his arms around Uncle William's chest and his shoulders shook with his sobs. A tear rolled like a crystal drop from his cheek. It hit Uncle William's khaki shirt and made a moist spangle on the fabric. The statue drew in a great lungful of air and a pair of arms came around him and lifted him off the ground.

'You came for me, Phillip, you came. My favourite nephew came! It was a dream I've had for an eternity, or so it seemed to me.'

Dogstar's wail changed key to a yelp of joy. The colour flooded back into Uncle William's face and relief flooded through Phillip. His uncle held him out at arm's length and his eyes moistened with gratitude and emotion. 'What kind of boy would risk hell to find an uncle?'

'A boy with a special uncle — one he couldn't forget about!'

Julia began to cry. Willard Chase pumped Uncle William's hand. Coomber grunted. He went scavenging among the offerings, kicking over objects as if they were autumn leaves on the ground, bending when choice pieces caught his eye. He stuffed them into his pockets.

Phillip's uncle took a step forward with effort like a bas-relief figure tearing itself free of its background. 'What a joy to break free, to move again. I've ached for this moment! Come, Phillip, walk with me.'

Uncle William stretched his legs and Phillip and Dogstar went with him, Dogstar prancing and barking. The old man's limbs loosened with every step. 'You risked far too much for me,' Uncle William said, chiding him quietly.

'It was worth it.'

'Well, no harm has come to you, I see.'

'I missed you so.'

'And I, you.'

Uncle William looked saddened. 'I have missed so much. You and others I have known and the world. But above all, I have missed the sun — not the sun in the sky, although I have missed that too, but the sun of a special, warming, life-giving presence. That's what I truly long for. It was around me all my life and I didn't recognise it.'

'You'll see the sun again. We're going to lead you out of here, Uncle William, but first we must find the scroll.'

'You mean you don't have the scroll?' Uncle William went rigid and his skin turned waxen. He looked as if he was about to become a statue again. 'How did you get here?'

'We passed through the gateways. . .'

'And the guardians? And survived? How?'

'Only by our wits and a lot of luck,' Willard Chase said, joining them, along with Julia who was still sniffing and dabbing at her eyes. 'Unfortunately your grave was robbed by modern-day tomb robbers who got here ahead of us. No doubt they've come to strip the Field of Offerings of its treasures. They're the only ones who know the direct way back. We must find them and recover the scroll.'

11
Two fates

THEY SEARCHED THE FIELD OF OFFERINGS for the tomb
robbers. They found them crossing a sandy plain, a file
of men going like a modern safari through hell, two
European men and a party of Arabs loaded like beasts
with treasure. One of the European men pointed up
ahead.

'We'll need to ambush them,' Willard suggested.
'They'll have to pass through that hollow over there.
Let's wait on the other side.'

'They're armed,' Uncle William said. 'The Europeans
have holsters with guns. We can't hope to overpower
them.'

'I have an idea,' Phillip said. 'Where do you think
they're headed?'

'I saw one of them pointing up ahead,' Uncle William
said. He pointed. They followed his line of direction.
On a rise stood a small shining obelisk coated with gold.
Even in the grey light of the sky it shone like a pale sun.

'A landmark,' Willard said. 'They're obviously taking
their bearings from it.'

'We must find a way to make them stop and take out
the map to check it.'

'Why?' Julia said.

'So that Dogstar and I can try to snatch it from them and run. Here's my plan. We hide the landmark on the hill somehow while they're in the hollow. When they come out, they'll look for it. When it isn't there, they'll take out the map to check it. That's when I'll make a grab for it and toss it to Dogstar who'll run off with it. They'll never catch Dogstar.'

'I'll take care of the landmark,' Willard Chase said. 'Leave it to me.'

'Keep your head down,' Phillip said.

Willard set off for the rise, doubled over to avoid detection.

'You Julia, Uncle William and Coomber, head for that stand of sycamore trees,' Phillip said, taking control. 'When Willard's hidden the landmark, give him a wave and he'll join you there. Dogstar and I will meet you later.'

Uncle William, Julia and Coomber set off for the stand of sycamores, while Phillip and Dogstar crept to the edge of the hollow to wait for the tomb robbers to emerge.

They lay flat on the sand overlooking the ridge. Phillip turned his head to see how Willard was going. Willard clambered up the rise to the small shining obelisk. He put a boot against it and gave it a shove. It toppled and slid like a toboggan down the blind side of the rise. Uncle William gave him a wave from the trees and Willard ran to join them.

The tomb robbers, led by the Europeans, reached the edge of the depression and started to climb. Phillip heard their voices. They spoke in French. Phillip could not understand them. The leader squinted up at the rise and rubbed his eyes.

They pointed to the rise where the obelisk had been. One of them dug into a satchel at his waist and removed the scroll. He began to unroll it.

'Now, Dogstar!' Phillip whispered.

An Arab gave a warning shout, but they came down the steep side of the depression like tumbling boulders and took the Europeans by surprise. Phillip snatched the papyrus out of the hands of the man. 'Catch, boy — run!' He tossed it to Dogstar who caught it neatly in midair and ran up the other side of the depression.

One of the men made a lunge for Phillip but, when he saw that the dog had the scroll in its jaws, he joined the others who scrambled up the steep side of the bank after it. Phillip went the other way. One of the Arabs made a half-hearted grab for Phillip's leg as he climbed, but missed.

At the crest, Dogstar stopped to tease them, allowing them to gain ground to make more sport of it, but the crack of a revolver shot and a spurt of sand thrown up beside it changed its mind and it took off like a greyhound at a racetrack. They fired after it, but it was like trying to hit a wind in the desert.

The band of tomb robbers followed Dogstar until they dropped in the sand from exhaustion. Phillip ran for cover in the sycamores. Dogstar made a wide circle and returned to the spot where it had left Phillip. Phillip gave the dog a low whistle and it joined him in the sycamores.

'Good boy, Dogstar,' he said, patting the dog who allowed him to take the scroll from its jaws.

They had the scroll.

Phillip unrolled it on the ground and they all craned to examine it. It appeared to be a normal *Book of the Dead*, except for a lower register that showed a map of underground passages leading to the Field of Offerings, with sketches of landmarks on it and a thin unbroken red line showing the way.

'Here's the obelisk of gold,' Uncle William said, tapping the scroll. 'The next landmark is the exit from the

Field of Offerings. We must look for an alabaster sphinx on a hillside. We'll find a tunnel passage behind it. From here on it should be quite straightforward,' Uncle William assured them. 'There should be no terrors for us in these passages. The terrors lie in the other system. This is the way around the obstacles. From now on the only problems we'll have will be ones we make for ourselves.'

'Let's hurry before the tomb robbers come after us,' Phillip said. Willard agreed. 'They'll want that scroll back and you can be sure they've looked at it often enough to remember some of the details.'

They found the alabaster sphinx and the passage behind it leading into the rock. They set off along it, Uncle William and Willard leading the way, Uncle William consulting the map as they went. Dogstar walked at Phillip's heels. Willard and Julia came next. Coomber, dragging his feet, brought up the rear. He was loaded down, Phillip thought, glancing over his shoulder. Coomber's pockets bulged. Coomber had not changed his light-fingered habits.

As he walked, Phillip became aware of a far-off shimmering or hissing sound. Insects, here? It was more like the sound of escaping air.

'Come on, Coomber,' he called over his shoulder. 'Do you want those characters to catch up? You're walking in slow motion. Why don't you empty your pockets and you might move a bit faster?'

'Why don't you stop turning your head around and mind your own business?'

'Fine.'

The hissing sound grew behind them, but he resisted the urge to turn. Was it Coomber puffing and hissing with the effort of carrying his stolen load? A loud hiss cracked the air like a gas cylinder springing a leak. 'Hey, you people!' Coomber yelled. 'Look behind!'

Phillip turned and so did the others. A serpent with a squat, diamond-shaped head almost as broad as the passage and eyes that shone like headlights slithered behind Coomber. It was the serpent that had followed them in the desert of snakes.

'What do I do?'

Julia screamed.

'Do what you did before,' Phillip said, going back to join him.

'What was that?'

'Throw something at it — throw the things you've stolen.'

'Not again. I want this stuff. I'm not going to throw my things away!'

'They're not yours. You stole them.'

The serpent opened its wet trap of a mouth and unsheathed fangs the size of swords and unrolled a tongue like a split red carpet-runner. It rose in the passage, gaining height to strike, puffing a blast of venom-reeked air.

'Get rid of it! Throw it!' Phillip said. 'You've brought this on yourself. You have to give up what you've stolen — give up stealing things. Don't you see? This is your monster. It appears every time you steal things!'

'Let me past.' Coomber tried to push his way past Phillip, but Willard and Julia blocked his way.

'Do it, Coomber. Once and for all, give up your stealing. Remember the tablet of destiny. It had a picture of a serpent. This is your doom and there's only one way to avoid it.'

'My family needs the money. My brother's in gaol; my dad's out of work.'

'Stealing isn't the answer, Coomber. You've got to solve problems the right way. Throw it all back.'

Coomber was torn. Stubbornness shone in his eyes. Phillip saw the struggle going on in his face. The serpent extended itself to a height where it looked down on the boy. The ridges of scales on its belly looked like tank tracks.

'What's it to be, Coomber? Precious things aren't going to do you much good in eternity. Remember the people in the Field of Offerings. Do you think they were enjoying them?'

Coomber dug into his pocket and came out with a handful of golden rings, amulets and pieces of jewellery. He drew back his arm like a baseball pitcher making a pitch and flung them up to the open mouth of the snake. The serpent widened its mouth to capture them, swallowing them whole, but it wasn't satisfied. It slid nearer, preparing to strike.

'All of it,' Phillip said. 'Your pockets are still bulging.'

Coomber, shaking with anger and disgust, dug deep into his pocket. He threw things wildly. Pieces of gold and jewellery tinkled against the walls of the passage. He dug into his pockets again, releasing a glittering hailstorm at the snake. It stopped its advance, licking up the pieces with its forked tongue.

'Is that all?'

'Every single piece I took from the Field of Offerings.'

They ran. The snake came after them. 'You're lying,' Phillip shouted as they ran. 'It's still following. You've kept something back!'

'I told you I've given back everything I took from the Field of Offerings.'

'Then you've kept something from another place.' A memory of Coomber's trial with the twelve dwarves and the missing emeralds flashed through his mind. Had the crafty Coomber pocketed one of the stolen gems? Phillip remembered how Coomber had sealed the pouch with its drawstring and thrown it to the overseer.

He stopped Coomber and spun him around. 'You kept one of the stolen emeralds.'

'Leave me alone. What are you trying to do — get me eaten alive?'

'That thing will never stop following you until you get rid of the emerald. It's been after you all this time.' Phillip shook him. 'Coomber, wake up to yourself. Your life — eternal life — may depend on doing the right thing now!'

'All right, all right!' Coomber said, despairingly. He dipped into his back pocket and removed a large green droplet that gleamed like a green light. 'Have everything. You might as well take the lot. I've never been allowed to have anything!' There were bright tears of anger in Coomber's eyes.

He tossed the emerald through the air and it disappeared into the pink, wet mouth of the serpent. The reptile let out a hiss like a blast of air escaping. The hissing grew in pitch and, as it did, the snake shrank in size. Coomber blinked. The shrivelled serpent flew off down the passage with a rasp like a balloon untied.

They pressed on through the passageways hour after hour. They began to tire. Odd, Phillip thought. Their bodies felt tired, yet they never once wanted to eat or drink. Julia called for a rest.

They squatted in the passageway in a place where it widened a little. Phillip sat next to his uncle. Uncle William put an arm around Phillip and gave him an affectionate squeeze. 'How's my favourite nephew?'

'It's so good to see you alive again, Uncle William.'

'Alive? I'm not too sure about that.'

'Why? Do you think you're still dead?'

'Maybe. Nobody should expect a second chance, Phillip.'

'Did all this happen because of the scroll? Is that why

you ended up down here? Because the *Book of the Dead* was a passport to the netherworld?'

Uncle William shook his head sadly. 'Magic didn't send me here, Phillip. I condemned myself to it. There is a saying: 'Where your treasure is, there will your heart be also.' My treasure was the past. Hell, I have discovered, is being given the things you treasured most in your life and then being sentenced to keep them for all eternity — only to discover that your treasure is worthless. The real treasure is love and living in a moment-by-moment relationship with your Maker, living in the here and now.

'I made a ghastly error, Phillip. An obsession with the past may seem harmless, but the gossamer threads of romance and mystery have the power to bind you like chains and hold you back from living effectively. Don't make my mistake,' he said, patting Phillip's shoulder affectionately. 'There is no coming forth by day as the Egyptians believed, no revisiting the world they loved — just eternal stillness, an arrested half-life in a stone-cold setting.'

Phillip was curious to know about the mummified ibis bird. 'Did you know that the sacred ibis bird you gave me had magical powers?' he said.

'Birds don't have magical powers.'

'Oh, but it did! It brought me here to find you.'

'The gods of Egypt have no power over us, Phillip. They are lifeless statues carved in stone. Don't make that mistake, either.'

'I've missed you,' Phillip said, squeezing his uncle's hand.

'And I, you,' Uncle William said. 'You were always like a son to me.'

Julia, who was watching the display of affection between them, sobbed.

It was a soft, choking sob. At first they ignored it. The

sobbing grew louder. Dogstar growled. Phillip turned at the sound of a rasping, dragging noise. Julia's sobs turned into a scream of terror.

It stood, squat legs outspread, just behind Julia, bulking in the passageway, a jagged mountain of green scales, a crocodile of heart-stopping proportions. It opened its mouth and its teeth were like a jagged coastline of white rocks covered with spume.

An image of the tablet of destiny reared in Phillip's mind. Next to Julia's picture had been the image of a crocodile.

Her doom!

Julia's sobbing had brought it here. Her envy of the love of others.

A memory of an incident ran though his mind like a length of film. It was the night they boarded the ferryman's boat.

'Did you love your uncle that much?' she had said.

'Yes,' he had said, 'and I believe he loved me.'

'I envy you,' she had said with a shake in her voice. 'Nobody ever loved me that much!' As she had spoken, there had been a startling rustle in the reeds as if something heavy dragged itself towards her. Julia had stiffened. 'What was that?'

'Probably a crocodile,' Phillip had said. 'Move away. We must climb into the boat. . .'

It had been following her all the way, just as the serpent had been following Coomber.

Envy of the love that others enjoyed. This was the monster following Julia. 'It's your monster, Julia,' Phillip said, calmly. 'Only you can get rid of it. You must deal with it.'

'Mine?' The crocodile dragged its heavy body closer to Julia. Julia flattened herself against the wall, sliding back along it until she bumped into Phillip. 'What do you mean mine? Shoo, go away!'

'It's your envy of others, like me, others who love their parents. You've got to let go of it. You've got to forgive your real mum and dad. It wasn't their fault what happened. They didn't want to leave you alone in the world. You've got to stop fighting it and let go. You've got to start appreciating the love you already have and those who care about you.'

'I can't forgive them!' Julia said. 'They left me as a little baby. Did I do something wrong to make them go?'

'Accept what's happened in your life. There are other people who love you!'

She sobbed, a frightened little girl now. 'Do they really?'

'Of course they do. Let go!'

'Must I?'

'Completely.' The crocodile was almost at her side. 'Do it now and not just because of that hideous creature next to you. Do it because you want to, because it's always been a monster that you had to get rid of.'

She blinked through her tears. 'All right. If you say so.'

'Say it to them. To your mum and dad — as if they were here.'

'I forgive you, Mum and Dad. I do, I really do. I don't know why you had to leave me, but I couldn't be loved more than I am now. . .'

She had sobbed before, but now she cried enough tears to wash the crocodile away. Phillip watched the crocodile. Its eyes were streaming. Was it crying because of the meal it was missing, because it finally had to let go of a small girl — or was it crying in some kind of reptilian sympathy?

'I forgive you, I forgive you!' Julia shouted, her young voice ringing in the stone passageway.

The crocodile burst like an exploding water bag, releasing an ocean of tears that ran in a wave up the length of the passage.

They had eluded the doom snake and the doom crocodile. Only the doom dog remained.

Phillip looked anxiously at Dogstar. The dog whined. Although Dogstar walked beside him, another hound dogged his footsteps — the spectre of the doom dog.

The tablet of destiny had shown the image of a dog carved next to his name. His fate had still to be played out. He recalled the ancient Egyptian story of the prince and the doom dog, about a boy destined by fate to meet his end through a snake, a crocodile or a dog. The snake and the crocodile were gone now. But an invisible shadow dog still loped behind Phillip, sniffing, waiting. He could feel its eyes measuring him, weighing him in unseen scales as the jackal-headed god had weighed his heart in the Hall of Judgment.

There was no ignoring the danger after what had happened to Coomber and Julia. Could Dogstar turn on him? He found himself wishing that this real-life story could break off suddenly, like the crumbling papyrus that told the story of the prince and the doom dog, suspending an ending that he did not want to face.

'Don't do it, 'Star boy,' he radioed silently to the animal. The animal must have felt his mood. He felt its tail slap reassuringly against the side of his leg. How could a friend like Dogstar turn?

If it did, if the unthinkable happened, when would it strike? Little time remained. Before long they would be emerging from the mountain and crossing the river to the other side.

Phillip patted the dog's head. If it did turn, it would not be because of its own choosing, he felt sure, but because it was in the power of something else.

He would have to be vigilant. He hoped it would not come to a choice between himself and Dogstar. The big-hearted dog had led them through the perils of a snake-filled desert, through a giant beetle's maze, along endless passages. It had been their compass as they ran blindly through the tomb-land of the underworld.

They stopped to check the map, comparing an inscribed stone at a branch in the passage with a sketch shown on the map. They pressed on. The last landmark had been a shattered pillar. There were landmarks all along the way, taking them on a route through the underworld that bypassed the guardians and gateways that had confronted them on the journey to the Field of Offerings.

They turned a bend in a passage and found their way blocked by an army of Nubian archers in a pillared chamber. It was a miniature army of models mounted on wooden pedestals. They had round black eyes set in brilliant white orbits and they carried unstrung bows and quivers full of arrows at their waists. They were larger than most models found in tombs — about half life-size, Phillip estimated.

The tomb travellers went among them to examine them.

'Nubian soldiers, along with Shardanas, were the secret weapons of the ancient Egyptians,' Uncle William explained. 'Like the British army with its ghurkas, they relied on these mercenaries to safeguard their empire.'

Coomber relieved one of the bowmen of his bow and a small quiver of arrows. A bowstring was attached to an end of the bow. He bent the bow, stringing it. He nocked an arrow to the string, took vague aim and let the string go. The arrow stuck in the chest of a wooden Nubian who fell over with a thud like a plank.

The tomb robbers must have committed more of the map to memory than Willard had suspected. A shot rang out, knocking another Nubian archer off its pedestal. The tomb robbers appeared at the end of the passageway.

'It's war,' Coomber said. 'Arm yourselves!' They made grabs for miniature bows and arrows. They ran for cover behind some pillars and here they made a stand, loosing off a hail of tiny arrows that stopped the tomb robbers' progress.

Phillip nocked an arrow to his bow, a bow no larger than an African bushman's bow. He drew the string to his cheek and let go. He saw the arrow fly and stick, quivering, in the tea-cloth-style headdress of an Arab and saw the man's eyes roll up to contemplate the nearness of his escape before he beat a hasty retreat, his white robe flapping around his legs like a tent in a gale. The tomb travellers fired another salvo and another. Julia cheered.

Phillip's bow snapped. 'Let's run!' he said.

The others followed him, firing the last of their arrows as they went.

The ceiling rose in the passage until it was lost in gloom over their heads. Something passed low over Phillip's head, brushing his hair. Was it a bat? He thought he heard the whistle of birds' wings.

'What was that?' Coomber said as another flitted past his ear. Phillip looked up. A winged creature sailed over his head and he almost stumbled when he saw a downturned human face on the bird's body, a small, Egyptian face with a beard and painted eyes. Then it was gone. Had he imagined it?

More birds swooped. He noticed a ledge running along the top of the passage just before it disappeared into darkness. Birds settled on the ledge to watch them go by. Another bird swooped low, its wingtips brushing Phillip's ear.

'Go, false shades who do not belong!' it said. It gave a piping laugh as it climbed into the blackness.

'Ba birds,' Uncle William said uneasily. 'Soul birds with vulture's bodies and human heads. Watch out for their claws and ignore what they say. They can be spiteful to the living and quite malignant.'

One dived too close to Dogstar who snapped its jaws and took a few feathers out of its wing, making it crash-land further down the passage. It got up and hopped grotesquely on the floor. Dogstar broke free from Phillip and ran after it.

'Leave it, Dogstar,' Phillip shouted after it. 'Here, boy!'

The soul birds sitting on the ledge above picked up his cry and parroted his words. They mimicked Phillip's voice perfectly, although at a higher pitch. 'Leave it, Dogstar! Leave it, Dogstar! Here, boy! There, boy! Here, boy!'

Dogstar twisted its head around in confusion. The injured bird made a run before achieving a wobbly take-off. 'Here, boy! There, boy! Here, there, everywhere, boy!'

Dogstar yelped and ran around in circles, baffled. They dive-bombed it, calling out its name, streaking off down the passage. 'Here, boy! Here, boy!' Dogstar snapped at the flitting missiles. The shrill cry of its name ran in spiralling echoes down the passage. Dogstar took off after the sound.

'Dogstar! Here, boy!' Phillip shouted after it, but it was just one more sound to confuse the dog.

The tomb travellers broke into a run. Phillip expected to find Dogstar around every turn of the passage, but empty passage after empty passage flung its disappointing length ahead of him. Tiring, he slowed. The birds had gone now.

Where had the soul birds led it? Into another system? Back into the horrors of the gateways and guardians?

12

The third fate

DOGSTAR WAS LOST and so was Phillip without it.
Maybe the Egyptians were right about the heart being
the seat of the soul. Phillip's heart felt heavy enough to
topple the balance of truth right off its stand, memories
of Dogstar adding an unbearable weight. He remembered the dog as a puppy when Uncle William first gave
it to him.

'I have named it for you,' Uncle William had said.
'Dogstar. After Sothis, the Egyptian name for Sirius, the
Dog Star, the most important star in the ancient Egyptian
constellation, the star that marked the inundation. One
day it may guide your life like that star. . .'

It *had* guided him, Phillip thought. It had run like a
living arrow through the Egyptian underworld, pointing
the way for the tomb travellers. Now it was lost and
needed his help. He could not leave it. He could not
repay the dog that way. And yet, in leaving the dog, he
might avoid the fate pronounced on him by Thoth, the
ibis bird.

'If you journey into the land of the dead, you may
meet your end through a crocodile, a serpent or a dog,'
the sacred ibis bird had said.

'A dog? You don't mean — not Dogstar! My own dog wouldn't turn on me, would he?'

The bird shrugged its wings. 'Who knows? Dogstar may turn out to be your doom dog. . .'

If he saved Dogstar, he might be saving the dog that would be his doom. Phillip remembered the milky smell of it as a puppy, the warmth of its body when he first took it from Uncle William's hands and the soft amber eyes that looked up at him, accepting him as a friend without question.

He would take the risk, he decided bleakly, whatever the risk to himself. If he had to spend eternity down here, he would risk it rather than abandon Dogstar. He saw Julia watching him.

'I won't leave here without Dogstar, either,' she whispered as if she had read his mind. 'Don't fret.' She patted his shoulder. 'We'll find him. We must. He risked his life to save me from the beetle. I haven't forgotten what he did and I never will.'

'We're not stopping to look for a dumb dog now,' Coomber said.

She turned, eyes flaming at him. 'You wouldn't have survived this long if it weren't for that dumb dog, you dumb boy!'

Coomber flinched at her ferocity and drew back half a step. 'I just want to go home.'

'We all do, but not without Dogstar.'

Phillip felt he had done well to control his own anger. He had wanted to hit Barry Coomber at that moment.

'The tomb robbers can't be far behind us,' Willard Chase said, reminding them of the threat that followed. 'We'd better find the dog quickly and move on.'

Julia stepped aside and waved him past. 'Go!' she threw a glance at Willard. 'Go!' she threw another glance at Coomber. She included Uncle William in her glare.

'You can all keep going if you like! Phillip and I are not leaving this place without Dogstar!' Her scalding anger at Coomber spilled over onto the others. Willard raised his hands in playful surrender. 'Easy, Julie girl. I'm as grateful to Dogstar as you are. Nobody's suggesting we abandon him.' Barry Coomber looked the other way.

'Well, good,' she said, softening. 'I'm sorry.'

Uncle William fell in beside Phillip. 'You're lucky to have a friend like that. She's a fine-spirited young woman,' he said softly. Phillip already knew that.

But his mind was on Dogstar.

Numerous passages ran off from the main one they were following. Dogstar could have been led by the soul birds along any of them. Phillip stopped at each one and called out hopefully, but with growing despondency in his voice. The echo of his own voice was the only thing that bounded back to him. Sometimes the echoes twisted cruelly into yelping sounds and his heart gave a hopeful leap.

'Dogstar!' Julia called down another passage. 'Come back, boy!'

Willard Chase looked uneasily over his shoulder. Was their shouting giving away their position to the tomb robbers?

Phillip went ahead down a ramp that led to a dimly lit chamber. The ramp was steep. It forced him into a run over the last few yards. Uncontrolled, he ran into the body and folded arms of a mummy. It broke under his impact with a soft snap like crust breaking, and gave off a cloud of dust. It happened before he had time to warn the others, who met the same grisly welcome.

It was a storeroom crammed to the ceiling with mummies. They were not stacked in an orderly fashion, but abandoned like a mountain of old tyres. Was this place the last refuge for the dead, chosen by the priests when the old order crumbled and they saw every tomb in the land lying empty and desecrated?

The tomb travellers moved uneasily through the chamber, hemmed in by the stacks of mummies. They passed so close that frayed edges of mummy wrappings brushed against them like cobwebs.

'Don't be afraid,' Uncle William said, calmly. 'Just try not to breathe in the dust. We've unsettled things a bit.' The mummies were powder dry. The sound of their approach dislodged a mummy. A grinning head with blindfolded eyes craned to look at Willard who was passing by.

A shot cracked and a new eye opened in the mummy's bandaged head. Willard dropped, twisted, and the others followed him. The tomb robbers stood at the top of the ramp.

'Stop!' one of them shouted in English.

Willard signalled the travellers to keep their heads down and made a run for the back of the chamber. They went after him. He stopped at the chamber's exit. 'This won't be pleasant work, but I need your help,' he said, urgently. 'Let's build a barricade of these bodies to block the exit.'

'Yuk,' Julia said.

'I'm not touching them,' Coomber said.

'A bit of body-building won't do you any harm, son,' Willard joked.

He dragged a pair of mummies by their feet off the pile and rested them together to start a new heap that would block the way out of the chamber. Phillip joined in and so did Uncle William and, more reluctantly, Coomber. The mummies were remarkably light, Phillip thought, grabbing one by the toe. It broke off in his hand. He heard the running feet of the tomb robbers approaching. Another warning shot ricocheted around the chamber, making their eardrums cringe. Stung to action, even Julia joined in, distastefully using her shoe to nudge a mummy onto the pile.

Willard produced a lighter from a pocket. 'These mummies are dry and impregnated with resins and natron. They burn quite merrily.'

He flicked the lighter and put a small yellow flame to a trailing twist of bandage. 'Light grey mummy wrapping and stand well back,' he quipped, pretending to read out instructions on a firework packet. The scrap of bandage gulped the flame as hungrily as a fuse. The whole mummy ignited, spreading flames to neighbouring ones and within seconds the chamber was ablaze.

Phillip saw the tomb robbers running down the ramp. The mummies sucked flames into themselves as if gulping in air. A mummy sat up, its limbs and wrappings twisting in the heat of the flames. Phillip felt ants run over his scalp. The men were quite close to the pile now. Phillip saw surprise jump into the faces of the robbers. A skeletal, badly decaying mummy sat up from the pile as if to challenge the new arrivals, the revivifying heat of destruction giving the mummy one last, mocking appearance of life before it disintegrated forever. Flames swept at the tomb robbers like an advancing bushfire.

'Now that's what I call a warm welcoming committee,' Willard Chase said.

'Let's go,' Uncle William said.

The tomb travellers moved on. Hope was fading for Dogstar. Was it trapped on the other side of the burning hall of mummies?

Phillip felt an empty whirring inside himself. More passages opened up on either side off them as they went.

'Dogstar! Here, boy. Come back — please!'

A soul bird flew past Phillip's face and laughed maliciously. It settled on the lintel of a darkness-filled doorway and turned to look down at him. 'You seek the pointy-faced one?'

'Where is it? What have you done with my dog?' Phillip shouted. The bird laughed, or at least the man's head on top of the bird's body laughed, making the wispy black curl of beard on its chin shake.

'The pointy-faced one is within,' the soul bird said, its painted black eyes shining with malice.

Phillip made for the doorway.

'We'll go together,' Julia said, stepping forward.

'No! Only the dog's master may enter here!' it said shrilly. 'If any other false shade sets foot inside, we will call the dog away and lead it on a dance through all eternity. The master — alone.'

Phillip shook his head. 'We can't risk it. I must go alone.'

Julia nodded and drew back.

'Be careful,' Uncle William said. 'Soul birds are full of spiteful tricks.'

Phillip walked eagerly into the black square of shadow that filled the doorway. The soul bird leaned over the lintel to watch him pass underneath. It spoke to him in rhyme:

Discover the truth that lies in the room.
Meet your dog — or meet your doom!

It took a while before Phillip's eyes grew accustomed to the gloom. He found himself in a painted chamber. Painted frescoes of shadowy human and animal figures sat up to watch him. It wasn't totally dark. A dim light picked out a familiar black profile against a painted wall. It was a pointy face with erect ears like spear tips.

'Dogstar?'

The familiar silhouette turned to face him. 'It's all right, boy, I'm here,' Phillip said soothingly.

Phillip went closer. There was something in the room, an inquisitive presence that brushed itself against him exploringly. It wasn't a friendly welcome. It was like stepping through a cobweb. Phillip shivered. 'Come to me, 'Star boy,' he said.

Was it Dogstar? It was hard to tell. The figure sat in shadow. He bent, hand extended to pat the dog's head. He saw the gleam of teeth and heard a rumbling, warning growl. It crouched low to spring. 'It's me, Dogstar. It's okay; I've come to get you.'

The growl grew to a snarl of rage and it leapt for his throat, or where his throat would have been if he hadn't kept bending. The animal swept over his head. He spun around.

A huge night-black jackal with unsheathed fangs stalked him, dripping saliva. Dogstar flew at it. They tangled like two buzz-saws of flashing fang and claw, rolling around the chamber in an unholy dogfight.

The jackal was bigger and more powerful, but Dogstar was as fluid as a snake, wriggling out of reach. The black-faced jackal snapped its teeth with a loud click. Dogstar danced around it, sinking its teeth into the jackal's thigh. The jackal rounded, giving a cry of pain and filthy rage.

Dogstar circled like a satellite using the slingshot effect, the way it had run around Phillip's mother with the bird in its mouth, and took off in a new direction. The jackal snapped at empty air. Dogstar ran at a wall. There was a deeply cut bas relief on it, with ridges like the rungs of a ladder. Dogstar ran up the wall to the jackal's surprise.

The jackal went into the wall, banging its snout with a force that made it yelp. It stood up against the wall, pawing it uselessly. Dogstar was halfway up. It dropped like a boulder on the jackal and grabbed it by the scruff of the neck, tipping it over, shaking. The jackal fell heavily, Dogstar still hanging on. The jackal gave a yelp of defeat. Dogstar wouldn't let go.

The black jackal, the god of the wrappings, went off like a detonation in a streamer factory. It exploded in a howl of rage and threw streams of bandages into the air. They fell in a pile of empty wrappings.

The attacker was gone.

Dogstar jumped into Phillip's arms and together they made nearly as much noise as the dogfight, but it was a joyful wrestling match of loving, squeezing and licking. Phillip was met at the door by an anxious-looking Julia. The others peered around her.

'Dogstar's back! You found him! What was all that noise?'

'The black jackal. Anubis. The god of the wrappings.'

'What jackal?'

They looked at each other blankly, but they soon shrugged the matter aside to join in making a fuss of Dogstar. 'We'd better keep going,' Phillip said.

They had survived the serpent, the crocodile and the dog of doom. Did all three fates now lie behind them? Phillip expected to feel a surge of relief, but a shadow loped behind him — further back, it was true, but still there — weighing him in unseen scales.

He tried to chase the shadow away by turning a bright light of examination on it.

Something had been different about his crisis. While the others had conquered their monsters themselves, Dogstar had fought the battle for him. The others had been compelled to change — Coomber to stop stealing and Julia to stop envying — but he had not been made to change. Why had it been different for him?

What was his monster? The problems of the others

had seemed so clear to him by comparison, but his own was more elusive, like the unseen dog behind him, slinking in the shadows of his imagination.

He remembered the ferryman's words: 'Be warned. Looking back isn't such a wise thing to do. One day you'll look back on my words and agree. Before too long, I'd say. Take care that you are not lost in the past — forever.'

Was a love of the past his monster? He sensed that his fate was linked with Uncle William's. He and Uncle William were more than kin; they were kindred spirits. Uncle William's experience was some kind of warning. If he did not change. . . Was his rescue of Uncle William also a rescue of himself? He needed to think more about that.

The passageway opened into the cave system that he remembered entering earlier.

They were nearing the opening. They were in darkness again. The lamps had ended. Willard produced his torch from a pocket and Phillip added the beam of his bicycle lamp to comfort himself. As they continued, the silence that had followed them gave way to the *plink plink plink* of water dripping. It cooled them. They bent to clear a low, saw-toothed roof. They met the undergound stream and there, beside a cluster of wild helictites that pointed like a hand, they found the place to cross, a series of slippery, soapy-textured stepping stones.

Once across it, they followed their torchlights along a gallery beside the water.

Then around a bend, the opening yawned in the dim light of the western desert. They were almost out of the system.

Uncle William stopped Phillip before they reached the opening.

'I can't go out with you, Phillip,' he said.

Something in his voice caught at Phillip like a cold hand.

'What are you saying?'

'Go out of the underworld exit alone and don't look back.'

'I'm not leaving without you.'

'You must go out, but don't turn around and look back. Whatever you do, don't look back.'

'Why not?'

'Because looking back is your problem. You've spent too much of your life looking back. It could be your undoing, just as it was mine.'

'Are you just going to give up, when I've come so far to save you? You must come out.'

'Let's be grateful. We've had one last journey together. I've been given a chance to say goodbye and, more importantly, to warn you not to make the mistakes that I made. Goodbye, Phillip.' He hugged the boy. 'You can have this if you'd like it; it's no use to me now.' He gave Phillip the scroll. 'Just keep it somewhere safe, a bank vault perhaps, so that it never falls into the wrong hands.'

'Uncle William. . . '

'Remember, go straight out. Don't turn around. None of you must turn around.'

'All right,' he said, dubiously. 'But don't you turn around and run away.'

'Go. . .'

Phillip tore his eyes away from Uncle William. He looked at the others. 'You go out first,' he said to them. They filed past him. Julia looked pale. Willard, sober-eyed, patted Uncle William on the shoulder as he went. Coomber looked puzzled.

Now Phillip was alone with Uncle William and alone with an aching fear. Dogstar whined.

'Go now.'

Phillip went towards freedom like a boy going to prison. Uncle William couldn't leave. That was it. He was probably turning to go already, to disappear back into that rigid world of the dead.

Don't look back. Whatever you do, don't look back. Why?

Uncle William didn't want the parting to hurt Phillip. That was it. He wanted the final break to be as clean and painless as possible. But it would end with Phillip losing him, just the same.

He didn't want to let go of Uncle William. He wouldn't. Memories of what they had been through to reach Uncle William came back to him — the goddess with the swinging swords, the struggles against the great beetle and the great ape, the weighing of their hearts in the Hall of Judgment. What had it all been for?

He remembered the loss he had felt at Uncle William's funeral as they turned the squeaking screws that sealed his coffin. Had he suffered all this merely to let his uncle go without even a backward glance?

He listened as he walked, hoping to hear Uncle William's footfall behind him. Nothing. Uncle William wasn't there any more. He was already melting into the dark.

'I'll go back after him. I'll go through it all again if I must. But what if he hides from me? What if I lose him?. . .' He was near the exit now. The others had stopped outside and in accordance with Uncle William's instructions, were keeping their eyes turned away.

The air from outside was sweet in Phillip's lungs, but it did not comfort him. The taste of freedom only tantalised him, like a glimpse of sunlight through prison bars. It wasn't freedom if he couldn't share it with Uncle William.

He remembered good times he had enjoyed with his

uncle in his house, especially late at night when his uncle's study was as quiet as a tomb and the old adventurer would translate ancient scrolls for Phillip's delight and wonder.

He did not much like the idea of shadows in his life at that moment. He wanted Uncle William back. He would have traded a museum full of treasures from the past just to have his uncle with him in the here and now, to see the humorous gleam in his eyes again and to hear his voice fondly reading out some text.

Uncle William was getting away. He was giving him time to hide. If Uncle William wouldn't come out, then he would drag him out.

His fingers tightened around Dogstar's collar as he prepared to turn and go back after Uncle William. Dogstar growled warningly.

Phillip turned.

Uncle William had not disappeared.

But he soon did.

He was no more than a step behind Phillip, but as soon as Phillip's turning eyes fell on him, so did a paralyzing beam of light that halted the old man in mid-stride. He began to fade away in front of Phillip's eyes.

'I can't go after you, Phillip,' he said in a voice that rapidly thinned away. 'Nor can you come after me now. Don't blame yourself. There are no second chances. This time our goodbye must be for good. It's forever. . .'

'Uncle William, come back!'

Dogstar squealed in distress. Phillip threw his arms around the glowing collection of atoms that was Uncle William, but his arms met nothing but themselves.

'Goodbye Phillip. No man ever had a better nephew. . .'

Then Uncle William was gone and this time Phillip knew that it was forever.

No words and no looks from the others could comfort him. They went down the cliffs to the sandy desert below. He walked behind them mechanically, not even feeling the sand under his feet.

No giant serpent chased them across the sandy desert this time although the sands still shifted with the wriggled signatures of innumerable small snakes. Phillip could not have cared about the snakes.

He had failed. He had put them all through the trials and terrors of the Egyptian underworld for nothing. Why? Why had he stupidly turned his head around to look? He was always doing it. It was his great mistake.

The Boy Whose Face Was Turned Backwards. The ferryman had said it. You paid a terrible price for living in the past. But would it have made any difference if he hadn't looked around? Would Uncle William really have been allowed to leave?

He remembered Uncle William's last words. 'Don't blame yourself. There are no second chances. This time our goodbye must be for good. It's forever. . .'

But no words and no excuses could comfort him.

They reached the cavern. The ferryboat waited at the quay after making its nightly voyage across the river with the souls of the departed.

'An Old Kingdom papyriform boat, here? Now I've seen everything,' Willard said.

'This is how we came over,' Phillip said. 'How did you get across, Willard — you and the tomb robbers for that matter?'

'I crossed in a *felucca*. The tomb robbers used a powerboat.'

'Where's their boat now?'

Willard Chase shrugged. 'Hidden somewhere on the riverbank. If they do manage to find their way through the underworld, they'll be trying to get to it so that they can stop us crossing.'

'We must board this ferryboat. It's our only way across. We must sneak on board — but be careful of the ferryman, the Man Whose Face Is Turned Backwards. If he sees us, he'll make sure we don't leave here. I'll go and renew my acquaintance with him, while you sneak on board. It worked last time.'

Willard Chase looked dubious. 'You're going to face a guy whose head is turned backwards — alone?'

'Not face him exactly,' Phillip said. 'He's twisted around the other way, you see. Don't worry though; we're quite good friends.'

Julia tugged Willard's sleeve. 'Come on, Phillip knows what he's doing. We must make our way to the prow where the ferryman can't see us.'

They left Phillip and Dogstar and crept towards the prow, staying in the shadows of the cavern, out of the torchlight that illuminated the ferryboat.

Phillip still had the scroll. He looked at it. It might not be wise to walk up to the ferryman with the scroll in his hand. It might arouse suspicion. As a denizen of the underworld, the ferryman might even try to seize it. Phillip stashed it behind some loose stones near the wall of the cavern, then walked into the pool of light shining from the boat. The ferryman was mending a net.

'Hi! Remember me?' Phillip gave him a cheery smile.

The ferryman had his broad back to Phillip, but his head was twisted around to face him.

'Looking back, yes, I do. How did it go for you? You are a rare one to have been there and back! Did you find what you went to find, Boy Whose Face Is Turned Backwards?'

'I have found what I wanted and I have some amazing memories to look back on.'

'Memories. Beware of those. Did I not warn you of the dangers of looking back? Haven't you learnt your lesson?'

'What lesson was that?'

'Not yet, hmm? Well, it can't be long now. You want a lift across, I suppose? Come on board.'

'Would you do that?'

'Of course, I've been waiting for you. You're late and I must cast off. Hurry up.'

Looking over the ferryman's shoulder, Phillip saw first Coomber, then Julia and finally Willard clamber over the side of the vessel and hide behind the deckhouse.

'You must be quick. I see others coming and they are not shades; they are the desecrators,' said the ferryman.

Phillip looked behind him. The tomb robbers were running through the archway towards the boat.

'Start casting off,' Phillip said. 'But first there's something I must fetch.' He ran back into the shadows to the place where he had stashed the scroll. Dogstar darted ahead of him. Before he could reach the stones, the animal turned on him, its teeth bared, its eyes shooting sparks of anger.

'No, Dogstar, out of my way. . . the boat's leaving.'

He reached out to pat the dog and it snapped at his hand. Loathing blazed in its eyes.

The doom dog.

Dogstar had become the doom dog.

The tomb robbers gave a shout and he heard the rush of their footsteps.

'Hurry,' the ferryman shouted. 'You must let go of the past. You must not try to take it with you. Hurry! See, I am raising the gangplank.'

Phillip heard Julia's muffled scream. The dog seemed to swell in a ball of hate in front of Phillip, its back arched. Dogstar had become like the seething, gnashing jackal that had stalked him. At any second it would jump at him and tear out his throat.

The scroll.

It was the last thing his uncle had given him, a key to the past. He could use it again to go back if he chose. He had to get it back.

He heard the rumble of the gangplank being dragged on board. Dogstar crouched lower to spring. He saw no glimmer of recognition in its hate-slitted eyes.

'Let go of the past and stop looking back!' the ferryman called. 'Turn your face around, Boy Who Looks Back!'

This was his doom. He was trapped between two choices. Run and leave the scroll forever. Stay and be caught by the tomb robbers. Coomber had let go of the stolen jewels. Julia had let go of her envy. Phillip had to let go of the map to the past.

He turned his head around and ran for the boat. The gangplank had already been raised so he made a dive and landed in a pile of fishing nets. Dogstar landed beside him, his old Dogstar, licking his face happily and yelping for joy.

A breeze blowing through the archway of rock filled their sail and took them away. The tomb robbers fired shots from the quayside. Phillip saw holes punched in the fabric like stitches.

'I envy you, boy,' the ferryman called to Phillip, 'for now your head is turned around, while mine is just the same. Maybe my head will turn around, too, one day,' he said hopefully.

'That's something to look forward to, Ferryman,' Phillip said.

Phillip patted Dogstar. The shadow of the doom dog had gone now, he felt — left behind in the shadow world of the other side where it belonged.

They sailed through the lake of fire just as before and though the flames raged around them, the ship passed through unscathed. Then they were out of the flames into a broad stretch of the river.

Phillip heard a whine floating on the breeze, like a far-off insect. A powerboat no bigger than a water bug began to grow in his vision. It was heading towards them. The tomb robbers had seen them and were trying to head them off.

'Turn your head around and look ahead,' Phillip said to the ferryman.

'Look ahead? Do you think I can?'

'You must. The tomb robbers are trying to ambush us. They have come around to head us off. We must take evasive action.'

The ferryman closed his eyes and, with a great concentration of will, turned his head. There was a ghastly cracking sound like a spar snapping and Phillip suddenly found himself looking at the back of the ferryman's head.

'You've done it, you've turned your head around.'

'It was your action that inspired me!' the ferryman said. 'But there's no time to celebrate now. I see them coming. We must turn back one more time, back into the flames.'

He turned the steering oar and shouted some orders and unseen hands adjusted the sail.

He turned the boat about and they drifted back into the lake of fire. The powerboat cut its engine and stopped to watch as they passed back into the flames. The tomb robbers had guns in their hands, but they did not use them. They watched spellbound as the ferryboat reached the flames. Did they expect to see the flames leap up the ropes and sails and engulf the boat?

When the ferryboat drifted on serenely, unharmed by the flames, they shouted. The one at the stern gave the outboard engine throttle. If it was safe for the ferryboat to go into the flames, then it was safe for them to do the same, they assumed. The nose of the speedboat lifted as they roared into the flames. The flames closed around them like red waves.

Their fuel tank exploded.

Phillip and the others watched as the boat burnt to the waterline. There was no trace of the tomb robbers.

13

Thoth

THE FERRY TOOK THEM to the far shore and unseen hands ran out the gangplank.

'I think I'll give up this work,' the ferryman said. 'I look forward to a new future. A man must look ahead. Maybe I'll take tourists on tours along the Nile. There's good money in it, I'm told.'

'Thankyou, Herhaf. You have not only helped turn my head, but also my life around and I owe you one. Goodbye.'

'Your stowaway friends may leave by the gangplank,' the ferryman said. 'They needn't sneak over the side.'

'You knew they were there?'

'All along. You don't have your face turned around for thousands of years without developing eyes in the back of your head!'

Phillip called the others and they came guiltily out of hiding.

'Thanks for the lift,' Julia said.

'We'll pay if you like,' Willard Chase said.

'I don't think you could afford it. There aren't many ferry services to the other side and I charge accordingly.'

'Name your price,' Willard said, reaching for his wallet.

'Five deben.'

'Would you take five dollars?'

'Seven,' said the ferryman.

'Five-fifty?'

'Six.'

'Done.'

'What's a dollar?' the boatman said.

'You don't know?'

Herhaf shrugged. 'No idea, but I can't resist haggling.'

Willard riffled through some notes in his wallet.

'Six dollars each; that's twenty-four dollars.'

'The dog's fare will be another dollar,' Herhaf said. 'Make it twenty-five.'

'I don't suppose you'd accept a tomb traveller's cheque?' Willard said, half-jokingly. The ferryman looked blank. 'No, I guess not.' Willard pulled some more notes out of his wallet.

He handed them to the boatman, who fingered them admiringly in calloused hands. 'It's exceedingly fine papyrus, but I only accept cold cash.'

'I don't have any.'

'I have very sharp eyes,' the boatman said. 'I saw those metal pieces in your purse.'

'That's only small change.'

'Small to you, but so are pieces of gold. I'll take them,' he said with a gleam in his eye.

Willard shrugged and shook the loose change out of his wallet. He dumped it all in the boatman's hand.

'Thought you could fool a simple peasant boatman, did you?' Herhaf said.

'Thanks again.'

'Goodbye, Herhaf,' Phillip said. Herhaf was busy counting his coins.

The tomb travellers stepped off the ferry and pressed their way through a crowd of tall papyrus reeds that clamoured in a breeze at the edge of the river, their heavy umbels bobbing like heads trying to gain a glimpse of new arrivals. Phillip and Dogstar went down the gangplank last, following Coomber, who parted the wall of reeds ahead of Phillip and the dog. He let them go and the reeds swished shut like a prickly curtain in Phillip's face, blocking Coomber from view.

Coomber hadn't changed, Phillip thought, in spite of all they had been through. He parted the reeds and slipped through. Coomber and the others had gone. Phillip found himself in a clearing. Dogstar growled. In the centre of the clearing, in profile like a tomb carving, stood a brilliant white ibis bird with black head and neck. It stared unblinkingly at them with a single, stone-hard eye.

'The boy has returned, I see.' It cackled as it had done that night that seemed so long ago when lightning had flashed in Phillip's bedroom. 'And so has his doom dog. You survived.'

'Dogstar wasn't my doom dog. And yes, we've survived all three fates.'

'You are a very resourceful and wily youth, Phillip. I see you have learnt your lesson though. This adventure has turned your head around.'

'Don't you start,' Phillip said impatiently. 'I've had enough talk about heads turning around. I want to go home, please.'

'That's not up to me.'

'But you have the power to send us home again,' Phillip said, feeling a coldness in his stomach.

'I have no power and never have had. The only power I have is the power others give to me. You must ask another for help.'

'Who?'

'Him. The power who has watched over you all this

time. One of your companions has been in touch with him from the beginning.'

'What power?'

The bird cackled spitefully. 'If you don't know about him, don't expect a pagan Egyptian ibis bird to tell you. Ask her.'

'Her?'

'The bird's eye hardened even more. 'That pestilent girl who plays such a mean game of senet. She has called on him constantly from the start.'

Julia.

Still Phillip did not understand. 'But you brought us here, didn't you? You were the one who granted my wish to come back to the land of the dead?'

'It may have seemed so, but it was your own will that made it happen. I was only a trigger.'

'Then you can't send us back?'

'I'm afraid not.'

'So we're stuck here,' Phillip said.

'Yes, and stuck here alone,' it said. 'The others have already gone. Perhaps they were never really here at all.'

The waving heads of the papyrus thicket seemed to crane their stalks to look at Phillip. 'You're trying to fool me,' Phillip said to the bird. 'The others are behind those reeds, waiting for us. Come on 'Star boy, find them.' Phillip took the dog by the collar and led it through the thicket in search of the others.

The papyrus reeds seemed to close in. He called out. 'Julia! Willard. . .' The wall of reeds muffled his cries. 'Coomber? Can you hear me? Where are you? Wait for us!'

He stopped, listening for a reply. The reeds rattled harshly against each other in the breeze, making a sound like dry laughter. Phillip went on, leading the dog in ever-widening circles through the head-high reeds. How far ahead could they be? Was there no end to this sea of green? He called out again. Perhaps he'd better fight his way through the reeds to clear ground. Perhaps the others were on the far side, waiting for him in the desert. The reeds marched in against him, throwing themselves against him. The giant umbels butted against him. Phillip felt smothered.

'Come on, Dogstar, we're going to have to fight our way out!'

Dogstar went at the reeds with a will, adding traction power to Phillip's step with its sinewy muscle. The reeds stretched endlessly, like the sea the Egyptians called the Great Green. They seemed to roll in like waves as if there were currents among them, holding him back, tiring him. Phillip felt perspiration trickle down the inside of his shirt.

When he reached a clearing, he fell down exhausted to rest. Dogstar flopped at his feet, resting its head on his legs. 'This is hopeless, boy. Let's get our strength back for a moment.'

What a spiteful turn of events to lose the others now, after all they had been through together.

Phillip's body felt limp with exhaustion. How long had it been since he had truly rested, let alone slept? He felt his muscles, bunched up from the effort of pushing through the reeds, relax. His breathing lost its raspiness and steadied.

Who was the other power who had watched over them from afar all the way?

A picture of his grandmother formed in his mind and he imagined he felt her touch again and heard her creaking voice as she read to him from a Book that had a soft, wrinkly leather cover that felt like the skin of her hands. That other Book of power. Julia had spoken about it.

Did he have a right to ask for help now, when he had not asked for it before?

He saw a large white bird fly across his patch of sky. It was the ibis bird. He wondered sleepily where it was going. Where did it belong? In myth?

The morning sun felt good on Phillip's skin. It was something he had missed in the Land of Shades. Uncle William had missed it, too. What Uncle William had said was true — it was not just the sun in the sky, but the sun of a special, warming, life-giving presence. That nagging unease had left him.

14
Saturday

THERE WAS A TAPPING SOUND QUITE CLOSE BY, at a
window perhaps, and answering it like a far-off echo,
more knocking. Was it somebody downstairs at the
door? He heard Dogstar barking at a distance.

Julia.

Phillip opened his eyes. The light was still on. A
knock at the window turned his head and he saw a
mummy's head with shiny eyes staring at him and he
saw the bandages part in a grin as the mummy face took
pleasure in his fright.

'Go home, Coomber,' Phillip shouted.

The knocking at the front door went on. Phillip threw
a pillow at the window and ran downstairs. He was
joined by Dogstar who whined and danced around him.

Phillip opened the door and shivered as night air
wrapped itself around the legs of his jeans. 'What took
you so long to answer the door?' Julia said. 'Did you
fall asleep? I've been knocking for ages.'

'Sorry, I must have dozed. It's all right now, Julia, I'm fine.
Thanks for coming, but I don't need you any more. I'll walk
you home again, but first I have to deal with a mummy who
keeps peering in at my bedroom window. . .'

'A mummy? Phillip, you're saying creepy things again!'

'Come and take a look for yourself if you don't believe me.' Phillip switched on the outside light and went across the porch and onto the lawn, with Julia and Dogstar in tow. He went to the peach tree that stood against the house underneath his window. 'You can climb down now, Coomber; you're not frightening anybody up there, except yourself!'

'Coomber!' Julia said. 'What's he doing here?' She peered up into the darkness of the tree. It was Coomber all right.

'Acting like an idiot. He came dressed as a mummy to scare me.'

The leaves of the peach tree rustled and the branches gave a shake. Barry Coomber slid heavily down. 'What's she doing here this time of night?' Coomber said, going straight onto the attack.

'I'd like to ask you the same question,' Julia said. 'Don't you think Phillip's upset enough about his uncle without your playing juvenile tricks in the middle of the night?'

'Don't expect me to cry for him.'

'You'll never change, will you, Coomber?' Phillip said.

'Why should I?'

'I just hoped you might. I hoped we all might change. Especially after tonight.'

'What's so special about tonight?'

They didn't remember. They didn't know. They hadn't really shared his nightmare, it seemed.

'Tonight's as good a time as any to change,' he said, disappointed.

'What a lot of rot.'

'I think you ought to change,' Phillip said. 'You ought to stop taking things that aren't yours.'

'Me, take things that aren't mine?' Coomber said innocently. He pulled a large ripe peach out of a pocket. He had taken it from Phillip's peach tree. No wonder he kept going back up there.

'No, perhaps you'll never change,' Phillip said. 'But I hope I've changed. I need to change. I'm sorry for what I said about your brother. I said it to hurt you and I shouldn't. I've got nothing against you, Coomber.'

'No hard feelings then,' Barry Coomber said. 'Here, have your peach back.'

He tossed the peach to Phillip and walked away.

It surprised Phillip. Perhaps it was a good sign. Barry Coomber didn't usually give things back. The peach was warm from being in his pocket. Then Phillip heard a soft crunch in the dark as Coomber bit into another peach. He had kept one. Well, at least he had made a gesture, Phillip thought.

'Why do you want me to change?' Julia said when they were alone.

'Don't you know?'

'Tell me.'

Phillip wondered how she'd take what he wanted to say, but he decided to say it anyway. 'I thought you might stop hating your real parents so much and start appreciating the only mum and dad you've got — also that you'd stop thinking nobody cares about you, because they do.'

Julia looked guilty.

'I suppose I'm wrong to think the way I do. I should try to change.'

'You must.'

'You really want me to change?'

'Yes, I do.'

'Then I'll try.'

'Come on, I'll walk you home.'

She nodded. 'Yes, I'd better go home. I don't really want to worry Mum and Dad.'

Dogstar walked beside Phillip, slapping its tail against the side of his leg.

'What's all this about changing, Phillip? Do you think you've changed?'

'I hope so, Julia. I've got to stop looking back. I've got to live in the here and now.'

She was still puzzled about his earlier phone call. 'What's the mystery about your uncle?' she said. 'Did you really visit his grave?'

'I thought I did. At least I tried to. Maybe I found the wrong grave in the dark. . . I thought my uncle had been swallowed up. . . Maybe it was a newly dug grave I came across. It was dark. . . and yet. . .'

'What?'

'There was an associate of Uncle William's at the graveside who also thought my uncle's coffin had disappeared. His name was Willard Chase, an archaeological detective.'

'Maybe he was lost, too.'

'I suppose it's possible,' Phillip said. 'He had a pretty hopeless sense of direction.'

Julia touched his arm. 'I've been worried about you, Phillip. In fact I've been thinking a lot about you.'

'Not just thinking. I know you've been doing more than that. I've never had anyone say prayers for me before.'

She stopped him, turning him around to face her.

'How did you know?'

'A bird told me,' he said.

Phillip woke the next morning and stepped out of bed, shedding dreams like a snake sheds its skin. He went to the window to look out at the morning sunshine.

Dreams, so alive a moment earlier, began to dissipate like morning mist in the sun. He spotted Dogstar running back from a nearby park.

He remembered the ibis bird.

He checked the bookcase shelf. The mummified ibis bird had gone. Dogstar came up the stairs and slipped into the room. The pharaoh hound had muddy paws. It had been digging.

'Where's the bird, Dogstar? What have you done with it? Buried it for good this time?'

Dogstar slowly wagged its tail and rubbed itself against his leg. 'You're hungry and want to be fed? Oh well, at least you didn't eat the thing,' he said. 'I'll tell you what. I'll feed you and then we'll take a good, long walk. What do you say?'

It was time to stop thinking of the past, he thought; it was time to be out in the sunshine enjoying the day. It was Saturday. Perhaps he'd call Julia and ask her to join them for a walk in the park.

Other books by Roy Pond
published as Albatross
teenage paperbacks:

PLAYING DIRECTOR

Dave loved reading choose-
your-own story books. He
didn't like others deciding
which way his favourite
stories should go.

Then one day he met a
movie director while on the Ghan train to Australia's
centre. 'You can pretend I don't exist if you like, but I'm
here and I plan to share the journey with you.'

Dave looked up from the page of his choose-your-own
story book into the eyes of a bearded stranger.

'You like being in control?' the movie director said.

What an exciting, yet scary possibility! Dave could
play director of his own life — choose his own path, his
own endings. No longer the humdrum, the boring, the
same old routine, but adventure in the mysterious red
heart of Australia, riding a legendary desert train.

But what if he chose the wrong track?

REMOTE CONTROL

'What if I said you were looking at Flite Madison in the flesh?' the flier said.

'I'd laugh. He's a book hero.'

'Maybe. But the books could have been written about me. I'm just like him. I fly anything, anywhere, and never ask too many questions — just like Flite Madison.'

Was the flier Nick's long-sought hero? Who better for a model plane enthusiast? And didn't Nick's English teacher say he needed more experience of life to write? Should he stay on the ground and 'play it safe', or join the flier and take a few risks?

PYRAMID VOYAGERS

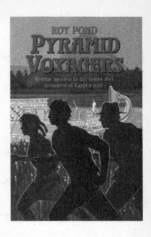

In this sequel to *Tomb Travellers*, the rich heritage of ancient Egypt — its tombs, treasures, pyramids and papyrus scrolls — is mysteriously vanishing. Can it be rescued before it all disappears? Tomb travellers Phillip, Julia, Barry and Willard take up this fresh challenge.

They must take a nightmarish voyage down the Nile in a 4 500-year-old sunboat, confronting the creatures of Egypt's dangerous underworld. . . Maybe they have taken on too much after all!

Samantha Alexan[...] son, husband and [...] animals including her thoroughbred horse, Bunny, and a pet goose called Bertie. Her schedule is almost as busy and exciting as her plots – she writes a number of columns for newspapers and magazines, is an agony aunt for teenagers on BBC Radio Leeds and in her spare time she regularly competes in dressage and showjumping events.

WINNERS 2

Crossing the Line

Samantha Alexander

MACMILLAN CHILDREN'S BOOKS

To my dearest husband.
For your endless love, support and encouragement.

First published 2001 by Macmillan Children's Books
a division of Macmillan Publishers Limited
25 Eccleston Place, London SW1W 9NF
Basingstoke and Oxford
www.macmillan.com

Associated companies throughout the world

ISBN 0 330 48439 7

A CIP catalogue record for this book is available from
the British Library.

Phototypeset by Intype London Ltd
Printed and bound in Great Britain by Mackays of Chatham plc, Kent

One

♘

"He's not picking up! He's not quickening!"

Horses thundered into the home straight. Jockeys shouted, a couple of loose horses ran with the main pack. The roar of the crowds, the smell of bruised grass, the fear, the adrenalin . . . I breathed in the race.

"Come on, Murphy!" I clutched the spectators' rail and prayed him home safe. The last fence loomed up.

Horses bunched together, lunging forwards. "Murphy, come on!" My whole being was fixed on the big, chestnut horse travelling on the outside, hating every minute. The jump was two strides out. He had to lengthen.

What I saw next made my words die in my throat. In desperation, his jockey, Rory Calligan, pulled through his whip. "No!" I managed to yell, knowing the consequences. "Don't hit him!"

I was haring along by the white rails, crazy with panic. Murphy's huge ears snaked back flat to his neck. The fence, it was upon them. Rory hit him

1

again down his flank but to no effect. The horse shouldered into the stiff black birch and somersaulted over it with a sickening thud.

"And Murphy's Law has fallen at the last, Heritage Bay takes up the running . . . It's Heritage Bay from Climate Change . . ."

I didn't stop to think for an instant. I shot under the rails and tore across the racecourse, heaving with fear.

He was up. No dangling legs. No horrific injuries. Just dazed and surprised.

"Rory!" His jockey was still down. "Rory!" He was curled in a tight ball, helpless in the cut-up grass. My stomach writhed with panic. If he was badly hurt, paralysed, unconscious . . .

The ambulance rattled along closer and closer. I could hear the siren. I knew I mustn't touch him but, like a moth to a candle, I had to run my fingers down his cheek.

"Justina!" Wild with fury, he leapt up. He grabbed the tops of my arms and yanked me down into the grass. Then his weight was on top of me, bearing down on my head and chest until I couldn't move. I could feel his heart hammering through the thin racing silks, his breath on my neck, the apprehension running through him. And then I realized.

The pounding hooves made the ground vibrate. The race wasn't over. It was the golden rule of

2

racing – never get up until the last horse has gone by.

How could I have been so stupid? And now they were upon us, a torrent of horse flesh, sliding, slipping, crashing through the fence. Any minute one could be a faller.

I pressed my head into Rory's chest. He was squeezing me tightly. A rain of legs came down and skidded to each side, inches from our heads. It was like being stampeded by a herd of buffalo. And then, nothing. The danger passed. Just a crow cawing and the ambulance crew rushing to the scene.

I was shaking but I didn't know whether it was from being so close to Rory or nearly being trampled to death.

"What the heck were you playing at?" Furiously, Rory flung off his jockey skull cap, glaring at me with his dark, piercing eyes. "I saw someone killed by standing up in the middle of a race. Have you no brain in that thick head of yours? How can you call yourself a jockey, a professional?"

"Don't speak to me like that." A lump sprang into my throat. "If you hadn't hit Murphy in the first place—"

"Don't mind us," a Red Cross man grinned.

"Oh, you make me sick," I yelled, on the defensive because I knew I was wrong. Rory was nineteen and an ace jockey who had been in line for

3

the Jockeys' Championship until he had broken his leg last season.

I was sixteen and had ridden in four races to date. It was my ambition to win the Grand National but nobody took me seriously. Racing was a man's world and getting rides was like getting blood out of a stone. I was cut up with jealousy because the Guv'nor, Kenneth Brown, had put Rory on board Murphy instead of me. He owned the stables out of which we raced and what he said went.

"You'll never win a race on that horse," I spluttered, swallowing back a torrent of tears. "Because you haven't got a sensitive bone in your body."

Murphy was back in the overnight racing stables being examined by a vet, as was routine procedure. I cast my eyes frantically over his legs but he seemed to be all right. Mandy, one of the lasses from the same stables as me, was holding his head collar, while Scottie – the travelling head lad – had Gertie, a miniature black-and-white goat, pinioned at the back of the stable. Gertie was Murphy's companion and travelled everywhere at his side. She'd happily die for him and was at present eyeballing the vet who was moving in with a syringe and needle.

I took the rope from Mandy and pressed my head against the big, chestnut horse. He was everything I'd dreamed about since I was six years old. Even though he hadn't tried today, and he wasn't the best-looking racehorse in the world, I knew he was capable of anything.

"He'll be a bit stiff but he'll live." The vet packed up his case. Another horse had come in with a nosebleed.

"Everybody's talking about how you ran out on to the racecourse to save Rory," Mandy gushed, popping with excitement. Mandy was my best friend at the racing yard. At first we hadn't got on too well. Her only ambition was to marry a famous jockey, but by sharing a house we'd become close, especially as Shona, the other girl with whom we shared, could be so awful.

"It was for Murphy," I snapped. "And as for Rory Calligan, he's just an ungrateful pig."

"He only shouted because he cares." Mandy bit her lip. She had obviously been reading too many psychology books. "He hasn't even noticed that I exist."

I suddenly remembered that Mandy had a thumping great crush on Rory herself and guilt automatically kicked in.

"Anyway," she visibly pulled herself together. "It's not Rory who's going to be doing the shouting. It's the Guv'nor."

"Rory rode a good race, the horse just didn't try."

I did a double take. The Guv'nor, who'd watched the race at home because his arthritis was playing up, seemed to think he'd seen everything.

Rory smirked with relief and lowered himself into a leather chair. Chelsea, the Guv'nor's wire haired terrier with bushy eyebrows and a psychotic nature, dived on his shoelaces.

"If he hadn't used his whip—" I started.

"Oh come off it, the horse was travelling backwards long before then," Rory cut in.

"Don't talk to me about who should or shouldn't have been doing things," the Guv'nor flared up. "Channel 4 Racing had a field day filming my apprentice jockey bobbing about the racecourse in a miniskirt and trainers. What the hell did you think you were doing, exactly?"

I blushed brick-red and desperately tried to change the subject.

"You can't tell Murphy what to do," I burst out. "You have to coax him and, more important than anything, you have to believe he can do it." I glared at Rory who still thought the chestnut horse should be in a riding school and not on a racecourse.

"All right, Justina, I heard you the first time." The Guv'nor knew I was right. It showed in the way he nervously smoothed down his hair, which always stuck out like electrified steel wool.

The Guv'nor had come to believe in Murphy. He'd seen his talent, up there on the gallops, when he could cruise past anything on four legs and jump five foot for fun. He knew he could get the four and a half miles round Aintree. He just didn't voice it like I did. But it was there – a dream, germinating and growing. A Grand National winner. There hadn't been one at Dolphin Barn, his stables, in years.

"It seems that the horse responds best to a female touch." The Guv'nor shredded a form book out of nervous habit.

"What are you saying?" Rory's gorgeous mouth clamped into a tight line. The temperature had suddenly turned Arctic-like.

"I want to put Justina up for the rest of the season."

I collapsed on a pouffe in the corner, my mouth open. This is what I'd prayed for day and night. I could hardly believe it.

Rory looked as if he wanted to commit murder. As stable jockey he should have all the best rides. Murphy was scheduled to run in the King George Chase on Boxing Day. It was one of the most prestigious races in the calendar.

"I think you're making a big mistake." He stood up, stiff with shock. "The horse is dangerous, he could kill her."

Rory had been the one who had taught me how to ride races. When he was in hospital with his broken leg, he'd spent hours going through videos with me and drumming in tactics. We'd both wanted to oust an apprentice called Jacko who had been head lad but was cruel to the horses. But, since then, I sometimes felt that a competitive edge had developed between us, that Rory resented my success, especially with the most difficult horses in the yard. I'd been in love with Rory Calligan for longer than I could remember, but I found it hard to work in such proximity to him.

The front door closed with a sharp snap. I was still rigid with shock when his sports car roared out of the drive.

But nothing could spoil the delirious, mounting elation. It only took one extra-special horse to make a jockey famous. And I knew I'd found him . . .

Two

"What did *he* swallow for breakfast, a hand grenade?" Scooby, one of the stable lads, fought to settle a stroppy filly on the gallops and rolled his eyes in the Guv'nor's direction at the same time.

"Don't even ask," I wailed, wanting to defrost my toes with a hairdryer, it was so cold. "He even had a go at Mandy for putting more lipstick on herself than hoof oil on her horse. Honestly, if one of us falls off now, we'll be sacked on the spot."

I patted Murphy's solid neck, reassured that he was the last horse on earth who would chuck me.

Rory Calligan hadn't been near the stables for three days and the Guv'nor was spitting sparks of fury. He wasn't answering his mobile and there was no trace of life at his flat. It was so unlike Rory. He was the ultimate professional. He couldn't just disappear, not when he had a full card's racing at Wetherby in two days' time. Half of me felt responsible and the other half wanted to shake him by the ears for being so childish.

"I don't understand him," I moaned to Scooby,

who had become my agony uncle, older brother and close friend all rolled into one. "He doesn't even rate Murphy, he thinks I'm chasing a pipe dream."

"That could have something to do with the fact that he's raced him twice and had two crashes." Scooby waggled his eyebrows at me for emphasis.

"Are you just here for decoration, or are you actually going to do some work ride?" the Guv'nor blasted into my ear. I'd forgotten that he was mounted on an ancient cob he'd borrowed from an owner. It was obvious from the granite outline of his face that it was playing havoc with his arthritis.

"Bring back the Land Rover," Scooby muttered. The Land Rover, which the Guv'nor usually drove when we were out on the gallops, had temporarily died.

Murphy pounded up the all-weather track, streaking ahead of Scooby's filly. I never tired of this. Early mornings, freezing temperatures, steaming horses, the buzz, the speed, the power. It was an addiction. After racing, it was what racing people lived for.

Murphy bucked in protest when I pulled him back to a trot. He felt as though he could gallop for ever. Every day he was fitter and stronger. Scooby caught up with me, cursing that all he ever saw was my disappearing bottom.

"Don't knock it," I grinned. "When we win the National I'll sell it as advertising space."

The Guv'nor had an announcement. He wheeled the cob round to face the twenty stable lads and lasses, all desperate to get back to the hostel and breakfast. "As you know, since Jack Hughes left we've been short-handed."

Nobody dared breathe a word. The Guv'nor had sacked Jacko for beating Leonora, one of the horses, with a whip. One of the younger lads was riding her now, but she'd had her confidence badly knocked.

"We've a new member of staff starting this morning. Mickey Harwood," the Guv'nor continued. "I'm urging all of you to restrain yourselves from the usual infantile practical jokes which you all find so amusing." The Guv'nor glared at Jake and Harris who were known culprits. "Any pranks will be punished with a month on toilet cleaning and muck heap duty."

Twenty-odd faces dropped with disappointment.

"What about a month with Shona, sir?" Harris shouted. Shona was the stable man-eater. She promptly sliced Harris across the arm with her crop.

"Seriously though, sir," Harris wavered on to dangerous ground. "Who is this Mickey character who needs Guv'nor protection?"

If Kenneth Brown had looked like he'd eaten a lemon earlier, he now appeared to have swallowed a whole bagful, with maggots in.

*

11

There was still no sign of Rory later that day. Why did I feel responsible if he lost his job?

Murphy nosed at his hay net then swung round with a look which said, "For heaven's sake, what's up? You're putting me off my breakfast."

I picked out his feet and set his mane and tail with the water brush. Every afternoon each race-horse got an hour's intensive grooming.

Gertie rummaged in the corner, perfecting the art of head-butting the manger; an art which she often used to great effect on the back of my knees.

"Are you in there?" Mandy rattled the stable door.

"I've just met him. Mickey, I mean," she gasped, pink spots mingling with her blusher. "You'll never guess what."

"He used to work for Adam Valentine," I finished for her.

"How did you know that?" she gasped, outraged.

"Shona got there first," I grinned. "With a questionnaire six pages long."

Adam Valentine was the youngest and probably the most glamorous trainer in National Hunt racing. Mandy had a whopping great crush on his stable jockey Ben Le Sueur. It was bigger than her crush on Rory.

"Do you think he might organize a blind date for me and Ben?" She wrung her hands together hopefully. "I mean, jockeys like to take risks, don't they?"

But not stupid ones, I thought, and then wanted to slap myself for being so horrible. Mandy was a pretty, kind-hearted, funny girl – if only she wasn't so desperate to be like Shona.

After first lot, the first work ride of the day, all the stable staff had breakfast in the hostel. This was where the lads slept and played pool, darts and generally hung out. Shona, Mandy and I lived in a tumbledown cottage at the back of the main yard.

If we hadn't been short-staffed, Scooby would have missed first lot and cooked sausage, bacon and eggs. Instead mutiny had broken out over the last of the Crunchy Nut Cornflakes and Harris said he couldn't see how he could survive on a bowl of pressed cardboard. The milk had run out too.

"Would somebody tell Scottie that his feet smell?" Jake yelled across the room.

"What about your armpits?" Scottie was busy turning up Channel 4 Morning Line.

Saturday morning was always more relaxed than weekday mornings, even though a dozen horses would probably be out racing.

"Shhh, shhhhh." Scottie started waving his hands, gesturing at us to calm down. Harris had just broken the sugar bowl.

Adam Valentine flickered on to the screen.

"Quiet!" Mandy roared, pulling a chair up so close that she was nearly perched on the telly.

I noticed the stranger then, leaning against the back wall, casually observing and listening. He was stocky with streaked blond hair and a strong face. I couldn't help doing a double take. It was Mickey Harwood.

"Ben Le Sueur has been your stable jockey for six years. Is this split going to affect your chances at the championship?"

The noisy banter subsided, as if a teacher had walked into a classroom.

Everyone strained forward. "Turn it up, Mandy."

Adam Valentine sat in his farmhouse kitchen surrounded by dogs and a pot-bellied pig. He was smiling his easy, make-your-heart-tingle smile and shovelling sugar into a pint mug of tea.

"If Ben wants to go freelance, that's fine by me. My horses win because they're fit and up to the job. That's not suddenly going to change."

"Ooooh," Harris hooted. Valentine was as natural and confident on telly as a film star. Housewives always had a flutter on his horses.

The picture cut to Ben Le Sueur riding out the last Gold Cup winner in a tight finish, then to an interview after the race. Ben was surly and could barely speak to the interviewer. He had about as much charm as a boa constrictor.

"The traitor," Harris shouted, throwing a Wagon Wheel wrapper at the screen. "After all Valentine's done for him. What do you say, Mickey Mouse? A rotter, eh?"

Mickey Harwood stiffened against the wall, his face closing into a hard shell. Was it my imagination, or was he looking at Valentine with real hatred?

Abruptly he turned and left the room. I went after him. When I caught up, he was breathing heavily, his fist clenched into a ball. Something had really rattled him.

"Take no notice," I babbled, feeling unnaturally nervous. "They can't help themselves, they try it on with everybody. I had my riding boots superglued to the tack room floor and maggots put on my chair when I first came here. You name it, they did it, almost a full-time job to them."

I clammed up as a slow smile broke across his face. His mouth was twitching with amusement. I picked madly at my dirty fingernails.

"Superglue? Maggots?"

"Yeah, it was awful."

"I'll be sure to check before I sit down," he grinned. "Can't be too careful."

"I'm Justina," I blurted out.

"I know, I made a point of finding out."

Now that he had relaxed, there was something about him that was really, really nice.

But, as he headed back to the stables to join in second lot, a thought kept needling away in my head. If he'd worked for Adam Valentine as a stable lad, why were his hands so amazingly soft? They

15

didn't look as though they'd ever been near a yard brush, let alone a horse.

A shriek, which sounded like Mandy when she's seen a spider in the bath, came from the tack room. I leapt out of Leonora's stable, hobbling with one chap still half undone, imagining she'd disturbed a burglar. Scooby and Scottie were close on my heels.

Mandy appeared, white and angry. "Where's Shona?" she erupted, tight-lipped. "This time she's gone too far. Don't go in there." She made a grab for my arm but her fingers slid off my jacket.

I stared at the noticeboard and the newspaper cutting pinned haphazardly over the work ride schedule. A fuzzy black and white picture caught Rory coming out of a London nightclub with his arm draped round a pretty, blonde girl. He looked as if he was having the time of his life.

"Are you all right?" Mandy was carrying on as if I needed a stretcher. "Shona is such a cow. Just because Rory wasn't interested in her, she wants to spoil it for you."

"Uh," I gulped, dredging up false bravado. "He isn't my boyfriend, he can do what he likes." Secretly I wanted to rip his eyebrows off.

"Not on the Guv'nor's time, though." Badger, the head lad, peered over my shoulder. He was more dedicated to Dolphin Barn Stables than anybody. "The Guv'nor's already seen it in the *Sporting*

Life," he shrugged. "He asked me to pass on a message."

My blood froze.

"Get your silks ready for Wetherby. You're riding a full card."

Three

"Would you stop riding as if you're trying to break your neck?" the Guv'nor hissed. He was trying to rollick me without the owners noticing. We were in the parade ring, clumped together, and jockeys were mounting.

I was on The Fiddler, who tossed his head, flashing mean eyes in my direction. He was a small, dark bay horse with a lazy, peevish nature. I'd ridden him to fourth place in a race three weeks ago. He had ability but no spirit and I'd spent hours trying to get him to enjoy his job. He was so used to jockeys roughing him up that he just switched off and ploughed into his fences.

"Keep him covered up until the last furlong," the Guv'nor urged. "Don't make a run before then and, for God's sake, respect the fences." His voice rose with nerves. The lucky purple tie which he'd worn for every race meet for over twenty years blew over his shoulder, clashing with his red-threaded face. Faded denim blue eyes streamed in the wind. "Is

18

there a reason why you're determined to crash-land at every jump?"

"I'm not going to crash," I murmured. "I'm going to win."

We rode out on to the track, straight into a gale force wind. My face felt as dry as Ayres Rock. The Fiddler lived up to his reputation and hung back as if he was off colour.

"Come on, you old tyke." I kicked him forwards. "Less of the amateur dramatics."

I was desperate for a win. The last three horses I'd raced had all tailed off badly. I was one of the few jockeys to ride in every race on today's card and was about as popular with the professionals in the weighing room as a tarantula. Even worse, Jack Hughes was riding and doing his utmost to turn the other jockeys against me.

"Keep together, please." The starter looked in a foul mood.

A gust of wind blew rain into my mouth and The Fiddler hunched his back. My tiny saddle was slippery from the wet.

It was a two-mile hurdle race and my guess was that the field would go flat out from the start. You had to live by your wits and fight for survival otherwise you'd get cut up. I didn't admit to myself that I was exhausted from the other races.

The white tape flew up and a sea of horses leapt forward. For dizzying moments I couldn't function.

19

My brain turned to marshmallow. The gale was behind us, driving the horses on.

We rounded the second bend, tightly bunched. Too tight. I could reach out and touch the other jockeys. A mile and three furlongs. The ambulance accelerated alongside the rails, mindful of fallers. There weren't many jobs where you had an ambulance follow you around permanently.

"Get over!" A tussle for space broke out as someone tried to push through a gap. With a sickening feeling I realized it was Jack.

"Come on, boy, just keep going." The Fiddler was close to the rails. He was listening to my voice, taking comfort as I stroked his neck. Into the home straight. The last hurdle. Two fallers. A groan from the crowds. The Fiddler stumbled and righted himself like a cat. He shot nimbly up the inside rail, trying for the first time in his life. I'd got through to him.

"Come on, boy. Come on!" I started riding him out, hands and legs, on the tail of the leader. He could win, I knew he could. He wanted to. I had to pull out from the rail. The leader was drifting. Now! Now! Now! I opened my left rein.

Jack Hughes blasted his horse upsides, crashing into The Fiddler's shoulder. I couldn't function for rage. He had no other horse to his left. It was deliberate obstruction. I felt The Fiddler shudder and his confidence and spirit die. Jack had ruined him.

"You pig!" I yelled, turning sideways into the

20

battering wind. His horse was cooked and losing ground. It had all been for nothing. "You pig, pig, pig, I'll get you for this."

Tears poured from my eyes. I'd had the race. I could have won. Now we crossed the line a poor third with The Fiddler's ears pressed into his neck. He was shaking from fright.

I wanted to pound Jack to dust. Ever since I'd first ridden on the Dolphin Barn gallops he'd had it in for me. Now he was bitter because his own brutality had got him sacked by the Guv'nor. As the horses came off the course, he turned and leered with stony eyes. He wasn't a bit bothered about losing. The triumph was purely in stuffing up my chance. I lost control. He'd terrorized The Fiddler. As we clattered into the gateway, and he was about to speak, I clenched my fist and swung out. He ducked and I didn't connect.

All I saw was a TV camera pivot round and zoom in. I'd forgotten Wetherby would be televised and I knew how important good coverage was to the Guv'nor.

"There's a stewards' inquiry." The Guv'nor was beyond anger. He seemed to have shut down mentally and was walking around like a zombie. I unsaddled The Fiddler. I didn't want to leave him. He'd tried his best but I couldn't tell him that in horse language. All I could do was pat him and rub his ears.

21

"I knew we should have got a more experienced jockey." The owner's wife, huddled in a fake fur coat, groused like a bad loser. I tried to ignore her. "Why did you leave your run so late?" She plucked at my sleeve, hardly bothering to conceal her irritation.

"Trainer's orders." The Guv'nor rocked on his heels. I knew he hated this. Owners who bought a racehorse and just expected it to win.

"Would jockeys number six and eight please make their way to the stewards' box."

If I was suspended, I'd never get a ride again.

"Go on." The Guv'nor prodded me in the back. I could have wet myself. I walked on wooden legs round to the building where they held the prize-giving. Just coming out of the swing doors was Adam Valentine, whose horse had won the race. He winked and tipped his trilby jauntily. "Good luck with the three big bears," he grinned, and then rolled his eyes upwards. Stewards in racing were like a cross between headteachers and God.

A flicker of life came back into my legs. I braced myself. I could handle this. I focused on all the gruesome things I'd like to do to Jack and which I would do to Rory when I got my hands on him.

Jack stormed out of the building ten minutes later with a suspension and a fine. I tottered out, weak-limbed, after a warning and a lecture on professional behaviour. I'd managed to convince them that I hadn't actually been trying to knock Jack's teeth out.

Eleven minutes until the next race. Panic sent me catapulting towards the weighing room. Explosions of laughter filtered out as I wrenched open the door. Blast, this was going to be even worse than usual.

The silence was awesome. I wanted to die. But slowly, like a wave, a chorus of cheering built up, until even the valets joined in.

"Next time you take a slug at Hughes, make sure you wear knuckle dusters." Ben Le Sueur came forward. I thought he was going to shake my hand but instead he offered me a half-eaten piece of cherry cake and a lukewarm cup of tea. "You look absolutely perished," he whispered. I could see now why Mandy fancied him.

This was the first time any of the jockeys had acknowledged me. I felt like a long-lost daughter. I crumpled on to the bench underneath my peg and tried to stop my bottom lip wobbling. I was finally being accepted as a serious jockey. It was miraculous.

The Raymond twins, who were identical and always in the Championship top ten, shrieked from over by the television. News was coming in from a new racetrack in the south which was attracting big prizemoney. Red Robin, a brilliant steeplechaser, had been killed outright at the water jump, the third horse this season. Beside the television, a foreign

23

jockey called Davide went into a spiel of Italian, waving his arms around in a fit of passion. No jockey liked to see a horse hurt. Especially when it could be avoided.

"If somebody doesn't fill that water jump in soon, I'm going to get a JCB and do it myself." Ben flopped down on a plastic chair, raking his hair back in frustration.

Sharpie O'Hare, an Irish jockey, said we should stage a protest. I was still in shock. I felt as if my heart was doing a kind of drum roll in my chest. An entry form on the Guv'nor's desk came floating into my memory. He was planning to run Murphy over that same course – in his next race.

"Jockeys, please," a steward insisted for the third time. "I said, jockeys . . ."

We filed on to the racetrack for the last race, Davide losing a stirrup and delaying the start. The twins thought it was hilarious.

I was riding for the same owners, but the horse, although sweet, was a no-hoper called Milligan's Express. He couldn't jump to save his life but they persisted in thinking that he was going to be a champion.

All I could think about was the water jump that had claimed the lives of three horses. We lined up behind the tape. I couldn't let Murphy run in that race. It was too risky. I had to change the Guv'nor's mind. I couldn't let Murphy run.

Thirteen horses scorched down to the first fence. I was in the middle. I hadn't even picked out a good line. We crashed. Milligan sprawled over the top of me, narrowly missing my head, but catching me full in the mouth with a stray hind leg. Instinctively, I curled into a tight ball as the rest of the field ploughed past.

It felt like an hour before the last horse clattered over the hurdle top. A jockey shouted out but I couldn't hear. The blood was rushing to my head and my shoulder felt as if it had been refitted back to front. I wiggled my toes and arms and sent a Hail Mary up to the grey clouds. I was still breathing.

The ambulance jerked to a halt. If I'd been knocked out for over a minute, the doctor would have insisted on a racing suspension. I stood up wobbling. My lips felt like tyres. Something suddenly dropped from my mouth to the long grass. I'd lost a front tooth.

"You didn't even try," the owner was apoplectic. His wife stabbed the tarmac with an umbrella and shuffled and backed him up with frequent nods. The humiliation of having a faller at the first fence was clearly too much.

The Guv'nor fiddled with his purple tie and shot me black, meaningful looks. What he really meant was say sorry! Crawl! Suck up! Anything so they don't move their horses.

I managed a cheesy grin, showing off the gap in my front teeth.

"And as for you, Kenneth, I'm surprised at you, trusting valuable horses to hopeless, inexperienced girls. It's the last time we'll be taking your advice . . ."

I wanted to crush her frosted helmet hairstyle in a food processor. My temper shot up like boiling mercury. The golden rule of being a jockey was never insult an owner or his horse. But I'd had enough. I was wet and cold, my mouth was sore, and there was dried blood all over my chin. "He's forgotten more about racing than you'll ever know," I snapped. "And as for your horse, he couldn't win a Donkey Derby. He hates racing and it's cruel making him."

She let out a kind of strangled sob and screamed about Jockey Clubs and prosecution. The Guv'nor's face drained to a dishcloth grey colour.

A thin veil of dread started to drift down on my temper. I'd blown it, the Guv'nor would pull out all my teeth and make a necklace with them.

Gulping down panic, wishing I could rake the words back in, I did the next best thing and legged it. A St John's stalwart, seeing blood, bustled me into a First Aid tent and probably saved my life. I pulled down the flimsy canvas flap just to make sure.

"How long can I stay here?" I asked nervously. "I mean, could I possibly stay the night?"

"Well, hello again." It was Adam Valentine. His jockey must have fallen too.

"Another chance meeting, this must be an omen." His eyes danced with amusement.

I smiled despite myself, revealing the naked gap in my mouth.

"I think a gum shield would suit in future." He wagged his forefinger in mock sternness. "It's all right for the men to look like seventeenth-century relics but not the girls."

I had my reflexes tested and the medic in the tent referred me to a dentist. Adam waved away the fuss and said the only thing wrong with me was bruised pride. Then he asked me if I'd like a lift home. How could I refuse? The thought of travelling with the Guv'nor made having my fingernails ripped out sound like a pleasurable option. I couldn't spend the rest of my life in a First Aid tent.

"You're on," I gulped. I was still in my colours but I didn't dare go back to the weighing room.

We sneaked out towards the members' car park and a shiny, silver Mercedes with a personalized number plate.

"Nice wheels," I goggled, comparing it mentally with the Guv'nor's battered four wheel drive which had dog biscuits and mouse droppings on the back seat.

Adam Valentine's yard was within ten miles of Dolphin Barn. It was a modern complex with a full-time vet and a laboratory. All sorts of Frankenstein stories were told about blood transfusions and electrodes. In truth, his horses were super-fit, as lean as whippets and, although they always looked dull and poor in the parade ring, they performed on the track.

"Congratulations," I mumbled, the heat of the car suddenly making my bruising throb. He'd had two wins and one second place. It seemed to highlight my failure. My nose began to run with the effort of holding back tears of self-pity. I'd let the Guv'nor down, and the horses. My racing career was in tatters.

Clocking up ninety-five on the speedometer, one hand on the wheel, Adam offered me a perfectly ironed, spotted hanky.

"Thanks," I sniffed.

"I'm only going to give you thirty seconds to feel sorry for yourself," he grinned. I couldn't help noticing his immaculate suit, the perfect colour coordination, the conker-shiny shoes. The Guv'nor always looked as if he had just fallen out of bed. They were about as opposite as the Equator and the North Pole.

"You're a talented jockey, potentially the best I've seen for a long time." He casually overtook a long line of lorries, pushing a hundred. "Kenny Brown doesn't realize what a gem he's got under his nose. I'd like you to ride some of my horses. That's if you want to. Just pick up the phone."

If I want to? It was like being offered a golden

ticket to fame and fortune. People would take me seriously overnight. I'd be a pro, not a stable lass who worked all hours and got the odd ride. It was the experience and credibility I needed. But then reality kicked in. "I can't," I croaked, "let the Guv'nor down, I mean. He gave me my first chance. And I couldn't leave Murphy."

"You wouldn't have to, you'd be working freelance." He pulled the car in to the hard shoulder and switched the engine off. He looked at me with such intensity, I thought he was going to burn a hole in my head. "Brown doesn't own you," he said. "You need more than a small-time trainer to get to the top in this job. And you're young enough, for goodness sake. How old are you, anyway? Sixteen? You've got it all ahead of you."

My brain was zinging with new possibilities but despite the temptation, I knew that my place was at Dolphin Barn.

"I'll think about it," I said, suddenly feeling uncomfortable. He must have picked up on this because his expression softened at once. "You've got the same drive that I have," he smiled. "I know you'll come back."

My heart dropped like a stone when there was no sign of Rory at Dolphin Barn. I'd been kidding myself that he'd be sheepishly waiting for us to return, ready with some batty excuse which the

Guv'nor would half swallow and then we'd be back to normal.

I trudged up the drive, feeling as if I'd been run over by a steamroller. The silver Mercedes streaked off into the distance. There was only Mickey in the yard. The other lads were off playing football on the village pitch.

"They didn't ask you to be goalkeeper?" I joked, looking for Murphy's familiar chestnut head over his door. Seeing it instantly made me feel better.

"Nope, they think I'm a nerd," he grinned. He pulled off a woolly hat that was rammed down to his ears. "And I am now."

I gasped in amazement. Then I shrieked with laughter. Mickey had bright green hair. "How did that happen?" I broke into non-stop giggles, clutching my sides. As if I couldn't guess.

"Harris put some dye in my shampoo bottle. You didn't warn me about that. Superglue, maggots, yes, but not hair dye."

"Oh dear," I giggled, convulsed. "You're not going to report him, are you?"

"Nope, not a chance. I think it's quite funny, really. Anyway, I'm going to turn the joke back on them."

"Oh yeah, like how?"

"I've got some tickets for the Hallowe'en party at the Raymond twins'."

I gasped. Tickets for that were like gold dust. It

was to raise money for the Injured Jockeys Fund. I'd been hoping for weeks Rory would invite me.

"Would you care to accompany a dotty chap like me with green hair?" He cocked his head on one side appealingly.

What the heck. It was better than moping at home. "Only if I can dye mine blue," I answered.

Four

"He's here!" Mandy raced across the yard spilling dirty woodshavings everywhere, as the wheelbarrow collided with a pitchfork. "Rory, he's back!"

It was six-thirty in the morning and I was wearing a balaclava to keep out the cold. Now I pulled it off, and my ears nearly came with it. I fluffed up my hair, which felt like straw.

Rory's dog, Poppy, bounded out of the house. I ducked behind Murphy. There he was, going across to his sports car to fetch his jockey skull. Poser, I grumbled, chewing nervously on my thumbnail. He didn't even look as if he'd had a roasting from the Guv'nor.

"Aren't you going to talk to him?" Mandy hissed. We were riding first lot up to the gallops. Murphy was striding out, pretending to see dragons in the hedge. The cold scoured at my cheeks and made my eyes run.

Mickey rode upsides, huffing on his hands, his

reins loose. "What does a penguin wear on its head?"

"I don't know, what does a penguin wear on its head?"

"An ice cap."

"Is that supposed to make me feel better?"

"No, but you could have laughed just to humour me."

I caught a glimpse of Rory looking daggers in my direction and smiled widely at Mickey, despite the gap in my teeth. I couldn't believe the Guv'nor had let him off so lightly. He should be on toilet cleaning for a year. "I think it's so important to be professional at all times, don't you?"

Mickey looked blank. "Come again?"

The horses rocketed up the all-weather track, matching strides, eager to warm up their muscles. Murphy, as usual, bucked five times and squealed like a foal with excitement. I curled over his withers, letting him eat up the ground with lengthening strides. The Guv'nor watched from the top of the hill, binoculars trained on each pair of horses, ever critical.

Racing was an addiction, a daily fix. We were all exhilarated as the sweating, snorting horses pulled up in a bunch.

Back at the yard I quickly untacked Murphy and threw on his cooler sheet. The smell of cooking bacon wafted from the hostel kitchen. Scooby was back with the frying pan which was probably why everybody was so cheery.

I fought down hunger pains and escaped to the tack room. I wrapped myself in Murphy's exercise sheet, which was still warm and smelt of horse, and picked up the saddle soap.

"Don't think you can hide that easily." Rory stormed in.

The bridle fell off the cleaning hook and clattered to the floor. Rory bent and picked it up so I could see the soft downy black hairs on his neck. "I hate him," I told myself.

"I don't believe you," he started. "I give you the chance to ride a full race card at Wetherby, televised, good horses, and now you won't even talk to me. Have I missed the plot here or what, because I thought you badly needed race experience." His black eyebrows knitted together in frustration.

"Excuse me, but you let the Guv'nor down, went off in a sulk because I'd got to race Murphy, and were photographed gallavanting around London like a playboy. Talk about immature." I rolled my eyes for effect.

"Aaaah, now we're getting to the truth. Not that it's any of your business, but I took my sister out on the town because she'd just been cleared of having cancer. I went to the specialist with her and then she wanted to celebrate. And as for the Guv'nor, I sent him three e-mails. It's not my fault he's a techno-phobe with as much nous as the Flintstones."

"Oh," I gulped, dropping the saddle soap. It went skidding across the York paving and bounced off his boot. I'd kill Shona.

He pulled something out of his back pocket. "I've got two tickets for the Raymonds' Hallowe'en party, the one you've been raving about for weeks. I thought you might come with me, as a peace offering . . ."

He was asking me out. On a date. For the first time.

"I'm sorry," I croaked, wanting to cry. "But I'm going with someone else."

"What do you think?"

Mandy walked into the cottage just as I arrived back from the hairdressers in Cheltenham. She nearly fell through the floor. "It's – different."

I patted the back of my head and stared into the frying pan in the hope of seeing my reflection. I'd been to the dentist to have a false tooth fitted and afterwards spent three hours in the hairdressers being primped and poked at by a junior who had nearly singed my ear off with the hairdryer.

Before my first race I'd chopped off all my hair with a pair of kitchen scissors. I'd needed a decent cut and blow-dry more than Rory's dog did.

"Blue tips?" Mandy's eyebrows arched in awe.

"Electric blue tendrils actually," I corrected, feeling rather smug.

Of course, if we didn't do evening stables and get

changed soon, there wouldn't be a party to go to. The Guv'nor was deliberately late. He'd obviously heard about the Hallowe'en bash and that was his idea of a joke. We couldn't do anything until he'd examined each horse, which he did every day. All ninety-three of them.

I was responsible for Murphy and Leonora and I prided myself on them having the cleanest, deepest beds and mangers. The Guv'nor spent about two minutes with each horse, running his hands down their legs and asking questions. Each stable lad or lass had to be ready in the stable and woe betide anyone whose horse wasn't up to scratch.

Typically, Murphy was in the last line of boxes. Harris was in the next stable singing a song about a girl with blue hair, just to annoy me.

The Guv'nor arrived with Badger, the head lad, and scanned Murphy carefully as I folded back his rugs. I had worked hard to get a real shine on his chestnut coat and he looked hard and lean and ready for business. The Guv'nor obviously thought so too. "He'll be racing next week – at Sunningdale."

I felt as if a bucket of ice had just cascaded into my stomach. My throat went tight. "You can't be serious?" The words tumbled out before I could stop myself.

The Guv'nor had his back to me feeling Murphy's hocks, but I could see his shoulders stiffen. Badger looked as if someone had placed a large bomb in his hands. He was mouthing at me to shut up.

"You can't," I ran on. "It – it – would be like committing murder. That water jump isn't safe. All the jockeys say so—"

"Aaah, so a few friendly words in the weighing room and you're eating out of their hands . . ."

"Three horses are dead."

"And there's been a Jockey Club inquiry. Nothing conclusive."

"What's it going to take, more horses' lives, a jockey's?"

"You're being dramatic. If he can't take on a paltry water jump, how on earth is he going to cope with Becher's Brook on the Grand National course? The horse runs and I'll hear no more about it."

I bit my lip until I felt the skin break. The Governor marched out without giving Murphy his Polo mint. Badger scowled as if I'd really blown it this time, but I didn't care. Murphy pushed his nose into my pocket and begged with his foreleg, something I'd taught him to do ages ago.

"I'll find a way," I murmured, scratching his huge ears and pulling out half a biscuit which was stuck to my pocket lining.

A pumpkin lantern rose up over the stable door followed by Harris putting on a quirky voice. But I wasn't in the mood for a party any more. All I wanted to do was crawl into bed and hide under the duvet.

*

"Rory, I told you, I'm going with someone else." I opened the back door listlessly, still in my jodphurs and devouring a Lion Bar.

Rory stepped into the kitchen over a cardboard box containing Smokey our kitten. He was dressed as Dracula, with a black cape, fangs and a made-up white face. He looked great.

"I see the cleaning rota hasn't improved at all." He glanced round the kitchen, at the pots piled higher than the taps in the sink and the microwave chip boxes scrunched up on the units. Mandy's and Shona's clothes littered the floor in a trail up the stairs. Poppy, Rory's Great Dane, bounded past and up the stairs where we heard a shriek from the bathroom and a door slam.

"I'm well aware you've got a date," Rory grimaced. "I'm here to pick up Shona."

It was my turn to pull faces. Fury rocketed up and scalded my tongue.

Shona – of all people! How could he?

He was grinning with satisfaction at my reaction.

"Pig!" I wanted to yell, but at that moment Shona shimmied down the stairs in a tight black skirt and top. She latched on to Rory like a barnacle.

"Haven't you forgotten your broomstick?" I asked nastily, wanting to pull her hair out.

"I thought I'd leave it for you. You might need it to get to the party as it looks as if your date's going to be late. That's if he's coming at all."

38

She escaped outside before I could trap her in the door.

Mandy came down in a white tent of a dress with ringed black eyes and a desperate look. "Where's the Sara Lee chocolate cake?" She raided the fridge. "Ben Le Sueur's going to be there tonight. I can't go on an empty stomach."

Mickey arrived ten minutes later with a box of chocolates and his green hair stuck up in spikes. He too was dressed as Dracula, with a cape and fangs and carrying a mask. My heart instantly lightened.

"Love the hair," he admired. I gave him a twirl under the fluorescent light.

"There's room for Mandy, yeah?" I touched his arm. Luckily Mandy was too busy scraping the last of the Sara Lee up with a spoon to see his face drop like a brick.

The party was a typical racing affair, with jockeys who are usually on strict diets going haywire with the punch and *vol au vents*. The Raymond twins were dressed as identical trolls and halfway through the evening displayed their stupid party trick of swallowing a dry teabag whole. Sharpie O'Hare took bets on anything anyone suggested and Davide cheated and got doused with a watermelon.

Mickey never left my side, which was flattering, but meant I had to pretend to be happy every second. Whenever I looked round the room I locked eyes with Rory who seemed to make a point of giggling into Shona's ear each time he saw me look at him.

There was an auction which captured everybody's attention. I put a full week's earnings on a pair of riding gloves Bob Champion had worn to win the Grand National on Aldiniti.

"Isn't it marvellous how anybody, even if they've never been on a horse, can go into racing?" A woman I'd never met before, with dangly earrings, was clutching my arm. "My daughter went to racing school and now she's rubbing shoulders at parties with Zara Phillips. Before then she hadn't even looked after a guinea pig, let alone a racehorse."

I smiled politely and spotted Mandy sidestepping her way over to Ben Le Sueur, who was leaning morosely against the wall. Please don't let her mention marriages or babies. I crossed my fingers and toes and then groaned when I spotted a brown iron mark on the back of her white dress.

Mickey asked me for a dance but the music changed to Celine Dion and everyone evacuated the dance floor. We bumped into a man with ginger hair who Mickey introduced as Adam Valentine's head lad. My heart lurched.

"So you've found yourself a new position?" He scrutinized Mickey without an ounce of friendliness. "Let's see how long you hold on to this one, eh?" He narrowed his eyes until they practically disappeared into thin slits, then he vanished into the crowd.

"Nice guy," I breathed.

Not for the first time Mickey seemed really rattled. The niggling worry at the back of my mind started up again. Mickey was hiding something. Something big.

"Party games!" Davide sprang up in front of me, clutching an empty cornflakes box. Before we knew it, we were being dragged off to the kitchen where Shona had earned herself the name Bendy Barbie for picking a paper clip off the floor with her teeth, and an arm-wrestling tournament was in full flow between Sharpie O'Hare and a Raymond twin.

I completely forgot about Mandy until hours later when she gushed across the room like a love-sick puppy with smudged lipstick and grips hanging out of her hair. "Oh, Jus, he's gorgeous. He's the one. He's asked me out to the flicks and he says I'm the nicest girl he's ever met. He's gone home early because he's racing tomorrow. Jus – I think I've fallen in love."

"That's fantastic," I chirruped, but Mandy was too happy to listen.

Mickey gently but insistently led me across to the patio. "You've got to put her off," he hissed, panic crinkling his forehead.

I'd lost the plot completely. He hardly knew Mandy. What was he on about?

"You mustn't tell a soul," he bent in close,

41

brushing my ear, which tingled and throbbed. "Ben Le Sueur is up to his neck in race-fixing and bribes. The police are investigating him at the moment. That's why he got the sack from Valentine."

"If you don't stop staring your eyes will drop out of your head." Shona sashayed past with Rory.

I put on a false grin which nearly cracked my face. Two sets of emotions were hurtling round my head like racing cars: relief that Valentine was in the clear, and dread at what I was going to have to tell Mandy. How on earth did you tell your best friend that she'd fallen in love with a crook?

Five

"Would somebody remind me why we do this for a living?" "Pixie" Raymond took over his shift at the driving wheel from Rory with great reluctance. Rory sank into the back seat, looking exhausted after three hours' driving.

I flinched against the door handle as his arm accidentally rubbed against mine. With a lurch which sent my heart skidding into my ribcage, I saw the first yellow arrow pointing to Sunningdale racecourse. It was happening. My worst nightmare. I couldn't put it off any longer. Murphy would be in the pre-parade ring already, ready to race on the deadliest track in the country.

"Step on it, Raymond, we'll be fined at this rate." Rory nervously fingered his Rolex watch which he'd won in a French championship. If we were late, the stewards would give us a hefty fine, regardless of excuses. I could sense Rory regretting the decision to share a car and petrol money. With Davide and the twins it was like organizing a children's tea party. Jockeys travelled thousands of miles a year and usually doubled or quadrupled up in a car.

A speed camera flashed as we cruised past. Pixie cursed. I gazed out of the window at water skiers on a reclaimed gravel pit. Just the sight of water made me want to throw up. I quickly wound down the window for a blast of cold air but Davide and Ike Raymond shrieked like banshees.

One of the most common ways for jockeys to lose a few excess pounds quickly is to wear a rubber sweatsuit on the way to the races and turn the car heater up to maximum. Davide and Ike were doing this now. They resembled two Mr Blobbies with cherry-red faces. The sweat pouring down their faces was causing condensation on the windows. Pixie, under pressure from Rory, shot on to a roundabout, cutting up a police car.

"Oh great, that's all we need." Rory buried his face in his hands in despair as the police car flashed behind us. The sight of two jockeys in rubber suits was enough to throw any policeman into disarray. Pixie flashed his identity card and quickly explained what was going on but the police officer wasn't having any of it. Then he recognized Rory, and a signed photo for his daughter got us off with a warning.

"Go! Go! Go!" Rory yelled, by now demented with panic. The racecourse was overflowing with people, bouncy castles and some kind of Donkey Derby. We pulled into the jockeys' and trainers' car park and legged it to the weighing room, clutching race saddles and weight cloths. Jockeys had to be on and off the scales at least fifteen minutes before the race. We made the deadline by thirty seconds.

"Phew, that was close." Pixie fiddled with a pair of paper-thin riding boots weighing about two ounces each.

"Have you heard what's happened?" A jockey called Daryll Hamley came up, pulling on his colours. "Sharpie O'Hare's been taken to intensive care. Fell at the water."

We gazed at him for at least fifteen seconds before the news sunk in. No wonder the weighing room was like a morgue. Nobody said a word. I sat down heavily and felt a rush of blood to my head. This couldn't be happening. Poor Sharpie.

"How bad?" I asked, wondering if I really wanted to know.

"Not good. Looks like internal. Possibly a split liver. It's touch and go at the moment."

"This is crazy." I leapt up. "Why isn't somebody doing something? They should have roped off the area. What do they think we are, performing monkeys? Poor, poor Sharpie."

"Surely they'll do something now." Pixie pulled his left boot on to his right foot. "It'll make the headlines tomorrow."

Through the window I saw Murphy striding out round the parade ring, proud, determined, dragging Scooby off his feet. He didn't know what was ahead of him. He didn't know that his life was in danger. Bile rose in my throat and I wanted to gag. I had to do something. Find an excuse. Withdraw. But there wasn't time, everything was set in motion, owners, trainers, the betting public, all waiting to see the next race, probably queuing up now, ten-deep round the spot where Sharpie . . .

"Jockeys, please," a steward shouted.

The valet passed me my gloves and hat.

I followed Pixie out into the frozen sunshine and a sea of faces. Across the paddock Rory was already talking to his connections. For a brief moment he glanced across and I saw the worry in his eyes.

Murphy neighed as soon as he spotted me and charged across, stuffing his nose in my chest and waving his foreleg for titbits. A few people laughed and then scanned their programmes for the name of the ungainly chestnut horse.

"Take the lead from the first and keep in to the rails," the Guv'nor barked.

I checked Murphy's girths even though it wasn't my job. I was playing for time.

"Hold him together at the water and, whatever you do, don't go off on a long stride." I heard the cracks of doubt in his voice then. He was churned up like the rest of us. Sharpie shouldn't be in hospital. I wanted to yell out that this was stupid and we should go home. But Scooby legged me up, his arms as stiff as ironing boards.

"Take care," he murmured. Murphy half reared,

and plunged towards the exit. A bunch of horses scattered as he barged through. We were on the racecourse and heading down to the start. In ten minutes it would all be over.

"I'm going to deliberately fall before the water." Pixie trotted upsides on a scrawny horse of 15.2 hands. "At least yours can jump," he complained. "Mine can barely see over the fences."

Ben Le Sueur circled from the opposite direction and angled his horse so Murphy had to stop in his tracks. "What's up with Mandy?" He leant across on a rangy chestnut. "I've rung her five times but she won't speak to me."

He looked genuinely hurt. I was taken aback that he'd been so serious about her but then I remembered the race-fixing and I couldn't help spotting the air-cushioned whip in his right hand. These new whips were specially designed so that they wouldn't leave a mark on the horse, no matter how hard you hit them. Trust him to carry one.

"She's busy," I snapped. In truth, Mandy had been moping about red-eyed since I told her. "With a new boyfriend," I added for emphasis. "And she wants you to leave her alone, she's not interested."

His face seemed to sink into itself with disappointment. Maybe I'd gone too far but it was for Mandy's own good. He wouldn't be bothering her again, that was for sure.

The starter called us in. Murphy immediately stood on his hind legs and started prancing around like a Lipizzaner. A steward hastily dodged out of the way. I pulled down my goggles. Horses jostled for position. Jockeys cursed. Racing was the only sport where riders jumped on a strange horse and, within minutes, were galloping full pelt over enormous fences. It took nerves of steel.

"Close in! Close in!" The starter raised his flag. I curled my fingers round the reins and stood up in the stirrups. Adrenalin took over. I was hooked. I wanted to race. We were off.

Murphy belted forward. He'd die rather than be overtaken. Horses fanned out in a line and we were approaching the first fence. Steady! Steady!

"Get over!" Ben Le Sueur took it first, skimming through the top.

Murphy was hot on his heels and missed out two strides. My breath locked in my chest as he sailed over effortlessly and landed in the lead.

Anyone who has watched racehorses take on massive fences at thirty to forty miles an hour will understand the sheer exhilaration.

We scorched ahead by six and then seven lengths. His head came up and his ears flicked forward. He flew the open ditch. Come back, come back, steady, boy. The biggest fence on the course was looming round the next bend. Five foot two inches and uphill. The rest of the field tailed off behind us, burnt out with the sheer pace.

Not for the first time a delirious grin spread across my face. Everybody had called Murphy a no-hoper, a cart horse, a boat of a thing, a liability. But once again he was proving his worth. He was every inch a champion and I knew if I asked him to, he'd jump the moon. He could read my mind, and he knew I believed in him.

The solid black birch was upon us. Murphy lengthened his already enormous stride. I saw the TV car bumping along beside us. I knew there was a camera in the black hole of the ditch for the benefit of the viewers. They'd see Murphy at full stretch, the underside of his belly, the muscles, the sinews. He took off level with the wings. It was no effort. It was as if he could fly.

A great roar went up from the crowds. We turned into the home straight.

There was no better way to get noticed than out in the front, on a huge chestnut horse, decimating the competition, especially as I was a sixteen year old girl who'd only just got her conditional jockey's licence. The media spotlight would be on Sunningdale, a new course, big prizemoney. All around the country people would be tuning in.

A sickening weight caught in my chest. The water jump, officially known as the Pond Fence, was three fences away.

I was out there alone, with no lead. A roar went up from the grandstand as we rocketed over the next fence. People were clamouring to the rails, three- and four-deep. I didn't move a muscle but Murphy stepped up the pace, playing to the audience. I'd lost his attention, he was gawping at the crowds and forgetting his job. Panic seared through me as he stumbled clumsily. MURPHY! I swear he was more concerned about looking photogenic than he was about jumping his fences properly. I hauled on his mouth to keep a straight line.

The magic bond between horse and rider was broken. He was too busy playing the showman to listen to my frantic signals. He was running downhill and out of balance. I had to do something.

It was as if he could suddenly smell my fear. His ears flicked back and he changed legs. Then he grabbed the bit in his mouth and took off. I was out of control, the more he pulled the more he frightened himself. The Pond Fence drew ever closer. I was screaming now, hysterical with panic. He was going to break both our necks.

Then an idea came to me. Why hadn't I thought of it before?

There was a gap in the rails where the horses in the two-mile chase crossed over. With both hands I hauled on the left rein and prayed he would listen. It was our only chance.

"Come on, Murphy – turn!" I yelled.

He'd spotted the water glistening ahead and was lengthening his stride in anticipation. At this pace he'd somersault into it for sure. I couldn't let that happen.

A few more seconds and we'd miss the gap in the

rails. In desperation I threw myself up his neck and grabbed the bit ring. "Now turn, turn, turn!"

He responded. My breath flooded back into my lungs. And then it happened. My leg tangled with the rail and I was catapulted out of the saddle. I wasn't prepared. I hit the ground shoulder first and felt pain slam up my arm and across my shoulder blade. It felt like red-hot flames licking up my left side. I groaned and rolled over. The last thing I saw was Murphy hurtling towards the car park chased by two police horses and the TV car. I couldn't fight it any longer. A wave of blackness kicked in and I passed out.

"Fifty-six seconds," the course doctor smiled as I came round. Any longer and I'd have faced a three-week injury suspension.

But the relief didn't last long. A blaze of pain scorched across my left shoulder until I couldn't breathe with the agony of it.

"Dislocated collar bone. I can either put it back in here or you can wait for the hospital doctor." There was something in his eyes which didn't expect me to say yes. I was a girl jockey – a rare breed. Not as tough as the men, couldn't possibly be.

"I'd like you to put it back in now, please." I measured every word so it wouldn't sound punctuated with pain.

"I won't pretend this won't hurt." He cut off my

back protector and lightweight polo neck jumper using surgical scissors. "I'd like you to look across to the grandstand and try to count how many people have binoculars."

He didn't waste a moment. He'd obviously done it time and again on every racecourse in the country. "Feel better?" he grinned, reaching for some strapping.

"Much," I nodded. I hadn't even winced. But when I glanced down at my hands there was blood on the cuffs of my shirt where my nails had dug in.

"I've seen slugs with more colour." Ike put his head into the First Aid tent, licking an ice-cream, which would mean more time in the sweatsuit.

"You're not a proper jockey until you do your collar bone," he grinned. "Sharpie had one of his removed in the end, he smashed it so many times. Did you see his party trick?" His voice faded as we both recollected that Sharpie was in intensive care.

"It's not broken," I corrected, although from the pain, it felt as though it was in bits.

"Listen, I've got something to tell you," he leant in close, suddenly shifty and glancing towards one of the St John's crew. "Ben Le Sueur's organizing a sit-down protest," he whispered, dribbling ice-cream down his chin, "just before the last race, at the Pond Fence. Are you in?"

It took a while for the words to register. My brain felt like a squashed cauliflower. "Umm, yeah, of course I am."

"Meet in the canteen in a quarter of an hour." He winked and ducked out into the crowds heading for the prizegiving before I could ask any more questions.

Did I want to be associated with Le Sueur after what Mickey had told me? But I couldn't turn my back on something I believed in. I thought of Sharpie and the horses who had died and my mind was made up. First though, I had to check on Murphy.

"Justina!" Rory was bobbing through the crowds, still in his silks and waving a programme in the air. I had a premonition of what he wanted to say and dodged behind the saddling stalls.

The stable area was heaving with staff and horses. Two leading trainers were arguing with an attendant about roof trouble and lack of wood-shavings. A hosepipe was spraying water everywhere and nobody seemed able to turn it off.

"Hey, you, hang on." A grim-faced security man with a walkie talkie grabbed my arm. "Where's your pass?"

Damn, it was still in the weighing room. "It's all right," I smiled, "I rode in the last race."

"No way. No pass, no entry. They're my orders. Now let this gentleman through."

Of course it had to be Rory. "Why are you following me?" I glanced at my watch in panic and then down the row of stables for a chestnut head.

Something in the way he gripped my good arm made my eyes travel back to his.

"The Guv'nor's doing his nut," he hissed. "If you're OK, you're supposed to be in the sponsors' tent talking to owners or had you completely forgotten? He's threatening to sack you if you're not back in five minutes. Either stay in First Aid or get up there now."

"So what's new?" I rolled my eyes in exasperation. "When isn't he threatening to sack me?"

"Read this." Rory stuffed a beer mat into my hand. In a corner the Guv'nor had scribbled: *Don't you dare join protest. It will be the end. Repeat. The end.*

"What are you doing?" Scooby appeared at the other side of the barrier clutching a scoop full of horse feed and the dog lead which we used for Gertie the goat. He looked harassed and flushed and his red woolly hat had a large hole in the back.

"How's Murphy?" I rushed out. Scooby loved the chestnut horse nearly as much as I did. The security man gave me a sour look as I pressed against the railing.

"Not a scratch on him," he grinned. "Fine fettle. He's taken a fancy to one of Adam Valentine's mares though and he's doing his best to flatten the stable. I've had to put Gertie back in the horsebox because some of the other lads were complaining about the racket. How are you feeling?"

"All right, thanks, but will you do me a favour?

Take this and sling it on the muck heap." I stuffed the beer mat in his hand.

"You look like death." He peered into my face.

"Not now, Scooby," I wheeled round so fast I went dizzy.

"Justina!" Rory was livid. "Have you lost your mind?"

"Which way to the canteen?" I glared at him.

"Don't blame me when you're in the dole queue."

The canteen was a shabby, green portacabin tucked away behind the pre-parade ring.

"They're gone, lassie!" A toothless chap with bushy whiskers dribbled tea down his front. He was staring at my blue hair as if he was seeing things.

Searing shots of pain leapt up my arm as I ran full pelt towards the course. I nearly ran straight through an interview a jockey was doing for Channel Four. I caught a glimpse of Shona smoking with a stable lad under the grandstand. She was supposed to be doing Rory's horse for the next race. Maybe she'd heard about the protest. The stewards would go loopy when half the jockeys sat down on the course in front of sixty thousand people. A lick of adrenalin warmed my stomach. We were breaking the rules and it felt right.

The twins and Davide started clapping and cheering when I raced the last furlong towards the

Pond Fence. "And it's Justina Brooks well clear of the rest of the field, going strong."

Davide, fearful of getting wet, was sitting on an empty feed bag and the twins had somehow found two rubber ducks which they were pushing across the water. Ben Le Sueur was deadly serious, as were nine other jockeys I vaguely recognized from the weighing room.

Three vehicles in convoy were already driving towards us.

"Eh up, here comes the *Daily Mirror*," Daryl Hamley nudged my strapped arm at the sight of a press car.

A faint chorus of booing started from the grandstand. Three very angry-looking men were striding across the grass.

"Nobody get up," Ben Le Sueur hissed through gritted teeth.

Pixie Raymond's mobile phone rang. "It's for you." He passed it down the line towards me.

"Justina, if you don't get up this minute and come straight to the sponsors' tent, I won't be responsible for my actions." The Guv'nor's voice rattled out like a machine-gun.

Very delicately I pressed the red button and cut him off. The musical tone immediately struck up again.

"I'm not moving," I yelled, one finger stuck in my ear.

"I wouldn't expect you to." It was the silky voice

of Adam Valentine. He sounded amused. "I hope you remembered an umbrella, it's going to rain in a minute."

"I'll pass you over to Pixie," I breathed, panicking slightly at the number of cameras lining up in front of me.

"Oh no, it's you I want to talk to. It is Miss Justina Brooks, isn't it?"

I held my breath.

"Only I've got a ride for her on the twenty-first, the Beamley Novice Hurdle – at Ascot."

Six

"It's made headline sports news in all the papers." Scooby opened a copy of the *Daily Mail* to a half page picture of me and the other jockeys sitting cross-legged in front of the Pond Fence.

"Mum and Dad told me when I phoned them to let them know I was all right. But they didn't tell me how hideous I look." I squirmed, horrified at the state of my hair and the smudges of mud on my cheeks. Scooby slid three bacon butties across the table, which we devoured like wolves, and then he began to read aloud.

Miss Justina Brooks, age sixteen, apprentice jockey to Kenneth Brown of Dolphin Barn Stables, made her views perfectly clear at yesterday's sit-down protest at Sunningdale. "It's got to be filled in, it kills horses, the life of one of my best friends, Sharpie O'Hare, hangs in the balance. I'll do anything to protect my beloved horses and my colleagues."

Miss Brooks, National Hunt's youngest jockey, would look more at home in a pop band with her

*spiky blue hair than the conservative Kenneth
Brown's top jump yard. Miss Brooks is making
a name for herself on the talented front-running
chestnut, Murphy's Law, although in yesterday's
coveted three-mile chase she controversially missed
out the Pond Fence, resulting in disqualification.
Mr Kenneth Brown refuses to comment.*

*Meanwhile the Jockey Club has announced that
the course meets all of the safety requirements and
racing will continue there as part of the annual
calendar. The rest of the jockeys involved have
agreed to call off their protest.*

"They make it sound as if I organized the whole
thing!" I exploded. "There's hardly a mention of
Ben Le Sueur. What are they all going to think?"

Mandy visibly winced at the name but she didn't
say anything. I pushed my plate away, feeling as if
my stomach had suddenly filled up with lead.
Neither did it raise my spirits to remember that
somebody had crossed my name off the work ride
board with a red pen.

"That's the last time I'm going to the races with
that chestnut horse," Scooby moaned, feeding
scraps of bacon to Chelsea. "Something always
goes wrong. I'm like a jinx. Ouch!"

Chelsea nipped the end of his fingers and then
started attacking the chair leg. "That dog's a
psychopath, just look at him."

Mandy lifted her head out of her hands. She was
in an awful state. Anyone would think she'd been

59

ditched at the altar. I'd have to have serious words with her later.

"You know what that means, don't you?" she said in a voice of doom. "The Guv's in a really bad mood. Last time Chelsea bit somebody was the day the Guv sacked Jacko."

I smiled stiffly and started shredding bits of newspaper over the table. You could always rely on your best friend to make you feel a hundred times better.

Harris, Roy and Jake came in from first lot smacking their hands together against the cold. "Well, if it isn't our very own Emmeline Pankhurst," Harris grinned, ruffling my hair as if I was Rory's Great Dane. "I didn't think you'd got it in you, kid, I'm seriously impressed."

Roy, nicknamed Roy Rogers because he'd never been near a horse till he started at racing college and who now rode a bit like a cowboy, slapped me on the back, sending darts of pain across my shoulder. "You're famous at the Jockey's Rest. The landlord's even pinned your picture up on the wall."

I went out to get some fresh air. Murphy stood nodding his head irritably over the door. Frost glistened in a white carpet while shards of ice dripped off the guttering. I breathed deeply and ran my hand down his enormous face.

Dear, dear, Murphy. I'd never forget the first time I'd seen him, gangling down the road like a young colt. From a standstill, he'd leapt over a thorn hedge the size of Becher's and I'd known then that he could win the Grand National. He had the guts and courage of a hundred horses but nobody to believe in him.

I'd rescued him from that, put my racing career on the line, and brought him back to Dolphin Barn. I'd worshipped and cherished him until he realized he was special. Now there wasn't a jockey in the country who wouldn't want the ride on him.

"He'll only ever like the girls, that 'orse." Badger, the head lad, was pulling the feed trolley down the aisle towards us. "If one of us blokes tried to stroke him like that, he'd bite a hole in our head."

As if he understood, Murphy immediately put his ears back.

Badger was dedicated to Dolphin Barn in a way nobody else was. He'd still be checking the horses at midnight and he was up before daybreak. All the lads had a tremendous respect for him. He was the Guv'nor's right-hand man, his voice and ears.

"The boss wants to see yer." He sucked in his cheeks, scouring my face with eagle eyes for a reaction. Inside I was writhing with nerves. "I'd have thought you'd have wanted to keep your nose clean," he grunted. "What with your ambition."

Badger was one of the first people in whom I'd confided my dream of winning the Grand National. I braced myself for a lecture.

"You won't get to Aintree upsetting folk. Look at Rory Calligan, keeps his nose clean, totally blinkered and focused. He'll be the next Tony McCoy, mark my words." He seemed to have conveniently forgotten about Rory's recent disappearance.

"I have to do what I believe in, otherwise what kind of person would I be?"

"Seems a ruddy waste, what with a horse like that and the way you ride him. Better not stand there catching flies, the boss won't wait for ever."

I tapped on the office door. The slightest excuse and I'd have run off like the Cowardly Lion in *The Wizard of Oz*. Instead I concentrated on slowing my breathing which was rattling along at a hundred miles an hour.

"Come in."

He was sitting behind a mountain of entry forms with the television switched on to the Racing Channel and an electric fan heater whirring in the corner. Chelsea barged over my feet and ran under the desk, carrying one of Scooby's sausages.

"Take a seat."

Usually at this point he'd fire questions at me about Murphy. How did he feel? What did I think of his new diet? Was he right in himself? I stared at a picture of a racehorse called Dolphin who had been a Grand National winner for the Guv'nor twenty years ago. Since then another win had eluded him.

"You'll be pleased to know that Sharpie O'Hare is making an excellent recovery. He should be out of hospital in the next few days."

"That's brilliant," I gushed, wondering if that was all he wanted me for.

"However, what isn't so brilliant is your behaviour of late." Silence hung in the air for an eternity. I could see him struggling to restrain his temper, his face flooding purple.

A lump sprang into my throat. Suddenly it was stiflingly hot in the tiny office.

"First I have to put up with you scampering on to a course in the middle of a race and hindering Rory Calligan – right in front of TV cameras, I might add. Then you're impossibly rude to owners and disappear with another trainer. You dye your hair blue and run round in skirts the size of tea towels and then there's the whole matter of your dubious actions towards Jack Hughes."

My face was burning red by now.

"And to top all that . . ." He leant over his desk, knuckles glowing white. Chelsea growled, his bushy grey eyebrows twitching just like the Guv'nor's. "And to top all that you deliberately take the wrong course at Sunningdale which results in you injuring yourself." He was spitting his words out now in disbelief. "You snub important owners and sponsors to join a protest in which I had strictly forbidden you to take part. Is that the behaviour of an apprentice jockey who has been given a golden opportunity with a top jump yard? Is it? Is it?"

I thought he was going to have a heart attack.

"Less than a year ago you were a school leaver

desperate for a job as a stablehand. You win one race and now you think you can break every rule in the book. Is that how you repay my support?"

I squirmed in my chair wanting to shout back that it wasn't like that but I closed my eyes with a grimace and waited for him to calm down. He always did. We had that in common – a fiery temper that burnt itself out in minutes.

He sat back down and ran his hands through his hair, which stuck out at the sides in tufts. "You ride like nobody I've seen on a racehorse. It doesn't matter that you don't have a man's strength, you get under their skins, inside their heads. You create your own magic."

I felt my face flush at the unexpected praise. I'd ride my heart out for Dolphin Barn, he had to know that.

"But I can't have you riding roughshod over my authority. I'll have the whole yard rising up in mutiny."

A cold shiver suddenly ran down my spine despite the heat.

"I'm suspending you for a month from all stable duties and work riding. I'm handing Murphy over to Scooby and you're not to go anywhere near the yard."

My mind had gone blank with shock. I was transfixed with disbelief. He couldn't be serious.

"We'll review the situation in four weeks' time."

I felt as if my heart was cracking open. He'd never keep me away from Murphy.

There was a knock at the door and Scooby walked in. He couldn't look me in the eye, he was cringing with embarrassment.

It was true, then. It wasn't an idle threat. He was making an example of me. I felt as if every nerve in my body had been encrusted with ice. When it wore off I'd be aching with pain but for now I was just numb to everything.

"Aaah, Scooby, you'll be doing Murphy's work ride tomorrow, second lot."

I slid out of the office unnoticed. Somehow I got back to the cottage without breaking down. I sank into the one decent chair we had and turned on the television, which flashed up some children's TV programme in a grey haze. I stared unseeing until the credits rolled up at the end.

Mandy burst through the door. "I've just heard. It's terrible. How could he do such a thing?" She flopped on to her knees and grabbed my hand as if I was going to break into a thousand pieces. "All men are pigs," she moaned, animated now that someone else was feeling miserable as well.

"I don't want to talk about it," I whispered through wooden jaws.

But at that moment Scooby burst in, followed by Harris and Roy.

"I'm sorry, Jus." Scooby was squirming with

65

guilt. "I never thought he'd go this far. I didn't know what to say."

Of course nobody ever said no to the Guv'nor.

"Rotten luck." Harris leant on the telly and for once the picture cleared. "You'd probably get a job at the Jockey's Rest. I could have a word with the landlord. You could always help me do up my old Escort."

Nobody seemed prepared to go on strike to support me. The icy protection which had kept me together so far was starting to thaw. I felt gutted. Harris and Scooby were arguing about when Murphy would next race.

I wanted to scream and never stop. Instead I ran into the downstairs toilet and locked myself in. "Just leave me alone," I wailed through the door when somebody knocked.

There was much hushed whispering and then, finally, I heard everyone tiptoeing out and the back door clicked shut.

I gave way to racking sobs then. Tears rolled down my chin and on to my hands. My chest heaved until it hurt.

"Justina?" There was a gentle tapping on the door. "It's Mickey. I'm not going until you open the door."

I dabbed my eyes and fluffed up my hair. Then I pulled back the bolt.

He didn't say anything at all. His eyes just ached with care and concern. I felt so alone, and when he opened his arms and pulled me to him, I buried my head in his jumper like a scared rabbit.

"Shush, shush." He dropped tiny kisses into my hair and rocked me until I felt calmer. I pulled away, slightly flustered, and went and sat down in the lounge.

"Maybe he'll change his mind," Mickey eventually said, sitting down beside me.

"You don't know the Guv'nor," I answered. "He never says anything he doesn't mean."

"It's only four weeks."

"That's if he gives me my job back."

"You've got to be positive."

"OK, I'll work for Adam Valentine and ride *his* horse at Ascot." I said it without thought but suddenly I realized it was a possible option.

Mickey's face drained of colour. "You can't." His mood completely changed. A nervous tick started in his cheek. I was amazed at his sudden tension. "Promise me you won't agree to anything until I get back?" His eyes searched my face.

"Where are you going?"

"I can't say. Only that it's important." He left the cottage.

A wave of irritation washed over me. How was it Mickey and Rory seemed to come and go like hotel guests and the grumpy old Guv'nor didn't say a word? Anger rose inside me. I was sick of being told what to do and what not to do. Who did these men think they were? I plumped up a cushion, bashing it

67

so hard, dust flew out. The soaring, grinding pain in my shoulder forced me to catch my breath. Surely it shouldn't be this painful? Jockeys' injuries were par for the course. If I was to be taken seriously as a girl rider I had to grin and bear it.

A phone rang. I jumped out of my skin at the strange tone. Glancing around I spotted a mobile on top of the television. Mickey must have left it behind in his rush. It was probably him ringing from a call box to tell me.

"Hello?" I tried not to sound sulky.

"Hello?" I could sense the hesitation at the other end. "Is this Mickey Harwood's phone?" It was a girl's voice. She sounded upset, panicky.

"He's gone out somewhere," I explained. "Can I take a message?"

She didn't speak for ages.

"I'm a friend," I said.

"Tell him he's needed urgently. It's been brought forward – Burrows Lea has gone missing."

"Can I say who called?"

"Yeah," she answered. Her voice was thick with despair. "It's Diane. His girlfriend."

I sat down heavily and stared at the phone in its plastic case.

"Girlfriend. Diane."

I felt as though someone was pouring red hot lava into my veins. The two-timing rat. What was it with guys I met? Every time I turned round Rory was all over Shona. And now Mickey. Well, I'd show the lot of them. And the Guv'nor as well. I was old enough to make my own decisions.

I bolted upstairs to my room and with manic energy started flipping through a trainers' directory I kept under the bed. V. V. V. Valentine. I punched the number on Mickey's phone and wasn't surprised to discover that it had already been logged.

"Come on, come on." The ringing went on for ever. My hands were shaking with temper. It was two weeks till Ascot, the doctor said it would take that time for the muscles to tighten up fully in my shoulder. I could make it. Please, please don't let him have booked another jockey.

It was the head lad who answered. Adam was out swimming one of the horses. "Could you pass on a message for me?" I begged. "Tell him Justina Brooks will be available to ride his horse. You'll tell him? Thanks." The line clicked dead.

That would show high and mighty Mr Kenneth Brown. Maybe now he might stop treating me like a dogsbody. I rolled over on the bed and started dreaming about Ascot, one of the most prestigious racecourses in England . . .

Seven

"Look here!" Mandy came into the cottage brandishing a copy of the *Daily Mail*. "There's a letter from a reader congratulating you on standing up for horses' rights even if the protest has fizzled out."

I was more interested in the packet of custard creams she'd fetched from the village shop. Mandy looked exasperated. "You can't hide away in here for ever, clipping your toenails and watching repeats of sitcoms. Why don't you go and apologize to the Guv'nor and try to sort it out?"

"No way."

"The lads are going down to the pitch to play footie and want to know if you'll referee?"

"Nope." I stuffed a whole custard cream in my mouth. Shona walked in, looking as smug as Chelsea when she's bitten somebody. "Honestly, I can't get away from Mickey, I'm sure he's dying to ask me out."

"Join the queue," I spluttered. "Along with everybody else in the county." That shut her up. I'd sent Mickey's phone back via Mandy with Diane's

70

message pinned to the front. At least he'd had the good grace to keep away.

Scooby knocked on the half open door. I leapt up, forgetting everything but Murphy. "How is he? Did you put the molasses in his feed? Remember he likes his girth tightened at the end of the driveway otherwise he bucks. Did you put his extra blanket on last night? He always likes his eyes and nostrils wiping before he goes out."

"Shh." Scooby smiled calmly. "He's fine, OK? Don't be so paranoid."

I'd only been away from the yard for twenty-four hours and it already felt like a hundred years. What I really wanted to hear was that Murphy was pining away and the Guv'nor was begging me to come back.

The phone rang. "I'll answer it." Mandy leapt up, still thinking it might be Ben Le Sueur.

"No. I will!" I literally flew across the room and snatched it from her in a rugby tackle.

"Hello? Hello. Yes, speaking." A thin film of perspiration was breaking out all over my body. It was Adam Valentine's secretary.

"Yes, fine, OK." Scooby and Mandy were looking at me strangely.

"No problem. Yes, yes. Till then." I replaced the handset with shaking hands.

"Who was that? Leonardo DiCaprio?" Mandy asked suspiciously.

"The dentist," I squeaked. "My new crown's

ready. You remember this one's just a temp." I tapped fiercely at my top lip to make sure she understood. "Anyway, must dash, I'm supposed to be walking Rory's dog." I opened the back door and made to go out.

"What? In your slippers?" Scooby questioned in a dry voice.

That night, I was lying in a lukewarm bath when I had a brainwave.

I could easily see Murphy. All I needed to do was climb out of the bathroom window on to the flat roof of the cottage and then on to the adjoining stable block. From there I could sidle along to the third skylight and then drop down into the hayloft and climb down the ladder to Murphy's stable. The only thing was that it was freezing and I didn't have much to wear. I got out of the bath and pulled on my dressing-gown and slippers. Shona's dressing-gown was hanging on the back of the door and I put that on too.

Murphy was overjoyed to see me and went crashing into my bad arm in his enthusiasm. Gertie, who was asleep in the corner, looked sour-faced and wrinkled her top lip at the smell of lavender bubble bath, but didn't wake up. It was just brilliant to see the chestnut horse. I snuggled my hands under his warm rugs and chattered non-stop. He whickered noisily and stamped and tapped his feet as if he were off to the races.

The next night I did exactly the same thing, but as I was climbing back in through the window, I could hear Mandy practically breaking the door down. "Jus? Justina, what are you doing in there?"

Anyone would think I was trying to drown myself.

"Rory's here. He's been waiting to see you for twenty minutes." I tore off my clothes and threw on my dressing-gown, then bolted downstairs trying not to look guilty but I was so cold I practically had to sit on top of the electric fire. "No hot water," I said, teeth chattering. "Must be Shona hogging it all again."

Mandy handed me a mug of Ovaltine and I suddenly realized that Rory looked bemused. I followed his gaze and could see cobwebs and shavings caught on the hem of my dressing-gown. "How did those get there?" I said weakly, brushing them off.

I hadn't told a soul about my ride for Adam Valentine. The longer I left it, the worse it became. My mother has an old adage: act in haste, repent at leisure, and it kept coming back to haunt me. I was free to ride for other trainers, so why did I feel so guilty?

Rory seemed to be able to read my thoughts. "I'm riding at Ascot next weekend, if you want to come?"

I nearly choked on my Ovaltine. "Oh," I managed to croak.

Why did he have to keep staring like that? And why did he have to be so ridiculously good-looking? I plaited the draylon frill on the arm of the settee while my insides bounced around like a hundred yo yos.

"But that's not why I'm here." He threw a pile of postcards on to the coffee table.

I went bright red and snatched them up. They were advertisements for work which I'd put up in the village shops that afternoon.

"You and the Guv'nor, you're as stubborn as each other."

"I think my bed's calling." Mandy leapt up nervously.

"Don't you realize, you stupid idiot, *why* he's stopped you working?" Rory leant over the settee so I could feel his breath on my neck. "To protect your shoulder, you clot. If you ride too early you'll wear a groove in the end of the bones and every time you tap it it'll pop out of its socket."

"I don't want any special treatment," I yapped, but shut up when he looked as if he was going to strangle me.

"You'll end up riddled with rheumatism like nearly every retired jockey in the country. Did you know," he hissed, leaning in closer, "that there are jockeys who have to tie their arms to their sides before they go to bed at night because if they don't and they raise their elbows above their heads while they're asleep their shoulders dislocate?"

I didn't say anything, just blinked in amazement. I'd never thought, never considered. I must have looked shocked because Rory's expression softened.

"He's agreed to let you back in the yard providing you only do light work, a bit of tack-cleaning, cutting up the carrots, helping Scooby in the kitchens, that kind of thing."

Normally my mouth would immediately have opened in protest but now my pride seemed to have withered away. I just wanted to be close to Murphy and back in the hustle and bustle of the stables. I was touched as well that Rory had gone to so much trouble.

"And one more thing . . ." Rory got up to leave, which made me want to pull him back.

"The Guv'nor suggested that perhaps now you'd give up night-walking along the roofs and use the stable door instead. Harris is convinced that either we've got a ghost or he's spending too much time at the Jockey's Rest."

I howled with embarassment and hid my face behind a cushion until I heard the back door shut behind him.

"The Guv'nor's in a lousy mood." Mandy hacked back from first lot on an experienced hurdle racer who had picked up a stone in his hoof. "He's torn strips off nearly everybody for walking through an icy puddle."

I gulped back a wave of nausea. It was three days until Ascot and I had to tell the Guv'nor that I was riding for Adam Valentine before he heard from someone else. Just the thought of facing him made me feel as if I'd eaten rotten fish. There was something about the pressures of training racehorses that made governors extremely grumpy. Apart from Adam Valentine that is, who seemed to sail through everything with serenity.

"Why don't you just cancel the ride, say you aren't fit enough?" A voice kept hammering away in my subconscious. But another voice always answered, the voice of drive and ambition. Deep down I knew I wanted the chance, the exposure. I wanted to prove myself as a jockey in my own right, riding a strange horse for a leading trainer. Valentine was right, the hunger for success was eating me up inside until I could think of nothing but winning.

"Ouch!" Blood spread over my thumb as I sliced more than just carrot. I'd chopped enough carrots to feed ninety-seven horses for a week.

The rest of the string of riders came round the corner in a steaming, clattering mass. Everyone was unnaturally quiet and sitting very straight-backed, which suggested the Guv'nor was not far behind. Sure enough the battered four-wheel drive pulled into the main yard and the Guv'nor, defying his arthritis, marched straight into the stable of

Tralligan, one of his best chasers who was hopping lame at the moment.

"Stop it," Shona waved her hand, giggling at Harris who was mimicking the Guv'nor. He ran his fingers through his hair to make it stand on end, narrowed his eyes to slits, hunched his shoulders, held his breath so he went bright red in the face. The effect was quite startling. All the lads and lasses creased into laughter until they spotted the Guv'nor staring over the door.

Ten minutes later I forced myself to face him. All the life drained from my limbs as he kept his back to me, squirting purple wound spray into Tralligan's fetlock.

"I've accepted a ride for Adam Valentine." I was amazed I could unstick my tonsils. My voice sounded remote and unnatural. I was beginning to think he hadn't heard me. "It's just the once," I added, as lightly as I could.

He started whistling through his teeth and tapping Tralligan's racing plate with a hoof pick. I shivered and felt myself turn pale. It was ages before he answered.

"You didn't think Valentine would keep it to himself, did you?"

I realized then he'd known all along. "You'd better watch those Ascot fences."

I rocked back on my heels in shock. There was a sudden coldness in his manner which I'd never seen before. I'd hurt him. Badly. For the rest of the day, guilt gnawed at my insides until I felt like an empty shell.

The morning of the race I was sick three times but at least my shoulder felt better. Daryl Hamley and another jockey I didn't know arrived to give me a lift. Just carrying my race saddle made me feel weak at the knees. Fear tweaked every nerve in my body. The next few hours could make or break my career.

"Justina?" Mickey Harwood appeared out of the gloom.

"What's your problem?" The last thing I needed was to see him.

"Just take care, OK?" He stared at me for numb seconds until I thought he was going to bodily drag me back to the stables.

"You take care of your girlfriend," I snapped, and slid into the car.

The only thing that mattered now was riding the race of my life – and winning.

"You're odds on favourite." Ben Le Sueur deliberately sought out my peg in the weighing room. Outside, fog was descending like pea soup but the race was still on.

Adam Valentine's voice suddenly cut through the background noise as someone turned up the television. *The girl's got hands any horse can trust. She's an instinctive rider. I believe in giving new talent a chance.*

I couldn't believe it. I was being discussed on national television – like a top-flight jockey.

"You're ruddy famous," Daryl Hamley grunted. "They're laying money on with a trowel."

I couldn't look or listen any more. I buried my face in my hands and felt a wave of nausea wash up my throat. I was attracting the kind of attention most conditional jockeys only dreamt of.

"We're on!" Someone nudged my back. I hadn't even heard the steward call. This was it.

We trudged out into the gloom and one of the most famous parade paddocks in England. I had about two minutes to acclimatize myself to a horse I'd never even sat on, before I risked life and limb over three miles and twenty-seven enormous fences.

I spotted her straight away. She was a black mare wearing a white bridle, which was the Valentine trademark. She was as lean as a greyhound and arched her back indignantly as the paddock sheet was slipped off. I had to get inside her head and persuade her to run like the wind for me.

"Here she is!" Adam stepped forward with a dazzling smile and ushered me into his party. "We're changing tactics," he whispered, leaning close to leg me up. "Front run from the start. Put as much distance between you and the others. She'll stay all the way."

I swallowed back surprise.

"Hey, Justina?" A punter at the rails waved his

79

programme. "You're not going to let us down, are you?"

Daryl was right. I was famous. From that moment, the will to win kicked in. I gathered up the reins and edged out on to the track, more determined than ever.

The tape flew up. In a split second a cavalcade of horses rushed forward. Thundering hooves, excitement, fear, creaking leather, jockeys shouting: this was what I was born to do. The familiar fire lit up inside.

I asked for another gear and the mare shot forward. We rounded the first bend into a cloak of fog. It was eerie. Black, solid birch rose up as we met it on a perfect stride. I kicked on. We had to gain ground now – before the uphill slope. Pounding horses sounded on our tail. I asked for more. And more. Lengthening. Pulling away. The fog cleared, so did my view of the horses. The dense air had disorientated sound. We were fifteen lengths in front.

But something was wrong. The horse was labouring, great, rasping breaths tearing from her lungs. I knew from having studied her form that she had never won from the front. She needed to be nursed, asked in the final furlong. I'd gone against my instincts to follow orders. I'd have to pull up. I had no choice. But the next jump was upon us. There was no time.

She could have crashed through it. Most horses

would. But with a massive effort she climbed over. Sweet, genuine horse that she was, she tried her heart out for me.

We landed badly. I lurched forward, jerking on to her neck. Everything was OK for four strides after the fence, then she went down, skidding on her nose. Her neck concertinaed sideways and she slumped on to her side. I knew what had happened, something in her near foreleg had snapped like an elastic band. I'd heard it, felt it go as she floundered and fell.

Oh my God! It was my fault! My fault!

Crunching, shooting pain ripped up my shoulder but it didn't register. I had to reach her, keep her quiet till the vet arrived. The rest of the field skimmed past, a hair's breath from mowing me down. I was like a walking zombie, threading my way through a stream of galloping horses.

She was over by the rail, gingerly dangling the useless leg. Oh God, what could I do? Something, please. Her eyes rolled in terror. She tried to stagger forwards and scared herself more.

"Come on." An arm grabbed mine. I spun round to see Ben Le Sueur. He'd obviously fallen too. "She's broken down, there's nothing you can do."

"But?" He was dragging me off the racetrack.

"Let the vets do their job. She'll probably have a life as a broodmare, eating and having babies."

Like an athlete, a horse could break down at any

time, severing the delicate tendons at the back of the legs. It took months of rest to get them right.

"But it was my fault!" I half shrieked. "I knew she wasn't right. I should have pulled up earlier. I did this to her."

"No you didn't. It was . . ." Ben broke off, stony-faced.

I climbed into a medical car in a trance. I had to find Adam. "We'll take you to the weighing room. Just sit down in there for five minutes. You're in shock," the driver said to me.

I was shaking like a leaf. From the weighing room, I heard a cheer go up from the grandstand as the race finished. I was on my own in there when the television in the corner cut to Adam giving an interview. He looked angry and ashen-faced. Everyone wanted to know what had happened to the favourite. Crowds were clamouring in the background. *"The jockey completely disobeyed orders. All I can do is put it down to her inexperience."* He gave a regretful smile. *"Unfortunately Out Of The Blue has had to be destroyed. No further comment."*

I sat for ages staring into space. He'd told me to ride from the front – I hadn't imagined it. But I'd asked too much. I'd ridden her like Murphy and she wasn't in the same class. I'd killed her as surely as if I'd shot her with a gun.

One minute I'd hit the headlines for trying to save horses' lives, now I was doing the opposite.

Adam Valentine had announced to the world that I wasn't competent. I thought he was a friend, on my side. The horrible truth sank in like a stone. It was as though freezing hands were rising in my chest, gripping at my sides. The Guv'nor would never take me back now. My career as a jockey was finished. I'd never race ride again.

Eight

"I'm going home!"

"You can't!" Mandy grabbed the suitcase and tried to lock it in the bathroom.

"It's all over. I'll phone my mum to collect me and then I'm going back to college to become a riding instructor."

"You can't just give up."

"I can. I have to." I ripped open the wardrobe which was only ever full of screwed-up jodphurs and jeans. How could Mandy ever understand the dead weight in my chest? The guilt of having ridden a horse so badly I'd caused its death?

"At least talk to somebody."

"I can't."

"What about Rory? Scooby? You can't ignore them for ever."

"Watch me!" I picked up the plastic bag containing the lucky piece of turf I'd taken from Aintree when I was thirteen years old and slung it into my washbag. Somebody hammered at the front door. "Get rid of them!" I croaked, feeling as if my mouth was full of grit.

"It's Mickey," Mandy shouted up the stairs and then, to my horror, I heard his voice in the hallway. Blast. Why did he always have to see me when I was in a state?

"Justina? It's me, Mickey."

"I can see that." I bobbed down the stairs, pulling a jumper over my head as I went. He was standing in the hall with a girl.

"Justina, there's something I've got to tell you. This is Diane."

I didn't believe this. "Mickey, I really don't think this is the time . . ." then I paused, struck by the seriousness in his voice.

"I've not been honest with you. I'm sorry. I've never worked with horses professionally. I'm an investigative journalist working undercover for a TV documentary programme. Diane is my work colleague, not my girlfriend."

I blinked unbelievingly.

"It's true. We've been keeping tabs on Valentine for nearly a year. I had to move out of his yard when it looked as if I was going to be sprung. Diane still works there. I moved here so I could be close to hand. The Guv'nor knows exactly what's going on. He's doing all he can to help."

I collapsed sideways into an armchair with dodgy springs. My brain couldn't take in such staggering information.

Mandy gave a yelp of excitement and horror. "I always thought he was a smarmy snake! Television? My God, are we going to be interviewed?"

I was still frozen.

"He's been guilty of laying off bets, swapping horses, bribing jockeys, anything that helps him line his pockets."

I nodded but couldn't really understand a thing.

Diane leant forward, anxious we should hear everything. "Valentine took on a racing yard three years ago, even though he couldn't afford it. His partner pulled out soon afterwards, so he went to the bank and borrowed a vast amount of money. He started having winners but not enough. He resorted to cheating and then couldn't stop. The black mare you rode wasn't really Out Of The Blue. She was identical to the real Out Of The Blue, who Valentine has sold to a Japanese trainer for telephone figures. The horse you rode had been kept boxed and tightly bandaged. Before the race she was given a series of injections to weaken her tendons. Drug testing of horses is thorough these days, but they don't tend to check for that type of thing."

"There was no way that horse could win," Mickey took over. "Valentine sent her out knowing she wouldn't finish the race. He gave you instructions that ensured she wouldn't see another."

I shook my head in a daze. "But why a high profile place like Ascot? And why me?"

"Simple. He knew you wouldn't ask questions, just blame yourself. And Ascot has a huge audience. By criticizing you on television he created a smoke-screen which threw off suspicion. He actually looked like the good guy giving you a chance."

"Whereas a more experienced jockey might have challenged him?" Mandy asked.

"Exactly. Ben Le Sueur cottoned on to some of his scams and was having none of it. He couldn't prove a thing so he just left. When it looked like you and Ben were going to get together, I had to get Justina to put you off. I couldn't risk him telling you and spoiling the whole operation. I'm sorry."

I didn't look at Mandy. I knew how she must be feeling. But it wasn't anything like the humiliation tearing into me.

"Adam made a vast amount of money laying off bets that Out Of The Blue wouldn't win and then he cleaned up on the insurance when she had to be put down."

"Shouldn't you be taking all this to the police?" I felt my jaws tighten.

"The head of Cyber TV is in discussions now with CID. But there's something else which is much bigger. Valentine's been importing horses from South Africa, a couple every month, and then selling them off cheap at the sales. We're convinced he's been smuggling precious stones into the country via the horses but we still can't work out how. CID are planning a raid when he brings in the next lot."

"Why couldn't you have told me all this before?" I was struggling to stop my chin wobbling. I was asking sensible questions but my brain was whirling.

"Because you might have done something stupid, confronted him, anything."

"So why now? I presume it's still all top-secret? I might still do something stupid."

Mickey's face crumpled into a grin. "I knew you'd be beating yourself up about Out Of The Blue. You can't give up racing, you're a good jockey, even I can see that."

"Besides," Diane said nervously, "we need your help. Desperately. There's another racehorse that's gone missing and we're pretty certain Valentine's going to try the same trick up north. He says she's gone away for special training but we all know what that means."

The telephone conversation with Diane flooded back. "Burrows Lea?" I recalled, surprising myself.

"She's one of the horses I've been looking after." Diane looked upset. "The police and our boss have agreed to do nothing so they can collect more evidence." Her shoulders visibly sagged. "Valentine trained as a vet before switching to racing. He knows what he's doing. If he gives Burrows Lea the same course of injections as he gave your poor mount at Ascot, he'll damage her tendons for ever. I can't let that happen."

I could see the love in her eyes for the horse and knew that, in the same situation, I'd do anything to save Murphy.

"What can I do?" Nothing mattered more than saving Burrows Lea. It would somehow avenge Out Of The Blue's death and ease the rage building inside my chest.

"We have a plan," said Diane, "but it's dangerous and we're on our own. Neither the police nor the television station knows about it, but it's the only way to save Burrows Lea. We want you to search his house."

"Now, you know the plan?" Mickey pulled the car on to a grass verge and opened the door. "If he comes back unexpectedly explain how you found the key under the flowerpot and let yourself in. You act angry and hysterical and accuse him of ruining your career. Then get out as quickly as possible. I'll be waiting here to pick you up."

"Got it." I sucked in a deep breath to calm my jangling nerves. "I'm to look for anything that might tell us where Burrows Lea is hidden."

"It could be anything. Keep your mind open. An old receipt. Something scribbled on a newspaper. Go through the address book on the telephone table page for page."

"Right." My heart thumped so loudly I thought

it would burst. For a dangerous few seconds I couldn't move. I didn't think I could go through with it.

"You OK?"

"Yeah, fine." I knew what had to be done. Diane had already been caught in his office twice. I was the only one with a good reason to visit his home. Mickey gave me an awkward peck on the cheek and then opened the boot and lifted out my bike.

It was now or never. I climbed out of the car, into a thin drizzle of rain, and grabbed the handlebars of a bike I hadn't ridden since I came to Dolphin Barn.

It would be all right. All the stable staff would be having their afternoon break from two until four. Diane would be around to give the alert if Valentine came back from the races early.

I turned up the long drive to Hollingbrook Stables and pedalled under an arch with the outline of a racehorse etched into the stone. The yard was deserted. Horses nodded over open half doors and some white doves pecked at the bottom of a wheel-barrow. I guided the bike round to the front of the farmhouse and knocked on the glass door, even though I knew no one was in. Sure enough, the key was under a geranium pot by the side of a boot remover. I was in.

It was almost too easy. A clock ticked in the corner between the oak beams. Two dog baskets lay vacant under the table and a ginger cat lay curled up on a shelf beside a stereo.

Shaking, I tiptoed into the hallway where the phone rested on an antique, polished desk. In the almost complete silence, I started my search, hardly daring to breathe. I flipped open the spring-backed telephone directory and riffled through all the numbers. Then I checked the notepad and that day's *Racing Post*. Twenty minutes later I was back in the kitchen going through a pile of mail and I still hadn't found anything.

It looked as if Mickey would have to tail Valentine instead of depending on me for evidence. That had already failed once though, and the chances of getting caught were high. I moved swiftly into the sitting-room with panic starting to swell inside me. I couldn't stay much longer. Each passing minute felt like an hour.

A whole wall was covered in photographs of winners and trophies. There was the Gold Cup winner and the King George. Adam smiled towards the camera, the picture of confidence and success. Where had it all gone wrong?

Further along were two photographs of Adam as a younger man, posing next to a tiny two-seater aircraft with someone who looked like a flying instructor holding a clipboard. I scanned the heading. Adam was just eighteen years old. It had been taken at Stargate Airport, Cheltenham, which had closed down years ago. Somewhere between then and now the carefree boy with the charmed life had become a criminal.

The door into the kitchen slammed shut. I jumped out of my skin. The air locked in my throat. There was no escape. Whoever was in the house was talking on the phone and sounded pretty angry. It was a man but the voice was muffled. My thoughts darted around at a million miles an hour. It was a fifty-fifty chance that he'd come into the sitting-room. I had to think fast. Fear sucked the life out of my legs so I couldn't move. Heavy footsteps approached the almost-closed door. I was going to get caught. It was inevitable. Sick dread filled my mouth. The door swung open.

I looked up from the chintz settee and put down the copy of *Country Life* magazine I was holding, trying to look bored. The figure in the doorway jolted in surprise. Somehow I contorted my facial muscles into disappointment that it wasn't the boss. Instead it was the head lad, the one I'd met at the twins' Hallowe'en party. He had an oilskin pulled up round his neck but the ginger hair and hooded eyes were unmistakable. Surprise quickly turned to outrage.

"What the hell are you doing here?"

"One of the staff let me in," I snapped indignantly. I mustn't sound guilty or apologetic. "I'm waiting for your boss, he can't keep avoiding me for ever. I want to know why he slagged me off on television. He's got no right, I can't get any more rides . . ." I let my voice peel upwards with suitable hysteria.

Was it relief on his face? Just a glimmer before the jaw reset in a hard line? He was involved. I could practically smell it. His gaze darted around the room, checking that nothing was disturbed. "You'd better go." He put his hand on the doorknob. "He's got nothing to say to you. And I'd think twice about being a jockey if I was you, it's not a game for lasses." His tone was final.

I didn't need telling again. The nerve that had been holding me together caved in and I bolted like a rabbit before he changed his mind.

"What happened?" Mickey ran forward. "You've been ages." He picked up the bike and slung it into the car. "You're shaking."

"I'll explain later, take that road, the B26," I gasped. "The old aircraft hangar – we can get there in twenty minutes."

"You found something?"

"Not exactly." My chest was still heaving. "It's just a hunch. But hurry, there's not much time."

I didn't tell Mickey that the head lad would probably be talking to Valentine at this moment.

Mickey's phone rang. I picked it up. "It's Diane. What happened? Is Justina all right?"

"We're heading for the derelict aircraft hangar at Stargate," I shouted into the mouthpiece. "Can you organize a horse trailer to meet us on the road near the viewpoint?"

"Justina, what happened in the house? I couldn't get to you in time."

"The trailer – can you organize it?"

"Yeah, I think so, but—" The line crackled and broke up.

I was staking everything on a feeling. I hoped I wasn't wrong. Mickey crashed into fifth gear and zoomed past a line of lorries. The tension was unbearable. I crossed both fingers and just prayed I was right.

"Nobody's been in here for years." Mickey's voice echoed round the hangar. We'd climbed in through a loose sheet of corrugated iron. Pigeons took off from the rafters, shocked at the sudden intrusion. I'd been here once with my dad when I was about six. There'd been talk of turning it into an industrial unit.

"Where are you?" I wanted to scream. I'd been so convinced, so sure we'd find a racehorse hidden away. Rain pounded on the roof. The noise was deafening. Like a thousand echoes. Mickey froze.

"What is it?" I wanted to put my fingers in my ears as my voice boomeranged back.

"My God. Quick – at the back!" He tore forward.

"Mickey?"

He was squeezing past a twenty-foot tower of

beer crates stacked in the far corner. I ran after him, hardly able to hear myself think.

"There's a doorway!" He tugged frantically at the corroded metal which slid back on rotten hinges. The smell of horses filled our nostrils.

Burrows Lea was there, cowering at the back of an enclosure blocked off with straw bales, terrified of the thundering din above her head.

Mickey reached for her head collar. My eyes went to the pressure bandages on both forelegs. Diane had been right. This was the meaning of "special training", deliberately nobbling a horse to make her break down on the track. I felt sick at heart to think that Out Of The Blue had spent the last weeks of her life subjected to this.

"We haven't got much time," I shouted, and a shudder of tension passed between us. Torrents of rain bounced down harder on the corrugated roof. Burrows Lea rolled her eyes and hunched her back in terror. She was a lovely, rich, black colour under her rug and had a white blaze down her face. I could see why Diane had fallen in love with her.

"Stand back a touch." Mickey produced a camera from his jacket and grimly started snapping.

"We've got to get her out of here!" I glanced around, panic boiling over. Someone could be on their way at this very moment.

As quickly as it had arrived, the rain stopped and all we could hear was heavy dripping and an eerie silence.

"Mickey, what are you doing?"

He started punching a number into his mobile phone. I could feel precious minutes slipping away. His face hardened. "Change of plan," he grinned sheepishly but with an edge of excitement. "I heard from my boss while you were in Valentine's house. The raid's on for tonight. The horses have just landed. They're ready with a search warrant." His interest in Burrows Lea had vanished.

"You've got no intention of rescuing her, have you? You just set me up to find her so you could take your lousy photographs. You're going to leave her here alone and petrified and in pain. All you're interested in is your stupid story and your TV programme."

"That's not true."

"Prove it."

"Someone will pick her up tomorrow. I promise."

"It's not good enough."

"For God's sake, Justina, you want him to go to prison, don't you? Well, grow up. If we don't nail him now, he'll be out there doing this again and again. Is that what you want? Because if we frighten him off now, we've lost it for ever."

"I still can't leave."

My words hung in the air. I could practically touch his irritation.

"Well then I'm sorry, but I'm going to have to make you."

Nine

The cottage was deathly quiet. Even Smokey wasn't in his usual place. On the kitchen table was a message from Mandy – *Gone out with Ben. Won't be back till late, fingers crossed. Wish me luck.* Underneath she'd drawn lots of heart shapes dotted with their initials.

I was pleased for her, even though I desperately needed to talk to someone. I flicked on the television and sat there with my arms clamped to my sides, trying to stop shivering. I never even thought to turn on the fire. Five to eight. It should be happening now.

It was no good. I was going crazy over that poor helpless horse stuck in an aircraft hangar having God knows what done to her. I should have fought Mickey, been more insistent. I shouldn't have let him force me out of there. I could still feel where his fingers had grabbed my arm. He'd promised to ring as soon as it was all over, but when would that be? Was there even going to be a raid at all?

Coronation Street wound to an end and the

adverts came on and then the picture flickered and the telly went dead. So did the lights. Damn, that was all I needed, a flaming power cut. I searched for candles under the sink and lit them from the gas ring. Even having Shona there would have been better than nothing, but she was out in Cheltenham with a jockey.

The phone shrilled into life. I practically fell on it, knocking the whole thing on to the floor. "Hello, hello, Mickey, what's happened?"

There was a pause. "Umm, sorry to disappoint you, but it's Rory."

"Rory!" My voice came out as a yell.

"Are you all right?"

"Yes, yes, fine."

"Listen, I was thinking of coming over. We need to talk."

A warm, liquid feeling flooded my veins. Rory. He was just what I needed. I could pour everything out. He'd know what to do. "Yes, yes, marvellous. As soon as you can. Bring a torch, a generator if you've got one. The lights are out."

I couldn't stop a stupid grin breaking across my face. Maybe now we could be friends again. I stood up and decided I'd better have a look for some more candles. As far as I could remember, Shona had some that she used for aromatherapy.

The knock at the door came sooner than I had expected. I flung off the safety chain and peered into the shadows. But it wasn't Rory who pushed his way in.

"So you wanted to see me?"

Icicles of shock slipped down my spine.

"Adam," I croaked and cringed backwards. I could smell fear and drink on his clothes, his breath. He looked like a hunted animal, cornered in a cave.

"I think it's time we had a little chat, don't you?" he slurred.

I started trembling. Terror was working its way through my body. He looked completely unhinged, capable of anything. I'd have to stay clam, humour him until Rory arrived. When he demanded a drink I found an old bottle of sherry in the glass cupboard. Hopefully if he drained the lot he might fall unconscious.

"Sho, you're an interfering little busybody after all," he yelled, collapsing on to the settee and closing his eyes. His shoulders sagged and his head dropped to his chest. For a long time he seemed to forget I was there. I risked moving.

"Where you going?" He suddenly became alert, lurching up. His skin looked damp and waxy.

"Nowhere." I plopped down into an armchair. Rory, where are you?

"They're all over sher place," he ranted wildly. "They're on to me good and proper now. And it'sh awl your fault. Couldn't keep your nose out." He glugged back a tumbler of sherry and rubbed at his forehead.

Was this the great Adam Valentine? Trainer extraordinaire, suave, sophisticated, in control? He was broken and frightened and I felt sick that I'd ever been taken in by him. Just looking at him made me shrink back in my chair.

"Sit still," he shouted, and shook his head as if to clear a bad dream. I could see despair in his eyes. "What a mesh," he whispered. "Such an awful, terrible, mesh. Got to think . . ."

We sat in silence for long minutes. He lit a cigarette and pointed at the ashtray the Guv'nor had given to me. It was one of Murphy's racing plates encased in cut glass. I'd never used it because I didn't smoke. It was more an ornament, a keepsake. He turned it over and over in his clumsy hands, completely transfixed. I licked my dry lips, expecting him to smash it at any moment. Slowly his mouth began to twitch. Something seemed to be amusing him. How could I have ever admired him? He was a monster, a bully, a lying, filthy cheat. A swell of anger rose up in my chest.

"If I go down, I'll take you with me," he suddenly snapped nastily, lunging forward. "Don't think I wouldn't, I can pin anything on anybody." He swung out his arm towards me and the guttering candle on the coffee table toppled over and snuffed out on the carpet.

Just at that moment the lights flickered back on.

Rory, come on! Where are you? Adam frowned suspiciously, squinting into the bright light. His reactions were blurred with the alcohol.

"Of course, I've always looked up to you, Adam, you know that," I gabbled, desperate to keep him on my side. "You're the best trainer in the country." Sweat drenched my back and chest. Rory wasn't coming. He'd changed his mind.

"They're under the shoes, you know, between the pads," he muttered. "They'll never find them. It was a stroke of genius." He leant back, gloating at his brilliance. "Of course I know you'd never tell the police, you wouldn't dare. I like you, Justina. Together, with your riding skills, we could make a packet. You're wasted here. You've got to learn how to make racing work for you. It's no fun otherwise. I could teach you. We could work as a team."

Surely he couldn't be serious. "We need another drink!" I sprang up. "I'll be two secs." Rory wasn't coming. I had to reach a phone. I galloped into the kitchen. Where was Mandy's mobile? Please don't let her have taken it. Where? Where? Where? I spotted it plugged in, recharging by the toaster. Adam hadn't moved. Please let this work. I punched in the number. Come on, come on. Answer . . .

A glass shattered behind me. I froze, dumb with fear. A hand snatched viciously at my hair. "You double-crossing witch." Adam yanked my head backwards and leant close. I could feel his breath on my cheek. "You won't get away from me. Now get back in the front room."

I gave a tiny yelp of fear and did as I was told. I was desperately trying to wrench my thoughts into order. He was acting like a psychopath. He grabbed my arm and shoved me forward, his fingers digging into my flesh.

"Let me go, Adam! Stop it, you're hurting me." All pretence at friendliness left me.

"You won't be mentioning anything to the police will you, Justina? Not if you know what's good for you, WILL YOU?" He pushed me backwards into the wall. He came up close to me and I could see hundreds of tiny beads of sweat glistening on his forehead and upper lip. His eyes were level with mine. He looked desperate, terrifying. With the last of my courage, I opened my mouth and screamed at the top of my voice, "HELP!" Almost immediately the door opened. Relief gave me new strength and I wrenched myself free and flew across the room.

"Rory!" I shrieked and ran into his arms.

The coffee table crashed to the floor and I turned to see Adam making a dash for the door.

"He won't get far," Rory breathed. "The whole area's crawling with police." I buried my face in his neck. He felt so strong and safe. We stayed like that for a minute, clutching each other, holding on. I never wanted to let go.

"I've been so stupid," Rory mumbled into my hair. "You're so strong-willed and passionate and brave and talented. You scare me, Jus, you're not like other girls, I don't feel in control. But even when I'm out with other people, I can't get you out of my mind."

I think it was the most Rory had ever said about his feelings in one go. I buried my face in his jumper and grinned. I'd dreamt of this since he'd won his first race and I'd seen him on television. Since then he'd become every girl's pin-up.

"When I think what that creep could have done to you." He shuddered and lifted my chin gently away from his chest. My eyes felt as big as Bambi's. His lips found mine and we kissed, a long tremulous kiss, full of the sense of having been apart for too long, of having nearly lost each other.

"Whoops!" A figure in a red bobble hat appeared in the doorway. Scooby. "Sorry, folks, wondered if you knew anything about Adam Valentine being arrested at the bottom of the drive? The lads pulled him down in a rugby tackle. I think we're wasted on football." He was grinning from ear to ear. "Well, I can see there's no problem here." He backed out, looking pleased and embarrassed at the same time.

"You realize this will be all around the yard tomorrow morning?" I grinned. "Scooby's a great friend but he's a terrible gossip."

"He's also got a wager going with Harris that you'd pick me and not Mickey. It'll be drinks on Harris at the Jockey's Rest."

I raised an eyebrow in genuine surprise. "There never was a contest," I said.

"Well I wish you'd told me that, because I've never been so jealous in my whole life." And with that he wrapped his arms round my waist and kissed me until I felt I would melt.

I was chopping carrots in the feed room the next morning when Mickey came to find me. I didn't recognize him at first in a shirt and tie. He looked every inch a TV reporter now that he wasn't working undercover.

"I wanted you to know straight away. Burrows Lea was picked up an hour ago. There's no permanent damage, a few weeks and she'll be back in training."

"Good," I said matter of factly, still piqued at the way he'd treated me the day before.

"Also," he hesitated, "I've got an apology to make. I should never have involved you – when I think what could have happened last night . . ."

"But it didn't," I cut in, not wanting to be reminded. Late the previous evening two police officers had taken me to the police station to make a formal statement. A cache of stolen diamonds and emeralds had been found underneath the rubber pads on the shoes of the imported horses. Diane had suspected as much because the head lad had always insisted on doing the farriery on certain horses.

It was mind-blowing to think that criminal activities could be carried out so obviously without anyone suspecting a thing. There would be a long court case but enough evidence hopefully to send Adam and his head lad to prison on a number of fraud charges. Adam had the same addiction to adrenalin, to the buzz of danger, as most racing people, only he'd taken it a step further. That, and greed, had ruined him.

"The documentary will probably be out in the spring, I'll send you a copy beforehand of course," Mickey interrupted my thoughts.

I wanted to tell him not to bother. I didn't need reminding of how gullible and stupid I'd been.

"Diane's talking of staying on in racing," he said nervously. "I'm going to Bristol, to a dodgy pet food company. I'll be leaving this afternoon."

I picked up the feed scoop and started measuring out rations of oats.

"Of course, I could come back every weekend, if there was a reason . . ." he broke off, letting his eyes say the rest.

I knew he was serious. I knew I'd fancied him in the beginning, especially when I was so angry with Rory. But deep down we were like chalk and cheese. I couldn't forget how easily he'd left Burrows Lea in that hangar. He was all head and practical thinking, I was heart and spontaneity. So was Rory. We shared the same personality, the same dream. It tied us together.

"I'm sorry, Mickey," I began.

He looked sharply away to conceal his reaction. Apart from a sudden tightening of his jaw and fists, little showed. "I'll be off, then." He pecked me on the cheek and swivelled round.

"Where did you learn to ride?" I asked before he could walk away, suddenly curious.

"Pony Club showjumping," he smiled. "It was the only reason I was given this assignment. None of the other journalists could stay on a donkey, let alone a racehorse."

I smiled back. "You were very convincing."

The next few weeks passed in a blur. I took over care of Murphy again, which was like a tonic. The Guv'nor said very little and never referred to Adam. I'd hurt him and there was nothing I could do to change that. I was just thankful he'd kept me on as a stablehand. Race riding was never mentioned and Murphy didn't have any trips to the racecourse. Instead he fidgeted and brooded in his stable and got up to all kinds of mischief.

I thought of Out Of The Blue a lot. I didn't tell anyone, but I was scared that I'd lost my bottle for racing. I knew that I'd never be able to push a horse on again, and that was a jockey's job.

I saw Rory whenever I could but his racing commitments kept him on the road most of the time. He was determined to become Champion Jockey this season, which meant total focus and he was often travelling a thousand miles a week.

I took over looking after Poppy, who settled into the cottage and gave me loads of excuses to go for walks on my own. Mandy and Ben were joined at the hip.

I wondered whether, after Christmas, I'd have a place at Dolphin Barn.

"Hey, Mandy?" Jake shouted down the line of horses as we clattered along the road off the gallops. "He will survive a few hours without hearing your voice, you know." Mandy mouthed something rude and went back to riding with one hand and holding her mobile phone to her ear with the other.

We'd just finished first lot and were heading back to Scooby's breakfast. Murphy strode out in front, happy and eager to get to the warmth of his stable. I burrowed my hands under his mane for extra warmth. The temperature felt like minus a hundred and I could practically see my breath crystallizing in front of me.

"I wouldn't like to be a duck in this weather," Jake shivered dramatically, raising his voice so Mandy could hear. For the last few days, Mandy had been breaking the ice on the pond in the orchard and was now nursing a little drake called Bobby who was living in the feed room in a kids' paddling pool. Jake had kept threatening to pluck him for the Christmas staff party so Mandy had broken into the hostel and doused all his under-pants with itching powder.

Harris was convinced there were cockroaches under his bed and started to describe the latest trap he was going to set. I yawned and visualized Scooby's breakfast: fat juicy sausages with squirts of tomato ketchup.

"Message coming through!" Jerry shouted from the back.

"Message for up front." Horses jostled as it got passed down the line.

"It's from the Guv'nor," Roy's clipped tones rang out. I swung round.

Mandy was right behind. "The Guv'nor wants to see Justina," she shouted. Then sucked in her breath when she realized what she'd said.

All the warmth and normality drained out of the morning. This was it. He was going to tell me what I'd dreaded for weeks.

"Another day or two and we'll have to stop using these gallops." The Guv'nor stabbed at the frozen crumbly surface with his foot and snorted with annoyance.

I knew he hadn't called me back from the string just to talk about the weather. I waited apprehensively, hardly daring to breathe. "The chestnut horse, he's bang on form." He patted Murphy's neck and produced a Polo mint.

"Yes, sir," I croaked, feeling as if a fire had started in the back of my throat. Murphy skittered sideways, alarmed at my sudden tension.

"He needs a race." The Guv'nor sucked in his cheeks. The silence stretched on for ever. He looked irritable. "Who do you think I should put on board?"

"Well, er, I don't know, sir. There's Rory, he knows the horse." I was numbed by the question. "Davide has really good hands . . ."

"Have you hung up your boots or something?" he snapped, a purple welt of colour flooding into his threaded cheeks.

"I didn't think you'd—"

"You're his jockey, aren't you? I said I'd put you up for the season. Do you think I'm a man who goes back on my word?"

"I can't," I said, as calmly and clearly as I could. "It's not what I want any more."

A silence, tense enough to snap, stretched between us.

He eyed me fiercely through narrow, scrunched-up slits. "What did that warthog tell you, that you couldn't ride?"

"No, it's just . . ." The memory of Out Of The Blue flooded back. "I couldn't do Murphy justice. I couldn't push him on when it mattered."

"I see." He almost smiled. "Valentine crossed the line, Justina. You can't let one bad experience put you off. Do you think I'd send you out on a horse that wasn't up to the job?"

"No." I swallowed hard. I knew the Guv'nor had never done anything underhand in his life. Each horse was treated like royalty and given every chance. And so was every jockey because every race was a race to win. I'd scoffed and looked elsewhere because on the surface there was no glamour, no style, just endless hours of hard work and I'd been sulking.

"Do you not think if it was just down to technique and experience I'd hire the most successful jockey I could lay my hands on without a second thought?"

I cleared my throat but no words came out.

"There has to be instinctive communication between horse and rider otherwise they can't work together. That kind of partnership comes once in a lifetime. For heaven's sake, Justina, *you can hear that horse think*."

We stared at each other for a long time. My brain boiled over with a million thoughts.

"So," the Guv'nor rammed his tweed cap down with an air of finality, "do I declare him for the King George Chase or do we let the opportunity slip by and let the whole country think we're beaten?"

Ten

The King George VI Chase at Kempton on Boxing Day is a fast three-mile track over a flat course and attracts the best chasers in the country.

Nobody expected the chestnut horse and a sixteen-year-old girl to stand a chance. But as the big day drew closer, the press could talk about nothing else. *Kenneth Brown Chases Fairytale*; *Pigs Have More Chance of Flying*; *Will No-Hopers Even Get Round? They'll Break Their Necks*, shouted the headlines.

I snipped out each one and pasted it to the notice-board in the hostel. Each morning I'd read them and my determination to succeed would grow. They had the same effect on the Guv'nor. We had something to prove. Against all odds we would do it.

"Hold him steady, left rein, lean forward, sit quiet . . ." Rory rode upsides on Tralligan, shouting advice, fired up by the challenge the Guv'nor and I had set ourselves. There was no jealousy, no bad feeling because his ride had been withdrawn. We'd moved on since the early days and now there was just a solid, extraordinary comradery.

The rest of the yard was right behind us. Scooby went with me to the swimming baths every night and counted lengths as I battled up and down the pool, determined to get fit. Mandy did the cooking and washing-up when I came in too tired to stand up. Harris and Roy got into squabbles at the Jockey's Rest if anyone dared to make fun. We were united. The whole yard was buzzing.

"They'll not know how we're going to play our cards," the Guv'nor talked through the race for the thousandth time. "But as soon as they see you break for it, they'll be on your tail, nothing more sure."

We were sitting in the office poring over the list of runners. He rammed a tape into the video recorder. "Heritage Bay – the only horse who can match strides with Murphy."

A big, rangy, brown horse appeared on the screen. Murphy had beaten him last season but he'd come on in leaps and bounds since then. He'd won all of his races – easily – and was tipped to be crowned National Hunt Horse of the Year.

"The one to beat." The Guv'nor tapped the screen irritably. "Faster in a finish. You'll need to burn him up early. Set a hot pace. Disrupt his rhythm."

The Guv'nor rooted through piles of racing videos so we could analyse the rest of the competition. There was only one other real contender,

Scaramanga, a wiry, tough, little black horse with not much form but that always ran a blinder at Kempton. "Don't underestimate him," the Guv'nor ordered. "If the ground's fast, he could sprint past the lot of you. Level weights suit him. He's a threat. Mark my words. He'll sneak up if you're not careful. Yes, who is it?" he snapped into the phone.

It was impossible not to overhear. The great booming tones of a racing journalist who had been to the yard frequently filled the room. "Now then, Kenny, what are you doing? Coming to Kempton to take on Heritage Bay. You've no chance of beating 'im. No chance. Might as well save your petrol and stay at home."

The Guv'nor's face took on a purple tinge. I stared purposefully at the television and Scaramanga flying over an open ditch.

"How many winners have you trained, Bernard?"

"Well, none actually."

"Well, buzz off then and don't tell me how to train my horses." He slammed the phone down so hard I thought it would shatter. "Right, where were we?"

"Is this a private meeting or can anyone join in?" Rory pushed open the door. He had his usual smile in place but there was a tension around his eyes which I picked up on straight away. He hovered at the door instead of walking straight in. I arched my

113

eyebrows in a silent question, but his attention was fixed entirely on the Guv'nor.

"Come in, man, or have you taken a liking to chilblains and frostbite?"

Rory stepped into the room. "I don't know how to say this so I'll just come straight out with it," he said. He leant awkwardly against a filing cabinet at the back of the office. His knuckles were white. I wondered what on earth he was going to say. "I've just been speaking to my agent. He says Lawrence Oldham was in touch this morning . . ."

Cogs started creaking in my brain. Oldham was a top Newmarket trainer. "Davide had a fall on the gallops this morning. He's broken his wrist. He can't ride Heritage Bay."

The silence stretched on for an eternity. Eventually the Guv'nor cleared his throat. But Rory spoke first. "I've been offered the ride – I hope you'll understand. I can't pass up the favourite for the King George. It could mean the difference between winning and losing the Championship."

I drew in my breath. I didn't dare look at the Guv'nor.

"Of course you can't." He amazed us both. "You'd be a fool, a laughing stock." The nailbiting tension fell away.

"But we'll be in competition with each other." Realization suddenly hit home. The cosy teamship and camaraderie of past weeks disintegrated. When we rode out on to the racecourse on Boxing Day in front of a hundred thousand people, Rory would no longer be my boyfriend, my closest ally. He'd be my main rival. And, even worse, he knew every inch of my riding style, every tactic and ploy we'd discussed over and over to win the race.

He'd have the upper hand.

I didn't go home for Christmas Day. I couldn't tear myself away from the yard and Murphy. I felt that if I left Dolphin Barn, even for a day, I might lose my focus. My parents were disappointed, but I think they understood.

Rory stayed with us. He had steamed fish and boiled cabbage for Christmas lunch and spent the rest of the day in the Raymond twins' sauna, trying to lose weight. The Guv'nor made a special Christmas toast. "May the best jockey and horse win." The tension was sharp. Harris and Roy, who were the skeleton staff, made a few jokes but nothing was going to lighten the mood. We were psyching ourselves up for the biggest race of our lives. And it was due to start in less than twenty-four hours.

"He's going barmy!" Scooby pulled down hard on the lead rope in an effort to calm Murphy, who struck out with a foreleg and half reared in the tight stall of the horsebox. Sweat blackened his coat and ran down his back. We were at Kempton, getting Murphy ready for the King George.

"He knows what it's all about." The Guv'nor pulled down a corner of Murphy's eye to check the colour. "He won't settle until he's eating up those fences." He narrowed his eyes to the familiar slits. "You know, if I listened to my instincts, I'd swear this horse has the race won already."

People were piling into the course. The buzz was incredible. Everybody was in real festive spirit. I tacked back along the queues of people waiting to lay bets. Overhead, a large hot air balloon tugged against its moorings. TV cameras on top of cranes bore down, sharing the atmosphere with the people at home. Kids and parents in reindeer hats screamed excitedly as the second race came into the final furlong. I was here – it was really happening.

As if drawn by a magnet, I pushed my way through to one of the tic tac men chalking up bets for the King George. The atmosphere was electric, everybody wanted to pick the winner. I squinted down the list of runners to Murphy's Law. Then stepped back in amazement. "How long's the chestnut horse been joint favourite?"

The bookie shrugged, glancing at my hands to see if I had money for a bet. "Since this morning's papers," he grunted. "All in there apparently about that Valentine chap. The young lassie's become the housewives' favourite. Can't get cash on quick enough. Mad, I'd call it." He grinned greedily, anticipating a massive profit.

We've got to lose first, I thought, and turned

116

away with the weight of the whole nation on my shoulders. They were backing me to win.

"Hey, Justina? What's it like to be a fairytale jockey?" Pixie was reading from a newspaper in the weighing room. "'*Kenneth Brown recognized, as soon as he saw her on a horse, the extraordinary balance and the pair of hands that any horse could trust.*' Wooo! hot stuff!"

"Pair of what was that?" Ike joked.

I sat down heavily under my peg and the black-and-burgundy colours of Dolphin Barn. What if I'd lost my bottle? What if I couldn't ride with total belief? I couldn't do this.

The life drained from my limbs and I sat and watched valets struggle to clean the flow of muddy saddles as the earlier races finished. In less than fifteen minutes I'd be leaving the bright, cheering lights of the weighing room for the biggest riding test of my life.

Rory walked in with his saddle and weights. I wanted to run to him and throw my arms round his neck but his face was closed. He was riding for someone else and purposefully sat at the opposite side of the room. The divide was back. We were competitors. We couldn't think of each other.

As a wave of desolation crashed in, I visualized the five foot, unforgiving, birch fences which would come up thick and fast.

"Jockeys, please." A steward held open the door.

This was it. The moment of truth.

I followed Ben Le Sueur out into the fading afternoon light to the circle of racehorses brimming with
anticipation.

Murphy squealed with impatience as we waited our
turn to canter down the track. Scooby had him on a
tight chain, talking to him all the time. Scaramanga
fired off ahead for Ben Le Sueur. Murphy saw them
go and nearly yanked my arms out of their sockets.
Thank goodness my collar bone had healed. He
missed colliding with a TV camera by a centimetre.

"You'll lose," a familiar voice rang out above the
crowd.

I turned and in that split second caught Jack
Hughes' eye and the bitterness in it. He hadn't been
booked again to ride. I'd heard a rumour from
Harris that he was leaving the business.

Determination and new belief reared up inside
me. I'd show him. He'd never given Murphy a
chance, writing him off as a carthorse. Murphy
might not be the ideal racehorse but we were going
to win this race – for all the people who were
willing us on, especially the Guv'nor.

"Form a line, get up, get up," the starter urged.
Scaramanga sidled into Murphy who half reared
and squealed. I pulled down my goggles. "On your
starter's orders . . ."

My throat tightened and my jaw turned to iron.
We were off!

"Don't let Murphy's Law get away!"

I felt a stab of hurt as Rory shouted to the other jockeys. He was riding against me. Murphy lunged forward, determined to shake off his rivals. Mud splattered up and I could taste grit in my mouth. I guided Murphy over to the rail and let him drop his head. Scaramanga and Heritage Bay latched on behind. I urged Murphy on. He responded by taking the first fence in a flying leap, daring and reckless. We gained ground, we soared into the lead.

Go! Go! Go! He was jumping like a horse possessed. One, two, three, four jumps. I just saw the edge of the wings in a blur and we were airborne. I didn't check him. I believed he was the best National Hunt horse in the country. He was proving it to everyone.

The pace was frantic. There were no hills to wear down the others. We had to rely on speed and the will to win. Murphy threw himself at an open ditch as if it were a puddle. The TV car cruised along parallel to us, catching our every reflex. Not far behind was the ambulance.

The ground disappeared with every stride. We would soon be in the home straight. Scaramanga moved out to make his run. He relished the pace and ground. Murphy's ears immediately shot back.

We came to the next fence in a line. Scaramanga made a terrible blunder. He was going to cartwheel but tipped into Murphy on the way down. We were thrown off balance, corkscrewing through the air.

It wasn't fair. We couldn't lose the race by being pulled down by another horse. I stuck like glue. Murphy splayed his front legs, groping desperately to avoid Scaramanga's flailing body. He sank down on one knee but, amazingly, recovered.

I slid sideways. I couldn't get back. I'd slipped too far. I couldn't fall, I couldn't, I couldn't – not now. Rory was upsides. Deftly, without a second to spare, he stuck out a hand and shoved me back into the saddle. He'd saved my chances when he could have gone on to win.

I swallowed back shock and admiration and gathered my reins. The last fence loomed up in a blur. There was no time to set up. I sat quiet and let Murphy get on with it. He sprang upwards and, as he landed, I realized something. This was the King George, the blue ribbon. Murphy and I could win it.

The grandstand came alive with cheering. Rory and Heritage Bay thundered on abreast, but I knew in the last furlong that Murphy had the most to give. I leant into his neck and rode out hands and legs. We streamed away from a cooked Heritage Bay and crossed the line in a blaze of glory. Murphy had come to Kempton a novice, a no-hoper, won the public's affection and stolen the race with a spectacular performance. He was a superstar.

I collapsed on his neck and patted him over and over, tears of joy rubbing into his steaming coat. Rory rode up with an outstretched hand. He swung it round my shoulders and kissed my cheek. "I couldn't let it be an unfair race," he whispered. "You beat my horse fair and square."

We came off the course towards the police horses, with Rory holding my arm up in the air in a victory salute. I couldn't have been more happy. I had everything. I was living a dream.

A huge roar went up as we entered the winner's enclosure. Murphy pricked up his ears and there was a moment when a whole mass of people came running towards us. I thought he'd go bananas but he carried on walking as straight as a die. It didn't bother him at all.

Television reporters moved in as soon as I dismounted. The Guv'nor was already being filmed. "Murphy's Law is an extraordinary character," he shouted emotionally. "He has tremendous presence and determination. He's a marvellous horse, an honour to train."

As if in agreement Murphy stuck his head over my shoulder and gazed into the camera. I was suddenly aware of an old lady in a hat moving towards us among an entourage of other people. Murphy perked up and started nodding excitedly. Then it dawned on me – the Queen Mother! Best behaviour! We were about to be congratulated by royalty.

The next half hour passed in a blur. My head was spinning like a tumble drier. It was a wonderful occasion, a once in a lifetime experience. Scooby's face was bursting with joy. Mandy raced up for a congratulatory hug. Ben was with her, his fall forgotten. Relief poured out of the Guv'nor, which made me realize what a risk he'd taken by standing by me. He was now a public hero. We went up to receive the trophy all fingers and thumbs. It was too much to take in all at once. I gazed around at the cameras clicking and reporters elbowing for space. The Guv'nor winked and whispered that it would be the Grand National next. Murphy, as if he could hear, neighed in answer and marched around the winner's enclosure in his posh new champion's rug.

He's done it, I thought, brimming with pride. He's shown the lot of them. Nobody in the country could dispute his champion status. I wiped away tears of joy and turned towards the Queen Mum who was inviting us up to the Royal Box for a celebratory drink. Was there anyone I'd like to bring? she was asking.

"Oh yes," I nodded furiously. "Rory." I scanned the crowds in a panic for the familiar tousled head and coloured silks. "I wouldn't be here if it wasn't for him." I just hoped the owners of Heritage Bay weren't giving him a hard time.

Inside the Royal Box there was a whirl of people clamouring to shake my hand. I was shunted from one famous and influential group to another. Suddenly everyone was interested in Justina Brooks. "So, how does a sixteen-year-old female jockey sneak up and steal a classic from the pro-fessionals?" a television presenter asked me.

"It's all d-down to the Guv'nor," I stuttered. "He's a legend."

All the time my eyes searched the packed room for Rory. I had to thank him properly for what he'd done. Nobody seemed to have noticed, it hadn't shown on the cameras. But I knew in my heart that Rory had given me the race.

"What's your star sign?" A blonde-haired woman with bucked teeth leant in close. Suddenly the crowd parted and Rory was there. He looked straight at me with a lop-sided grin and mouthed, "I love you". My knees turned to jelly. Then a fresh batch of faces closed in. Someone was asking me about Adam Valentine and whether I'd been scared. The American accent made me look up into the most stunning face I'd ever seen. He was like a blond Robbie Williams with the most amazing eyes. "Hi, I'm Chester," he drawled, confident of the effect he was having on me.

I knew instantly he was a jockey. And a good one. What I didn't know was that he was going to turn my life upside down and threaten everything I'd achieved so far . . .

Glossary

box walker – A horse which paces round the stable endlessly, fretting and wearing itself out.

chaps – Usually made of leather, they are trousers as protection against dirt while ...

filling – Swelling.

first/second lot – The first and second w... the day.

furlong – An eighth of a mile.

guinea – The equivalent of £1.05.

racing plate – A lightweight horseshoe w... wear for racing.

seller – Also called a claims race, where ... can be bought for a set price after the ra...

steeplechase – A horse race with a se... obstacles including a water jump. C... cross-country race from town steep... steeple.

surcingle – A belt or strap used to ke... night rug in position.

upsides – Riding alongside another hor...